By Eva St. John

The Quantum Curators and the Fabergé Egg
The Quantum Curators and the Enemy Within
The Quantum Curators and the Missing Codex
The Quantum Curators and the Shattered Timeline
The Quantum Curators and the Great Deceiver

THE
QUANTUM CURATORS
AND THE
SHATTERED TIMELINE

EVA ST. JOHN

MUDLARK'S PRESS

First published 2022 by Mudlark's Press

This is a work of fiction. Names, characters, places, and incidents either are the product of the author's imagination or are used fictitiously. Any resemblance to actual persons, living or dead, events, or locales is entirely coincidental.

Cover art by Stuart Bache at Books Covered

First paperback edition 2022

ISBN 9781913628079
(paperback)

www.thequantumcurators.com

This one's for Al.

Here's to running around Oxford together and discovering the Quantum Curators before Covid struck! This should have been the dedication in Fabergé.

Chapter 1 - Julius

It was lunchtime and I was hungry. Had I known my days here were numbered, I might have paid more attention to the bigger picture, but my stomach was rumbling and a man has to eat.

Rami and I collected our food and headed over to the benches. Looking around, you wouldn't know that only six months ago the plaza had been the scene of a cataclysmic battle. An attempted coup made even worse by the appearance of quantum beings that looked and acted like gods. As with the ravaged buildings, history was being tidied up and smoothed out. Rather than face the reality of what had happened, it was being fictionalised.

'What's the matter?'

I glanced over at my friend and apologised. 'Still trying to get my head around what happened.'

I didn't need to explain. Rami looked about the place and nodded. 'Well, at least you come from an Earth that was more open to the idea of aliens and many universes.'

'Theoretically.' I thought about it. 'And then I turned up here, so I suppose I was already on board with the reality of multiple universes.'

'Exactly, whereas we were stuck on a notion of just the one parallel Earth.'

I took a bite out of my rice parcels and tried to catch the juice before it dribbled down my chin. Fennel seeds mixed with sumac and chilli made my mouth tingle and I grinned at the simple pleasure of a tasty snack. The food here was incredible although I still hadn't managed to bring myself to eat insects. I cleared my throat.

'Still, I just have a vague sense of things not being right.'

Rami laughed and waved a grasshopper at me, its crispy eyes staring at me accusingly. 'Of course, things aren't right. We found out that Earth is infinite and that extra-dimensionals exist.'

'And yet everyone is carrying on as normal.'

It was exasperating. We sat in silence for a while, watching our fellow citizens going about their business, eating lunch, catching up with friends, enjoying the fine weather. Maybe I was simply homesick. Since I had arrived in Alpha, I continually missed home, but it was mostly a background hum, and of course because of the stepper I had been able to visit home. Now I felt stranded, surrounded by strangers.

'You know what I think?' said Rami. 'I think that lots of people are desperately trying to pretend it didn't happen. Others like us are still attempting to understand what happened. Finally, some will be prepping.'

I blew my cheeks out. Prepping didn't sound good. 'How do you mean?'

'We didn't win the battle under our own steam, no matter how many people seem to have forgotten that. We may have neutralised the attempted coup on our own, but those gods,' he broke off and flapped his hand at me, 'or

2

whatever they were, were beating us. It took another extra-dimensional to get rid of them on our behalf. So yes, I imagine some people are prepping.'

It made sense. This wasn't a warlike culture, but war had come to them. An invading army had tried to destroy their way of life. They weren't naturally aggressive, but they weren't passive either. The Alexandrians were technological giants. I knew they'd be planning against the next potential strike. I wondered who was doing what.

'I guess you mean the engineers and custodians.'

'Who else?' Rami shrugged. 'It's their job to protect and to solve. In fact, I think even the curators are involved at the top levels.'

We'd been grounded for the past six months whilst the engineers worked on the new step technology, ensuring it was secure from anyone else trying to hitch a ride. I raised an eyebrow.

'Well, not us, obviously.' He winced and passed me a hanky as I wiped my chin on the back of my hand. 'But someone gave the command to release the banned Beta entertainment streams. I think that sort of helped people get a grip on things.'

He was right. Originally, when Minju had first mentioned that the pharaoh was keen to do it, it seemed a good idea. However, now the Alphas were confusing reality with fantasy.

'But that's fiction. E.T. didn't go home, the Force is not with us, Doctor Who is not real.'

Rami looked at me with concern.

I toned my voice down. 'I'm just worried that suddenly binge watching all of my Earth's SF and Fantasy offerings is blurring the lines between what they see on TV and what actually happened.'

Since the event, the engineers had lifted their ban on various topics. For centuries, they had tried to suppress the theory of multiple Earths. Now the cat was out of the bag, what was the point in the ban? What I found amusing was one of Alpha's responses. When they watched the programmes, they laughed at the inherent notion the Beta Earth were the superior species, when everyone knew it was Alpha Earth that was superior. They all seemed to be blissfully unaware of the irony that they themselves were recently pulverised by a species that could snuff them out in the blink of an eye.

'You're looking gloomy again. Take a leaf out of Minju's book, start whistling.'

I grinned. 'She really has blossomed, hasn't she? I think the reassessment of the Roman Empire is making her day.'

Along with SF and Fantasy, all history programmes and books were also permitted. So now the Alphas were watching and reading about the Beta empires. For many it underlined how dreadful empires were, but it was nuanced and people were beginning to also see the positives. The HBO show *Rome*, with all its sex and violence, was a particular hit. I wondered if anyone was going to study the actual history, not the filmmakers' take on it.

'Aren't you meeting her later? Ask her what she thinks about all this?'

'Seeing her tomorrow, and I know what she'll say. She'll tell me to stop overthinking things.' I shrugged. 'I don't know. I just feel out of sorts. And I think you do too. Honestly, we're missing something.'

Rami looked at his brace. 'Tell you what you are missing. It's thirteen o'clock.'

I stared at him. 'Thirteen o'clock?' I had heard him use the twenty-four-hour clock a hundred times, but this time it caught me out. No doubt because of our current conversation. 'Have you been reading *Nineteen Eighty-Four*?'

'No, is it good?' He smiled as he stood up.

'Very.'

'Well, I'll add that to my list of books to read. I could do with something cheery. Now—' he tapped on his brace '—as I said, it's thirteen o'clock and you are going to be late for Neith.'

After arranging to meet him later in the week for drinks, I headed off towards the hospital. *Nineteen Eighty-Four*, the comedy. Maybe I should have told Rami not to bother with it after all. If Rami needed cheering up, I guessed he was feeling the same unease I was. We were both missing something really obvious.

5

I would speak to Minju tomorrow. She might help put a finger on it. In the meantime, I needed to see Neith, and my heart sank further.

Chapter 2 - Julius

'And that, Neith Salah, is how you saved the day and became everyone's favourite hero.'

I was sitting by Neith's bedside, holding her hand as her eyes twitched beneath her closed lids. Occasionally she would twitch, but for now she was mercifully still.

Hospitals the two worlds over are basically the same. In the past six months of visiting Neith, I had realised that it didn't matter how many staff there were, how clean and welcoming the place was, how holistic the treatments, the fact was that the hospital was a place where you didn't want to be.

When Neith had first woken, she was in such pain and neurological distress that the doctors placed her back into a coma before we had the chance to talk to her. A bullet in the brain and temporary death can derail even the hardiest of individuals. Even Neith. I squeezed her hand again.

Three months ago, when they were confident that her brain tissue was properly regenerated, they brought her out of her coma. Whilst the doctors seemed happy with her progress, the rest of us were appalled. For the first few months, she was quiet and watchful. In the past month, she had become difficult. She would refuse to eat, as likely to hurl a plate at you as spit at you. Other times she just screamed at the ceiling until she was sedated. Funnily enough, as our optimism slumped, the doctors' soared.

They saw this aggression as a sign that she was getting better, that she was fighting to get past her blocks. However, now she appeared to have plateaued. The violent outbursts were few and far between. Mostly she stared blankly at the screens. Sometimes her eyes leaked, but her face was so passive it was hard to tell if she was crying.

The basic problem, as I saw it, was that Neith could no longer communicate. Or at least not in a way anyone could understand. The only language she had was Welsh, and it wasn't a Welsh that I could make head nor tail of. More importantly, it wasn't a Welsh that the Tiresias language algorithm could fathom either. And that was saying something. Tiresias made Google look like a card index. The problem was Neith spoke like Eric Morecambe playing Greig, all the right words but not necessarily in the right order. Actually, it was worse than that because most of the Welsh wasn't modern. There was dialect, slang, eighteenth century, twelfth century, and God knows what else.

In fact, Neith's language acquisition had been the cause of many papers. The linguist's department was buzzing with theories and I knew the academics looked at my head with undisguised avarice. I had permitted a few mind scans in order to help Neith, but they just made me sick and the researchers couldn't unlock the pathways that they theorised existed.

The prevailing theory was that Neith got her Welsh from me when we had spliced. So far so good, and I got it from my grandmother. All so straightforward and above board, but the twelfth century stuff? That was where my mind began to dribble. The idea was that we heard the language around us as babies, all of it, and absorbed it and it fed into our DNA as a genetic marker. It wasn't quite that. The researchers used terms I didn't understand. Something about the genetic inheritance of language. When I tried to question them, they would make disparaging comments about my lack of an intellectually robust gestalt. I may be too ignorant to digest the science. It irked, but I had to agree. What they were saying sounded like nonsense to me, but they had also shown me how a virus causes neurological degradation, and that cancer and bacteria go hand in hand. So what did I know?

Anyway, the idea was that it was possible for memories to be passed down genetically. They were in the early stages of this hypothesis, but my splice with Neith, and Neith's sudden accumulation of the history of the Welsh language, seemed to prove it. The fact that the bullet had torn through the location for language was causing the problem. As was her genetic adaptation to absorb other languages quickly.

Neith tossed and turned, and her eyes flicked open. She looked around the room, then clamped her eyes on me.

'Cwn, brad, angau, lollipops.' She glared at me, her eyes panicky and her breath laboured. 'Rhif tri deg dau, yn rhedeg yn las.'

The automatic translator unit started speaking from the loudspeakers. "Dogs, treachery, death, lollipops, number thirty-two, running blue." It was gibberish. I knew it, Neith knew it, and I suspected the Tiresias app knew it too, but it was doing its best. As was Neith. I smiled and said hello.

She threw her eyes to heaven, slapped her hand on the sheets and tried again.

This time I only understood *prick*. The audio monitors had begun recording her sentences, and I looked at the monitor to see if it had had any success at turning them into a sentence.

'Nothing,' declared Koda Bitsoi who had just entered the room. Koda was one of the tallest men I knew. Even I would crane my neck, and at six-foot-two myself, I wasn't what you would consider short. Today, his straight black hair was tied back and hung in a loose ponytail. When he was out camel racing, he would let it fly. If Koda was racing, I always bet on him. He was so good that he was banned from entering the horse races. Despite his height, he was unbeatable but had waved off all suggestions of going into sport, insisting he would rather be a doctor. Now, following Haru Githumbi's disgrace, Koda had been promoted and ran the entire medical facility for the quantum department.

10

Neith was shouting at us. Her expressions told me there was an alert mind in there, broken and frustrated. She was a long way from being a healthy Neith that just spoke funny. As was the pattern, she now struggled. She tore at the tubes that were feeding her and tried to slap away the drones monitoring her brainwaves. Restraints from the bed snapped up and pulled her limbs down to her side as her body thrashed in protest.

'Please don't sedate her.' I hated the way she was suppressed, even if it was for her own good.

'And how does letting her suffer help?' said Koda.

'Maybe she needs to suffer a bit to break through. Neith is a fighter. If you keep removing her from her fight, how can she get better?'

Koda stared at me compassionately, and I tried not to snarl as he continued speaking. 'We are close to the decision that we place Neith back into a long-term sleep until our science can develop to fully help her.'

Neith was properly shouting now, utter gibberish to us and maybe to Neith as well. But until we had the ancient Welsh language on our database, there was plenty of guesswork going on. Even Tiresias was struggling to translate. That said, no one needed a translation to understand that Neith was unhappy with the current situation as she thrashed and yelled.

'See, you don't have patient consent,' I pleaded.

11

Koda looked at me sadly. 'The patient isn't able to properly function. Tests have shown that she doesn't fully understand us—'

I stepped away from the bed and paced up and down the room. I was powerless to help, but at least I could advocate for her.

'She understood you want to put her back to sleep for good. She got that. Look at her.'

'Okay, but it could also be a coincidence. Observe.' Koda turned to Neith. 'Neith. If you can understand me, stop thrashing about.'

The thrashing continued, as did the swearing. I mean it wasn't bad language such as you would normally understand. I recognised the words puppy and cupcake, but their intent was obvious. Neith was swearing fit to make a sailor blush. But she wasn't lying still.

'Julius, this is not helping her. She is in distress.'

'But she is understanding us. Sometimes.' I looked at him hopefully. It was a weak case, but I had to try. 'Bits of it, anyway.' It sounded lame even to me and I could see Koda taking pity on me.

'We know that. We aren't unaware or unsympathetic. Neith Salah is a hero and we are all working night and day to understand her condition and heal her. Time solves—'

'-all. Yes, I know.'

God, how many times had I heard that? They were like archaeologists covering an important site because they didn't have the tools to properly excavate. Rather

12

than risk damage, they did nothing. Once upon a time, I had nodded along sagely, approving of the wisdom of that action. Now I was Charlie, champing at the bit. I wanted Neith saved. She was so close. Locking her away again felt like an abomination to me.

'Okay,' said Koda, checking his brace. 'That's five minutes.' I had bullied them into allowing Neith to remain agitated for five minutes, but that was the limit of cruelty they would tolerate. I winced as the fluid moved through the tubes and Neith's movements began to slow. A fish floundering on the deck of a boat. Her stillness felt like death.

'I know you hate this, Julius. And the counsellor is on standby should you need them. But Neith is a lethal weapon. Remember what happened last time you undid her restraints?'

She had broken my wrist and was out the door before an electric mesh had immobilised her and aerosol particles sedated her. I had watched as she was lifted back into bed and restrained before my arm was set and mended.

After that, I had to endure a week's compulsory counselling to help me understand my impulses were wrong and unhelpful. At the end, I nodded and agreed. I doubt they were convinced of my sincerity. The problem was that they weren't wrong. Neith wasn't in full control of her actions, and I was. So I had better grow up and start helping her.

I sat back by her side. She was mumbling and slurring now, her body becoming still. Holding her hand, I sang softly. I had done this early on and it had had an immediate effect on her. As I sang the lullaby that my grandmother used to sing to me, Neith relaxed. The language of my childhood holidays and visits to my mother's parents always made me happy. It was like our secret code, as I would chat to my grandparents in Welsh.

The words of *Suo Gân* soothed Neith and we sat in that hospital room, her lying prone and still beneath the antiseptic white sheets, me sat by her side singing softly into the silence, as the night fell outside

Chapter 3 - Julius

Three short sharp knocks on the door at seven forty-three precisely the following morning told me that Sabrina Mulweather had arrived. Since the Grimaldi coup, Sabrina and I had become friendly. I admired her bravery in action, but I was sorry to see how she tortured herself daily. Her partner had turned out to be working for the other side and she hadn't noticed.

I had suggested she swing by at a quarter to eight and we'd head to the meeting together. Now, two minutes early, she was precisely on time for her. Sabrina always liked to be ready for anything. Punctuality was just being lazy. You had to be there ahead of the game. Just in case. If you turned up at the allotted minute, you simply weren't putting the effort in. And those who were late? Beneath contempt. I regularly fell short. Which was why I suggested she call for me, rather than me for her. There was no point in adding to her anxiety. She had understandably become hyper-obsessive after the coup, taking the responsibility firmly onto her shoulders. God knows why she was spending time with me. My best guess was she either viewed me as a threat, or an ally. Either way, I was fine if I could help her settle back into her previous state of being the smartest student on the block.

I opened the door quickly, and it was all she could do not to salute. She was standing in formal uniform, as was I, and we were off to the first major address.

'Are you excited?' I asked.

She looked at me sharply, disappointed with my question, but trying to work out how to answer it.

'Yes.' She stopped and looked concerned. 'No. This is merely an announcement. An indication that things are getting back to normal.'

It was widely predicted that the engineers would announce this morning that the stepper was ready for use again.

'But don't you want to get back to work?'

'The holo-suites have provided perfectly excellent alternate work outs.'

I sighed. Poor Sabrina. She was a nice kid, but my God she could get so stuffy.

'Ah, come on. You had barely got into your stride as a curator before the proverbial hit the fan.' She liked Beta idioms, and indeed she paused and smiled at me.

'The excrement? Yes, that is a pertinent analogy. That's pretty much exactly what happened, isn't it?'

Originally, I didn't like them calling my Earth Beta, because I knew they felt we were inferior. Now, I had let it go. I couldn't change an entire planet. And as long as it didn't bother me, then so what? Over the past year, they had been rocked on their axis as they discovered their Earth was also far from perfect.

We were heading towards the main quantum building, as it held the largest auditorium. As other people were heading in the same direction, I could see that it was going to be busy.

'So few of us,' murmured Sabrina, and I looked again. She was right. There should be far more people. This was a full roll call of all quantum staff, from the ancillary workers to the engineers and curators. Only attending doctors and patients were missing.

'We have to be the very best for them.' Her voice was hard, and she had clenched her fists.

I looked at her, concerned. 'You can't do that, Sabrina. Be the best for yourself. You'll have a breakdown if you try to carry the entire loss.'

'What else do you expect me to do?'

'Well, you could start by forgiving yourself about Stefan.'

We'd had this conversation many times, and I wondered if she would ever get over her partner's betrayal. She picked up her pace and strode towards the agora. Sighing, I trotted to keep up with her and tried to engage her in small talk. Eventually I gave up.

'If you don't bend, you will break. And we have so few curators left, we can't afford to lose another.'

She glared at me and I rushed on.

'Besides which, I'd miss you. I only have a few friends, and I count you as one of them.'

Which I did. She might be officious and annoying, but when she wasn't trying to prove something, she was good fun.

17

'Curator Strathclyde—'

Oh God, she was trying to thank me.

'I mean it.' I hurried to cut her off. 'Rami is always tied up being big chief honcho. Stefan turned out to be a murderous traitor. Jack is permanently engaged on the new quantum innovations, and Sam spends all his time with his children. Which is as it should be,' I added quickly. I didn't want to sound like a whiney baby. 'And Neith is—' I shrugged. 'So, I have you and Minju.'

'I don't think you can name me and the hero of the archives Minju Chen in the same breath.'

'I can, I will. And I think you'll find, I just did.' I punched her arm. 'Now, come on. I'll get the popcorn.'

'Julius, we can't eat in there.'

'Joking, I am!' I grinned at her as she tutted in exasperation. Spending time with Neith speaking nothing but Welsh had brought back fond memories, and some days I went full-on Valleys. I hadn't been kidding, though. I was short of friends these days. Since Rami's promotion, he was regularly tied up in bureaucratic shenanigans. He and Neith had been my main companions, and I was feeling their loss. Hell, there were moments when I even found myself missing Arthur. I flinched and looked around carefully. In the past, just thinking about him had been enough to summon him. Now he was truly gone, and even that made me feel lonely.

We filed into the large auditorium. Something was off. An unpleasant echo bouncing off the walls.

Sabrina winced. 'They need to recalibrate the harmonic field. This is jarring.'

Everyone headed to the front and centre of the seating. How unlike my undergrad students back in Cambridge. They would hug the back row and the edges, all making sure they weren't sitting near anyone else. This lot all packed up. I longed to hold back, sit on the edge myself, but I followed Sabrina and soon we were surrounded by our fellow workers all chatting quietly and respectfully. Normally, any gathering that contained curators would be more boisterous, but we had borne the brunt of the casualties along with the custodians, and our numbers were heavily depleted. We were scattered across the auditorium, so few in numbers. I caught the eye of a few and returned sombre acknowledgements. Of course, we had been working together in the holo-suites, but watching everyone now simply highlighted just how many we had lost.

I was about to talk to Sabrina again when the harmonics in the room changed and the great and the good walked onto the stage.

The Egyptian pharaoh, Nolyny Cleeve, strode out in a slow majestic manner. As she paused in front of her chair, she acknowledged the crowd with dignified small bows. Despite having been hurriedly appointed after the recent coup, she seemed a steady choice. She certainly took the role seriously.

Behind her came the Chancellor of the Quantum Facility, or Sam to his friends. In my mind, a far more successful promotion. I thought Sam, with his kind heart and suspicious nature, was a perfect choice to run the whole enterprise. Even now his eyes were sweeping the auditorium, taking notes.

He was followed onto the stage by his replacement Rami Gamal, Captain of the Curators and I was proud to say, one of my best friends. Poor sod looked properly out of his comfort zone. Rami's skills came from blending into the background and watching. If he straightened his robes one more time they'd probably fall off. Well, it would give him something else to focus on.

They were followed onto the dais by all the other section heads, including Asha Giovanetti, Head of Security and Hypatia Smith, First Engineer. I smiled at Asha, but First Engineer caught my look and gave me a hard stare. Sabrina looked at me and glared. Trust her to blame me. I tried to sink down in my chair a bit. Asha was scary, but I liked where she was coming from. First — I couldn't bring myself to call her anything other than her title — was just terrifying. The fact that she had regularly contemplated my death didn't help.

Without further ado, Pharaoh Cleeve stepped forward and cleared her throat.

'Welcome, welcome.' She raised her hands in the air and smiled broadly as she looked around the room. 'Health to your heart and home. It has been six months since I was voted in as pharaoh, and I can honestly say today will be a highlight in what I hope to be a long and successful term of service.' She paused and dropped her tone, her face becoming serious. 'Alexandria, Egypt, and the entire world have been rocked by the events of last year, but it is time to move forward. And today we can do that, and once more it will be the quantum facility that will lead the way.'

She nodded at the applause and waited until we had quietened down again.

'The stepper is now operational, and I am pleased to announce that you shall soon return to your duties. I would like to thank the effort of the engineers, not only for fixing, but improving the quantum stepper, which I believe will herald a new golden age for Egypt and the whole world.'

There should have been stomping and cheering. Instead there was more polite applause. The pharaoh seemed nonplussed by the reception.

'I shall now pass you over to First Engineer to explain more. Afterwards, everyone is to report to their own sections where you will receive your new timetables and work duties.'

The pharaoh cleared her throat, and I realised she had expected more cheering. We would, normally, but she was a weak orator, and we just wanted to hear the fine details from the engineers.

'I will now ask First Engineer to speak.'

21

First stared out across the room. Today she was wearing a big skirt with layers of petticoats, a waistcoat and a pair of clogs. She looked ridiculous, but no one even raised an eyebrow. Engineers were famed for eccentric dress and liked to play with fashion to prove how little it mattered. She grimaced as she glared across the auditorium, and I wondered if she was trying to smile. It didn't sit well on her. She settled back into a suspicious glare and I relaxed. As did everyone else.

'We have been working on new theorems developed within the Engineering department.' I nudged Sabrina. We both knew it was Jack's meeting with da Vinci and Firenze that had fired up his neurons. He had finally understood what had been eluding previous engineers. The previous quantum stepper had been built on restrictive technology. It was full of fail safes and limiters. Now Jack had changed all that. Sabrina frowned and shook her head minutely as First continued.

'There has been a lot of speculation about the recent advancements. The ability to travel to other Earths, travelling along our Alpha timeline.'

A buzz of chatter broke out. This was ground-breaking stuff. It signified a great leap forward. First rapped her knuckle once on the rostrum and the conversations fell like heads at the scaffold. First carried on speaking into the sudden silence.

'For now, though, these developments remain theoretical. But as of today, we can announce that we are returning to Beta Earth.'

There was more clapping, but this time it was nervous. Would First rap her knuckle again? Would she glare out across the auditorium? Was someone taking notes? Despite the evidence of engineers' manipulation of society and technology over the past centuries, Alphas were still in thrall to them. It made no sense to me, but it was how this lot rolled. They were the power behind this society.

'And not only has Beta Earth re-opened...' The audience leant in. 'We can now go to any time reference of our choosing, again and again and again.'

Now that was news. There was no clapping this time, just excited mutterings as the implications rolled across the auditorium.

'We will now be able to save even more precious artefacts. Items that we failed to retrieve, we can return to immediately. We no longer have to wait for an appropriate window to be randomly assigned by the stepper algorithm. We will also be able to step back to Alpha then return to Beta during a mission.'

She was gripping the rostrum now, leaning forward and playing the room like Eva Peron.

'In a time of crisis, curators will be able to access further help or information. Curators will no longer be stranded on a single roll of the dice. We will once more save artefacts. And we will do so without loss of life.' She had been raising her voice and thumping the lectern with each point. And now, as she finished her speech, she shouted out the curator's motto.

'And yes, my friends. We will preserve!'

This time, as they say, the crowd went wild. I was laughing and cheering with the others and couldn't help but smile as I noticed a self-satisfied smirk on First's face. She knew how to play with a crowd.

In a buzz, we all filed out. Sabrina and I met up with others and headed towards the curators' briefing room. We'd already had a few sessions, but I was reminded again of how few of us there were.

My watch buzzed, and I turned to Sabrina.

'Jack says drinks later?'

Sabrina laughed and agreed. This was good news and, like good curators, we would want to celebrate. Even if Jack was an engineer, we all saw him as an honorary curator.

Chapter 4 - Julius

As we walked into the room, Rami was standing at the front and I gave him a friendly salute. Every time we had met, he couldn't talk about work. Now I understood why.

'Okay, settle down everyone.' He was grinning now. This was Rami in his element, small stage surrounded by friends. 'As you have just heard, we have exciting times ahead of us. What First failed to mention was that they are also dangerous times. But we can handle a bit of danger, can't we?'

'Care to elaborate, boss?' asked Ludo Bianco, the class joker. 'Are you leaving that for us to experience? Add some spice to the step?'

'After your performance in the Fakes Retrieval, I would have thought you'd want to avoid drawing attention to yourself,' drawled Rami, a good-natured smile on his face.

The Fakes Retrieval room was one of the many simulations that Rami had been occupying us all with over the past six months. In fact, the engineers had built a whole new suite of holo-rooms for us to train and keep our skills sharp whilst the stepper was unavailable. One room contained a variety of fakes and one genuine item. The goal was to retrieve the original.

'Remind me,' continued Rami. 'How many artefacts did you retrieve, Ludo?'

'All of them,' said Ludo, throwing his arms out wide. He leant back in his chair and acknowledged the laughs from the rest of the team. 'Let the archivists sort it out when I get back.'

'We don't send you over with a bloody suitcase!' said Rami.

'We should call him Suitcase from now on.'

'What about Luggage? Goes with his name, Ludo Luggage.' Manu laughed.

'He doesn't have enough legs,' I joked, joining in the fun. Everyone just looked at me puzzled, and Sabrina nudged me.

'He has two legs Julius, that's a perfectly acceptable number of legs to have.'

I sighed. Once again, I had made a funny that wasn't funny. I mean, it wasn't funny because it was bad. I'll grant you, it wasn't the best joke known to mankind. The problem was that Alpha Earth was behind on their Beta reading matter.

'Never mind. Captain Gamal, you were saying?'

Rami rolled his eyes at me. He knew I sometimes struggled with being the odd fish, and I knew he'd be buying me a pint later to commiserate, and get me to explain the joke. Or lack of.

'Very well. Initially, we will only do live steps. According to the engineers, they have had no failure rates with these steps. The technology is completely stable.'

'No more Washington Escapes for now,' said Ben Wakandi. He had retired but was now back on active service due to our number depletion.

'What's the Washington Escape?' said Ludo, tugging on his ear. I was glad he asked. I wasn't familiar with it either as I had missed so much basic training.

'Ah now, that was a cock-up and a half,' said Ben shaking his head. 'As you may all remember, the British were supposed to win the War of Independence.'

I sat bolt upright and Ben laughed at my sudden attention.

'Thought you'd like that, Blue. Anyway, Titus Silvanus, a curator before my time, travelled back on his own for a mission. It was more commonplace than it is now. He arrived as George Washington was pinned down in Brooklyn by William Howe. Trounced by the British, things were looking grim for Washington and his men. Their only option was an impossible retreat across the Hudson River but that was being monitored by British warships. Howe had the nine thousand men trapped with nowhere to go. Victory was his. He had taken New York and now he was ready to annihilate Washington.'

This was all news to me. History lessons back home didn't tend to focus on our losses. The rest of the room were enjoying Ben's story. He had a lovely slow way of telling a tale and we all listened as Washington and his troops crept onto their boats in the dead of night, whilst decoys wandered around the camp with torches, fooling the British into thinking they were still all in camp.

'I find it had to believe that the British wouldn't notice thousands of soldiers crossing the Hudson.' It had to be said and I was probably the one to do it.

Ben nodded slowly in my direction. 'You are not wrong. This should have gone in Howe's favour. Britain should have won, Washington died in battle and the War of Independence stuttered to an end. America remained a colony for another thirty years.'

This was fascinating and I knew I'd be looking this up as soon as I got home.

'So what happened?'

'Titus Silvanus happened. He'd meant to drop into New York city itself to save some artefacts before the British burnt the place down. Instead, he arrived in the middle of a battle. Panicking, he tried to step home but messed up the settings. He found himself on a quiet riverbank in the dead of night two days later surrounded by wounded American soldiers. Confused from the misaligned step, he attempted an immediate second step.'

The curators started to shake their heads. Two steps in close succession were always a dodgy move.

'In fairness,' said Sabrina, piping up in defence of the curator, 'the soldiers were startled to see him. Especially as he was wearing the British uniform. Our shielding technology wasn't what it is today.'

'Indeed it was not, Curator Mulweather. I too would have panicked had I found myself on the floor looking up into a sea of desperate American faces, all pointing their sabres and muskets at me.'

'So what happened?' asked Ludo. 'How did he cock it up?'

'He slapped his brace again and this time returned home safely.'

Those of us that didn't know the story stared at Ben in puzzlement. Clearly there was more to come.

'Curator Bianco,' said Ben, addressing Ludo. 'What's the last thing you do before you step?'

I could see the relief on Ludo's face. Even he knew the basics of step protocols.

'Check you are unseen and have left nothing behind.'

'Precisely, but poor old Titus was in a hurry and when he had fallen several whizz bangs had fallen out of his satchel. And unfortunately, those whizz bangs were clouding devices. A bank of fog covered the Brooklyn side of the river, leaving the Manhattan side in bright sunlight. The British were unable to see what was happening under the cover of fog. And that's how the Americans escaped and how we screwed up the Beta timeline.'

It was astonishing. I sat just staring at Ben as he gave me an apologetic glance. I know he wasn't apologising for the fact that we had lost, but for the fact that Alpha had messed up Beta's history.

'And that is why live steps are so much better,' said Rami, drawing everyone's attention back to our current situation. 'If we step into the present, we can't destroy the future as it hasn't been established yet.'

'Plus, if you get stranded at least the Beta's twenty-first century is moderately civilised,' said Ludo, which raised a few laughs.

'Very true,' agreed Rami. 'But that is only for the first few weeks. Soon we will be stepping back into the past. And what we can do this time is momentous.'

He leant on the rostrum, a broad smile illuminating his face as he looked across the room. Some curators like Ludo were brilliant at the action and adventure, smashing heads together, grabbing the artefacts and escaping. Others liked to slip in quietly and explore the surroundings, take it all in. Rami was one such and so was I.

'Now, it also seems that we will be able to direct the stepper to any point in time we wish to visit. Whenever we want. This has the following advantages.' He pointed at the display screen as the points came up. 'We can retrieve anything that we choose. No longer will we wait to see what artefact the quantum stepper has randomly opened a window towards. Now, we will decide.'

This was momentous. The old stepper's algorithm had been fed a list of artefacts that we were interested in saving. It would then open time windows, which we could use to try to save the item. The stepper had been built like this because of limited knowledge and deliberate obfuscation on the part of its original inventor, Leonardo da Vinci. But since Firenze had shared a few secrets with Jack, the technology behind the stepper had leapt ahead.

'As you may imagine, we can now plan and train better, rather than scramble to react. Imagine, instead of a Monday briefing where you are told that on Tuesday you will enter a war zone to retrieve an obscure item, you can now have months to study the terrain and consider the fastest and safest way to get in and get out. I know over the years we have brought the loss rate amongst curators down, but now we may even eradicate losses completely and eliminate the risk to the Beta timeline.'

Damaging their timeline was at the forefront of every curator's mind. Whenever we stepped into the Beta past, we risked spoiling their history and, therefore, their future. The room was very excited by the proposal.

Sabrina raised her hand. 'If a retrieval fails, can we try again?'

Before Rami had a chance, another voice called out.

'Can we go back to previous failures and retrieve the artefact or the curator?'

I looked around as I tried to come to grips with what this newfound flexibility could provide. Before we had one shot only. Now, it seemed anything was possible.

'The ethics committee is investigating that at the moment,' said Rami. 'We don't want to swamp the Beta timeline with multiple visits from us. Equally, we need to consider how to re-integrate curators who have been missing from our timeline for decades.'

'Couldn't we just return them to their own Alpha timeline?' asked Ludo. 'First said the technology existed to travel on our own timeline.'

Sabrina audibly sucked in air and a few other curators shook their heads vehemently.

Rami looked at him and tutted. 'Ludo. We spend years learning about the cause and effects of messing up the Beta timeline by displacing so much as a chicken. Now you want to lob an entire curator into our own past?'

Rami shook his head in horror at the idea. Hell, even I understood the time fractures that would cause.

'I'd like you to submit a full dataset showing the ramification of Marcus Caractacus returning twenty years ago. I want the dataset to fifty anomalies. On my desk first thing tomorrow morning.'

I winced, but at least it was an easy assignment. Caractacus was so famous that, had he returned, the knock-on effect would have been monumental. Not least that he was Minju's partner and fell in action, saving her life. Finding fifty changes would be child's play. Even for Ludo.

Rami carried on talking as Ludo looked mournfully at his desk. I felt sorry for him. He was prone to stupidity and now, with so few of us, there was nowhere for him to hide. That said, he was resourceful and fearless. Excellent qualities in a curator.

'Other improvements are that we can send out multiple teams to multiple points. In theory, we could rattle along, saving artefacts at a phenomenal rate.' Rami looked around the room as he let the ramifications settle in. 'That said, whilst the engineers have assured us that the technology is stable, there are only a few of us left, so we will take this nice and slow. Bast knows we are awash with new recruits, but it will take years for them all to be trained up. Even if we try to fast track them like we did with Julius.'

'Is fast tracking wise?' asked Sabrina. 'Julius had several unique advantages.'

Namely my splice with Neith, and the fact I came from my Earth, not theirs. Sabrina had always been opposed to my presence. It wasn't personal. No matter how much it felt that way. Sabrina was simply trying to protect the service.

'It's all in hand, Curator Mulweather. Very few will be fast tracked, but we have to be aware that our current numbers are heavily depleted.'

'How stable is the new technology?' asked someone from the other side of the room.

'No significant issues in the past month. The engineers have been successfully crossing themselves. Okay.' Rami decided to re-focus the curators. 'If you check your updates, you will find a list of the first hundred items we have been scheduled to retrieve, as and when the engineers deem it safe enough. Current forecast is another month or so. This will give you an unprecedented opportunity to prepare. I want you all to focus on these items, learn their history and the history of the period intimately. We will retrieve in the order detailed on the list, but as yet teams have not been assigned. Now.' He paused significantly, and the room stilled. 'There will be one step before these.'

We all looked at each other. This was it. We were about to get back to the stepper.

'As you know, one of our own is lying on a hospital bed. Struggling to recover. Neith Salah nearly died protecting a friend and saving our culture from extinction. She is still locked in a battle, and we plan to rescue her.'

Everyone was nodding, but what could be done?

'We are going to send a pair of you over to the National Library of Wales in Aberystwyth to download every data source in the Welsh language from its first recorded usage. All these sources will be used to repair Neith's language cortex and rebuild her syntax. Maybe if she can communicate, she can begin to heal. If this fails, she will be placed into long-sleep until our technology has progressed enough to heal her.'

The door behind me slid open and a tall person entered the room. I couldn't tell if they were male or female in their long, pale blue desert gowns. They were fully cloaked.

Turning back, I saw Rami nod at their arrival. He seemed unhappy. I couldn't tell why, but I was overcome with a sense of foreboding.

All I wanted was to be on that mission. I was the perfect candidate. It was my memories that were causing Neith the issues. It was my timeline. Hell, I even knew the library. Maybe that was the problem. Maybe I was too close. Would I set off alarms if I suddenly reappeared? I was panicking that I wouldn't be chosen and began rehearsing arguments as to why I should go.

'The two curators are Julius Strathclyde—'

I sagged with relief. Now I would get to save Neith. My friend who had had my back, had saved me, had made me laugh and had opened up a whole new world for me. I couldn't wait to find out my partner. At this point, even if Rami announced Ludo, I'd be happy.

'—and Clio Formerly-Masoud.'

Chapter 5 - Julius

The gasps in the room were audible as Clio removed her hood, walked forward and sat down. Her face was calm and passive, and she didn't look around.

I stared at her, my mouth flapping like a goldfish. This woman had killed my best friend, shot Neith, killed her partner, played footsie with Anansi, and taken part in an uprising that threatened to overthrow Egyptian society and establish a new order. I looked across at Rami, who gave me a very slight shake of the head as I realised I was standing up. I wasn't sure what I was about to do, but violence had felt like a good option.

Clio cleared her voice, then spoke softly, head bowed.

'Thank you, Captain, for the opportunity to begin my readmittance into the fold. We are a family, and I have wandered far.'

She sat like a Victorian governess, quiet and subdued. Her afro was tied back in simple braids. She wore no make-up or jewellery. No holo-tattoos flittered around her body. Calm and still. The embodiment of contrition.

The muttering was dark. Rami cleared his throat.

'Curator Formerly-Masoud has undergone full therapy training, re-acclimatisation and calibration.'

She could have gone under full electroconvulsive therapy for all I cared.

'What methods did you take?' asked Ben Wakandi. As Clio and Neith's original mentor, everyone wanted to hear what he had to say on the matter.

Clio started to speak, but then stuttered and hesitated. She apologised and started again, addressing Wakandi. 'I took the Monteagle method, the Hai-dan method, and the Bokbok method.'

Again, everyone seemed happy to hear this. These methods were regarded as the best ways of rehabilitating people. They ran all the way from phobias and bad habits, up to criminal activities. Alpha obviously didn't approve of physical punishments or imprisonment. Instead, people were talked into good behaviour and the occasional brain modification if the individual agreed. By all accounts, the "talking" could be brutal. And there was some surprise when she mentioned the extreme Bokbok method. This was usually considered severe and the cost rarely justified the cure. I didn't know anyone who had undergone it, but I understood it involved weeks of fasting, scorpion venom and needles. Lots and lots of needles. Most criminals chose exile or ending.

'It took three methods to heal you?' asked Wakandi.

Not likely, I thought. You don't heal a hurricane. Clio was not something that got fixed.

She cleared her throat. 'I was considered recalibrated after the Monteagle method.' Her voice trailed away again.

'So why the two further methods and why on earth the Bokbok?' Wakandi looked concerned, and the room was now hanging on Clio's every word.

'I volunteered. I suggested the Bokbok.' Her head was bowed, her voice subdued. It was a remarkable performance from the six-foot-tall arrogant swaggering warrior I knew Clio to be. 'I couldn't think of a better way to make amends for my dreadful actions. I wanted people not only to trust the system I have gone through, but to also trust me.'

Her words fell in silence, and I could see the others were contemplating them. Incredibly, everyone was going along with this charade, and the sense of hostility was receding.

'With all due respect to Curator Formerly-Masoud,' said Sabrina to Rami. 'Is she ready to return to work? I know we are short on numbers, but people who have experienced the Bokbok aren't usually fit for their previous careers. None of the rebel ministers who chose that option following the coup have returned to service?'

'I don't know.' Rami shrugged. 'Ministers are easily replaceable and not made of the same stuff as curators.' There were a few small laughs at this, but the tension was still running high. 'We need every curator we can get, and I have been assured that Clio is cured.'

She dipped her head, her eyes closed. An act of humble contrition. 'I know I'm a risk. And I can never begin to apologise for the pain I put you all through. I lie awake at night racked with grief about—'

'Horseshit.'

All eyes turned to me, and I realised I'd said that last bit out loud.

'Curator Strathclyde,' said Rami. 'I understand your concerns, but I can assure you that anyone who has completed three methods and been fully signed off from each course can now be trusted and received back into society. And it is our job as citizens to welcome them back with open arms.'

'Sir,' began Clio. Again, her voice faltered. 'I am prepared to step down from this assignment if Julius wishes it. I hurt him directly, and I know he isn't used to how we do therapy. I wouldn't wish to inflict any greater pain on him.'

Incredibly, the rest of the curators were smiling kindly at her. Somehow, they were buying this nonsense.

'I wanted desperately to go on this step to bring back the resources to help save Neith, my partner and best friend.'

Who you betrayed, I thought.

'But if Julius says no, then I will willingly step down.'

Rami had his poker face on. No expression was leaking out, and I felt bewildered that these curators were so quick to embrace the viper.

'There's no need for that, Curator Formerly-Masoud. If Julius wishes to stand down, he can, but the pharaoh

39

selected both of you for this mission. You don't get to say if the other goes or not. You can only speak for yourself.' Now he looked at me. 'Curator Strathclyde. Is it still your wish to go on this mission to save Neith, regardless of your companion?'

What could I say? Neith was dangerous. Without a cure, she would be shut away for decades. Maybe centuries. I would never see her again.

'I'm going.'

Sabrina gave me a small fist bump on the shoulder. 'Well done. I knew you had it in you to be one of us. Suspicion is so Beta.'

I fumed. It was my suspicion that had saved the day when Grimaldi had tried to seize power. How quickly they were reverting to peace and love. The fools.

'Captain,' said Clio. 'Is it okay if I leave now and spend some time in the contemplation grove before I prepare for tomorrow? I want to ensure I am at peak performance for the mission.'

'Of course,' said Rami, 'in fact, I was about to dismiss the whole class.'

'May I also be permitted to offer Julius the hug of reconciliation?'

Sabrina and Wakandi nodded in approval, and even Ludo was muttering to his partner with a smile.

I appeared to be the only person who thought this was a dreadful idea. I caught Rami's eye and, for a second, his expression gave way to one of total fury. He gave me a curt flick of his hand before he regained a benign expression.

'Very well, Clio. I think that's a remarkably generous gesture.'

Clio walked towards me and I grudgingly stood up. Were we really just going to hug it out?

'Julius seems unwilling,' she said in a sad voice and took a step back. I swear to God she seemed to shake. She was a sad, tragic figure and the other curators reached out and placed their hands on her arms in support and consolation.

'Julius is not unwilling,' snapped Rami.

I stepped forward and opened my arms. I felt like being sick. The idea of touching her without then hurling her across the room seemed impossible. In my mind's eye, I could see Charlie laughing as we staggered out of the pub at closing time. I saw Neith's head snap back as Grimaldi shot her in the head. How could I do this?

Clio wiped a tear from her eye, stepped forward and hugged me, ready to whisper the ritual words of apology. She twisted her mouth to my ear, her long plaits masking her lips as she whispered softly in my ear.

'Suck it up, Shitfly.'

I stepped away from her, invigorated. This was the Clio I knew. I looked at her as she stood there, looking at her feet, the beacon of contrition, and I spoke the ritual response.

'We are reconciled.'

Everyone clapped and cheered before I continued, looking directly at her.

'And now the game is on.'

There was more cheering, but this time I noticed Clio briefly raised an eyebrow as her lips twitched. The game was on indeed.

Chapter 6 - Julius

As the briefing ended, I made my apologies to Sabrina and high-tailed it over to Rami's office. I knocked on the open door and waited for Rami to wave me in. He already looked annoyed and I didn't want to push my luck.

'Close the door behind you.'

I closed the door, counting to ten, then turned around ready to explode.

Rami's hand was upraised. 'Spare me. I know what you are about to say and I agree with you.'

Temporarily derailed, I sat down. 'But Rami, this is insane. Clio is no more reformed than Genghis Khan. How has she fooled everyone?'

'I have no idea.' He drummed his fingers on the table. 'But she has, and we have to put up with it.'

'I don't like it.'

Rami gave a bitter laugh. 'So what? You don't have to like it. You just have to put up with it. If anything, we are at an advantage.'

I frowned, trying to see what he had already discovered.

'We know Clio hasn't changed. That means that she can't blindside us.'

'What do you think she's after?' I asked. If anyone had an insight into Clio, my money was on Rami.

Rami sat back in his chair and looked thoughtful. 'Honestly, I think she wants back in. She's lost Anansi, she's lost Grimaldi. She's a brilliant curator, and I think she misses the action.'

'That's insane.'

Rami paused and looked at me.

'Julius, I know you won't like this, but there's a lot you don't understand about how curators come to be. We are misfits. We are often too wild for our families. Standard education doesn't work for us. Some of us find a quick path into the quantum academy. Others are shunned and berated. We can suffer feelings of isolation and disgust if our impulses aren't recognised for the service we can provide. We are the closest you get to Beta individuals, and you know what this society thinks of Beta. Scary, dangerous, brave, impulsive, violent, selfish—'

I held my hand up. The compliments were too much.

'Sorry.' Rami poured us each a cup of mint tea. He had obviously been expecting me. 'It's just that Clio was always extreme. Her family pretended she was normal and refused to send her to the academy. Some old families view curators as undesirable. Her family shunned her as a child. She wasn't allowed to mix with other children, and that included her siblings in case she somehow rubbed off on them. It wasn't until she finally arrived at the academy that she found a place where she belonged. A new home.'

'And then she tried to destroy it.'

Rami shrugged. 'You have a saying about leopards not changing their spots? I think that works for Clio. She was brought into the fold too late.'

'So she gets rewarded for her actions. All is forgiven.'

'That is our way, when someone has recalibrated.'

'But she hasn't!' I stood up and started pacing the room. I needed to shake off this energy. For the first time in my life, I understood why people went out looking for a fight.

He frowned. 'She's a scorpion all right, but she is without protection or an exit strategy. So now she's our scorpion.'

I gave him a cold stare. 'I'm about to go on a mission with her.'

'I know it won't be easy, but remember this. Clio threw everything away to save Neith. She risked exposure when she rescued the two of you from the woods outside Rheims, and then, as Grimaldi was escaping, she killed him rather than run with him. She has never let Neith down.'

'She tried to shoot Neith once in Cambridge.'

'I am certain she would have only clipped her.'

'So, are you saying she's actually a goodie?'

Rami snorted. 'Clio Masoud, a goodie? When the Nile runs dry, maybe. No, what I'm saying is that, where Neith is concerned, Clio will protect her and save her. If Clio has a moral compass, it's Neith. She will do everything in her power, which is not inconsiderable, to get all the language files that Neith needs. You are probably going to have to bring your best game to keep up.'

I was momentarily affronted. The idea that Clio would perform this task better than me was offensive. Rami had the truth of it, though. Clio had been doing this for years, and was still at the top of her game. Added to which, she wasn't slowed down by ethical considerations.

'And what's to stop her from killing me?' I didn't want to come across all self-centred, but I had no desire to spend the entire mission watching my back.

Now Rami laughed. 'You're golden, don't worry. Clio understands how deeply entrenched your splice with Neith is. You remain the key to Neith's brain. It's a unique splice. You and Neith are each other's cranial first aid kit. Clio won't risk a hair on your head.'

I thought about it. 'And if Neith and I hadn't spliced?'

'I doubt you'd have made it past the week after she came back to Alpha. She certainly wouldn't have returned you when she rescued the pair of you in 1483. Believe it or not, you can trust her to have your back at all times.'

I looked at him and considered his words in silence. Eventually I gave up. I could see I was stuck with her.

'You're right.' I stepped forward and picked up the teacup, taking a quick sip. I noted the extra sugar. Rami had clearly thought I needed it for the shock. I needed to pause and think things through. 'Look, thanks for talking. I feel better knowing you can see this the way I do. I'd better get ready for tomorrow's trip.'

I felt fed up and worried. What should have been an exciting prospect, returning home for the first time in six

46

months, was now mired with concerns over Clio. I had expected him to say something and looked up. He was fiddling with the teapot and had now heaped about five spoons of sugar into the cup.

'There's something else you should know. I didn't want to bring it up in the meeting just now, although I will do later. I just wanted you to hear about it first on your own.'

I braced myself. Rami was a friend, but he never played pranks. Whatever he was about to say had upset him and it clearly affected me. He took a deep breath and looked directly at me.

'The engineers have been repatriating angels.'

Angels were dying Beta individuals who had no friends or relatives. They had been used as messengers in the past. It was a winning situation for everyone. The angels were cured and got to live their final years in comfort, and the stranded curator could send a message back to HQ. It didn't happen often, and now it wouldn't happen anymore. The repercussions from this new technology kept on reverberating.

'Why hasn't this been on the news?'

Rami looked miserable. 'Sorry Julius, I was only briefed this morning. It has been decided that as the technology now exists to return to set points in time, we can allow the angels to return home. It has also been suggested this will ease public fears about Beta threats.'

I was astonished. 'That will disrupt everything.'

'No, they are being sent back in real time.'

'And how will they explain their absence and their remarkable return to full health?' I was incensed. I didn't expect anyone to consult me about this, but I felt very protective of my fellow Betas.

'It's all been thoroughly researched, Julius. And no one is returning who doesn't want to. It was just proposed that it was better for them if they were sent home. If they wanted to.'

It all sounded so above board, but the phrase "send them home" sent chills down my spine. How many times in history had groups of people been sent home? Displaced, thrown out. Sometimes they never made it home at all.

'And what about me? Am I to be sent back as well?' I tried not to sound emotional.

'Not at all. It was the first thing I asked.' Rami looked straight at me, his expression earnest. 'Unless you want to go. In which case, it would be barbaric of us to stop you. But I, for one, would miss you. Not just as a friend, but as a valued member of the team.'

'Okay.' I picked up the tea and took a sip, barely registering the appalling sweetness. 'Okay.' I knew I was repeating myself but faced with the threat of banishment I discovered just how much I did enjoy it here.

'By the way,' said Rami, 'what was with the joke about Ludo's legs?'

I looked puzzled, then smiled, glad to have a change in the conversation. 'Luggage is a character from a series of books by Terry Pratchett. It has hundreds of legs and follows its owner around.'

'Wouldn't a GPS tracker be easier?' said Rami with a puzzled frown.

I sighed. How to explain the entire genre of Fantasy and Science Fiction?

'Instead of reading *Nineteen Eighty-Four*, try *The Colour of Magic* instead. It might be more instructional.'

I left the office smiling. The clacks were open and Terry Pratchett was ready to live on. However, considering what was happening all around us, we should have both been studying *Nineteen Eighty-Four*. Things were changing, and we weren't looking in the right direction.

Chapter 7 - Julius

'Curators Formerly-Masoud and Strathclyde,' Rami's voice called down from the loudspeakers. 'Pharaoh Cleeve is coming in to inaugurate this step. Please be mindful of the occasion.'

Which meant play nice. Which was difficult knowing I was about to go on a mission with someone I loathed.

I was standing in front of the stepper. It always felt odd, just looking at a solid white wall. All my nerves from my first step came flooding back. I knew that the technology had been substantially altered, but also knew it had been rigorously tested. This was still scary stuff, trusting my atoms would be thrown into a quantum state then reassembled in another space and time. I tapped my brace for the umpteenth time. I had fallen out of the habit of wearing one, but now for the step it was essential. It was also an upgrade. We were on a tight quantum tether, which meant the engineers could monitor our signals through an open link and haul us back whenever they were unhappy with a situation. We also had a figurative big red button that we could hit. This would yank one or both of us back simultaneously.

Clio was standing a few feet away, calm and serene. She looked ready to attend a prayer meeting. The door swung open as the pharaoh strode in, ready to officiate on the first formal step of the new technology. She was flanked by a team of officials, who now stepped to one side as she approached us.

I knew this was safe and there were no real risks, but it still felt daunting. My already racing heart jumped up a step. I was not the stuff that pioneers were made of.

The pharaoh addressed Clio and spoke of her shining example of reform and citizen engagement. I thought the entire society was insane, or were simply better humans than I was. Both might be valid interpretations.

Clio nodded and smiled softly, not quite looking at the pharaoh as she replied. 'I live to serve.'

Nolyny Cleeve frowned at her, then walked back to her flunkies.

I walked across to Clio and whispered in her ear. 'You're coming across as a little too passive. You'd better be careful, or they'll think you've lost it. And we wouldn't want that.' I pulled away and smirked at her.

She leant forward, and it was her turn to whisper in my ear. 'Then you had better get your heartbeat under control. You sound like an entire marching band in a carnival.'

I stepped back, and her smile was as sour as mine. I returned to my zone and started on some breathing exercises.

'Now then, Masoud,' continued the pharaoh. 'We expect great things from you. Your mission is vital to the recovery of your old companion, Neith Salah.'

Clio's body snapped into a rigid posture and her face settled into the aggressive planes I was so familiar with.

'Yes, Ma'am.'

The pharaoh visibly relaxed and nodded over to the other heads of department before coming to say the same desultory hogwash to me: You who are about to die, we salute you!

'Strathclyde, you must be very excited?'

'Looking forward to it.'

'That's the spirit. So what are you expecting when you arrive?'

I could see everyone was paying attention. After all, this was my home and I was the expert.

'Let me think. It's July, which is high summer, and we're going to Aberystwyth, which is on the west Welsh coast, a popular destination for holiday makers, so I imagine it will be freezing and lashing it down with rain.' I grinned around the room, but everyone just looked appalled.

'Will the place be deserted, then?' asked one of the technicians.

'Not a bit of it.' I chuckled. 'People will still be on the beach, eating ice creams, wrapping their insubstantial raincoats around them as the wind tugs at their clothes.'

'But why would anyone choose to go there?' asked the baffled pharaoh.

'I think if you've chosen to holiday in Wales, you aren't the sort of person to be put off by the odd deluge. It's a gorgeous country and well worth the gamble.'

Clio snorted. 'Captain. Can you book a slot in the hot springs for me on our return?'

Everyone laughed. This was the old familiar Clio and everyone shared her sentiments. It was a regular Alexandrian lament that so many lost artefacts came from Northern Europe.

Clio suddenly became properly alert, and a split second later I felt the familiar buzz in the air. The quantum stepper was warming up. The technicians told everyone else to clear the room. As they filed out, a few of them rubbed the hair on their arms, commenting on the effect to their neighbours. Clearly, Clio and I were more attuned. And Clio more so than I. I may have loathed the woman, but she was, without doubt, a superior curator to me. The fact that I was going to have to rely on her brought me no comfort.

'Curators, engage your wrist braces.'

I wrapped my hand around the brace as it responded to my bio signature. Once I was satisfied, and more importantly, it was satisfied that it was linked to Clio and the main control panel, I set it to translucent. It blended into my skin tone.

Under my clothes, I was wearing a new body suit. Full of all the latest gizmos and gadgets the engineers had perfected. Short of being trampled by a stealth rhino, I could weather any explosion or attack. It might even be able to keep out some of the Welsh rain. But I wasn't prepared to bet on it.

'Clio, Julius, are you ready?'

I smiled at hearing Rami's voice and turned around to wave up at the balcony. Rami was smiling down at us, and I immediately felt better.

Out of sight, First's voice boomed across the loudspeaker.

'Strathclyde, Masoud. Engage.'

We both took a deep breath. It wasn't necessary, but I think it's a human response to potential peril.

'Walk forwards on the count of three. One. Two. Three.'

We walked towards the wall that was now a shimmering mass of lights. There was no depth to it as I walked into a cloud. Then my brain and body snapped.

And that was it. I was standing on the Aberystwyth sea front and the sun was shining. The sky was blue, the air was warm, and damn me if I didn't start bloody crying.

Chapter 8 - Julius

As soon as the tears started, I wiped them away and took a deep breath, turning to locate Clio. I prayed she hadn't arrived yet, or was half the town away. In my experience, it could take a few hours for a curator to locate their partner.

Typically, she was standing exactly two feet away and looking at me with undisguised scorn. I tapped the side of my eye, where the contacts had onboard cameras, and her expression turned to one of instant concern. If I was going to be saddled with the venomous snake, at least I could have fun watching Clio do her best to be the new shiny version of herself. When we got home, our footage would be monitored and assessed for training opportunities. It would then be added to the general database of Beta day-to-day life. Clio wouldn't want them to see her in her old persona.

'Right,' she said, 'let's find the library.' She called up directions on her brace when I cut her off.

'No need. I've been here before.'

She looked at me with a caring expression. 'Are you sure? You also said it would be raining.' She looked worried, and I was impressed by what a consummate actor she was. 'And you appeared emotionally compromised when we arrived?'

Saccharin solitude.

I smiled back with the same level of warmth and concern. 'I'm fine, and remember. Weather changes in the UK, and having a positive engagement with one's emotions is considered a strength, not a weakness.'

'How right you are, Julius. Lead on, then.'

We walked in silence, which suited me. Aberystwyth was as I remembered, and I was almost overwhelmed with the salty sea air and the smell of vinegar and ozone. We stepped around two students sat on the pavement reading poetry to each other and drinking cans of Coke.

How I loved this little town, isolated and glorious. Around me, people were chatting in Welsh and English. Tourists were taking photos under Welsh signposts. It was a day of smiles and laughter. Down on the beach, children were running in and out of the waves. Chairs and tables had been placed outside the cafes, and I could only assume we were in the middle of a heatwave, or what passed for one here. The frenetic activity usually associated with the first few days of good weather had passed. The *must-make-the-most-of-it* mentality. Now everyone was simply enjoying the gift of waking up, knowing that the day promised nothing but sun cream and barbecues, and the atmosphere was relaxed. In a few more days, the population would begin to mutter about the state of the lawn, wonder how the farmers were managing, and bemoaning the fact that they couldn't sleep at night. Then it would rain, and all would be well in the world again.

I had explained the cycle once to Neith, and she felt it was exhausting to be in the thrall of something you had no control over. I had never seen it like that before, and felt somewhat chastened.

'Julius, are you lost? The brace says it's straight ahead.'

The brace was right, but I loved to wind my way up to the library via the lanes of the town.

'You're surely not heading towards the old college?'

Of course I wasn't. As lovely as that building was, we needed the National Library of Wales, one of Britain's five legal deposit libraries. More importantly, it was the centre for the study of Welsh linguistics.

'I was taking the scenic route.'

Clio flashed a look of scorn at me then, remembering herself, scowled, and then tried to smother the scowl as well.

'We can go that way if you want.' She looked so doubtful, she was practically fiddling with her fingers. 'I am just so anxious to complete our goal in a timely fashion with minimal interaction.'

Now it was my turn to bite my tongue. 'You are of course right, Clio.' Sarcasm dripped from my mouth. It was petty, but she and I had never been on first-name terms. All this Julius nonsense was just for the recordings. Normally, it was Psycho and Shitfly.

As we walked away from the sea front, I could see we were attracting quite a few second glances. Clio moved like she owned the place. Everything about her screamed *look at me.* Neith had always made an effort to blend in, to move unnoticed through the population. Clio practically demanded their obeisance.

'Clio, knock off the Queen of Sheba act.'

She stopped and looked at me quizzically.

'Try to be a bit more circumspect. Channel Neith.'

I watched in surprise as her face softened and she laughed ruefully. 'Bast, she would be forever berating me for how I walked around on Beta.'

'Exactly. Try and blend in.'

She raised an eyebrow. 'I do not blend in. I stand out.'

I trailed off. This was ridiculous. I was actually about to ask her not to be herself. The dispassionate thing was that she was magnificent. Some people just naturally radiated power.

She shrugged. 'I'll try. But it's not just me, pretty boy. You've forgotten how much Beta inhabitants judge people on their appearance, and yours apparently is very fine.'

I winced, embarrassed. I had my contacts in to mask the two-tone irises, but I had always been uncomfortable that people were looking at me and approaching me simply because of the way my face was put together. An act of biology that I had no say over. And here I was berating Clio for her own presence.

'Okay. I guess we can't help it, but shall we walk a little slower, maybe drop the purposeful stride?'

Clio nodded then spoke into her brace, 'Compile a short briefing document on "Queen of Sheba."' She looked over at me. 'That was what you said, yes? Queen of Sheba?'

I nodded, and we walked on as Clio listened to her earpiece. I was simply enjoying the view as we headed up the steep hill out of town, towards the library.

The National Library of Wales was a huge edifice, complete with columns and pediments gazing down over the town and looking out to sea.

As imposing monuments went, it wasn't the worst thing I had seen, but I have to confess, the Alexandrian architecture with its fluid lines and harmonics was more appealing than this statement of dominance. I smiled, remembering the library building in Cambridge, an altogether different architectural embarrassment. That desperate desire to thrust itself upon the landscape.

As we climbed the steps leading into the building, Clio was disappointed to be directed to a side entrance rather than entering via the main doors.

'We're blending in, remember? Two students come to study. The front doors are for ceremonial use only.'

She rolled her eyes at me as we walked into the building, presenting our rucksacks for inspection. This was a new security feature, but one that didn't surprise me. In the offices behind the counter, I thought I heard a familiar strain of music from a radio. I looked at Clio in alarm, and was about to hiss at her when all the radios and public address speakers suddenly belted out Handel's most famous aria.

Clio strode into the National Library of Wales to the glorious strains of the *Arrival of the Queen of Sheba*.

Chapter 9 - Minju

Minju Chen walked towards the hospital facilities. The warm breeze was scented with lemon blossoms, and some children were laughing over on the air vents. She smiled to herself. Her long thick tail swayed in the breeze, cooling her body down as the leopard pelt trapped all the warm breezes. Over the years she had adjusted to her tail and on days like this her snow leopard splice was a blessing.

This was a good society where engineers took the uncomfortably hot air from the workspaces then vented it away at speed out into parks and play areas. Children, and sometimes adults, would bounce on the columns of air trying to see who could stay afloat the highest or the longest. But nothing beat her tail.

Despite her love of her home and all it stood for, it was being eroded by the complacency of its own successes. Minju feared for its future. Before the uprising, she had worried about her home's development. After the arrival of Anansi, Firenze and the other quantum beings, she knew her fears were well founded. Should an alien Earth visit them, they could be obliterated. They needed to prepare. For now, though, she was all but immobilised and it was killing her.

Grimaldi's coup had been a disaster. She had spent years manipulating the system, bribing officials through third parties, running a black market network in Beta goods, all to amass the finance and contacts needed for when she wanted to take control. She meant to steer it back to a position of strength. She had hoped to do so with minimal violence, but the quantum beings had spoilt everything. She wasn't ready, but Grimaldi had seen it as a green light and rushed, unprepared, into the fight.

Her plans, following the coup, were in tatters. Ironically, though, the quantum incursion had proved her point. Now, she was more determined than ever. It was no small coincidence that their chaotic and violent arrival had helped others to share her concerns. Society was ready to be led in a new direction. She could feel it all around her, and where she experienced resistance, she was prepared to manipulate or shove at those barriers.

A young couple approached her, interrupting her thoughts, and she quickly smiled at them. Looking at their robes, she decided they must be tourists up from the south. The Mediterranean breeze was clearly a little too chilly for them. They were grinning excitedly at each other. The woman nodded and addressed Minju.

'Good afternoon Adviser Chen, may we take your image?'

Although still an archivist, Pharaoh Cleeve had requested Minju work more closely alongside her. The woman said she liked Minju's calm counsel. The idea had been entirely the pharaoh's idea, which was exactly what Minju wanted her to think.

A side effect of being one of the heroes of the Coup was that people often recognised her from newscasts and stopped her. People found it hard to relate to the curators and custodians; those who had died, those who had killed. But an archivist who would not abandon her post? One prepared to defend her artefacts. That was a concept that Alphas could get behind and support.

'Oh goodness, I would make for a very boring picture.' Minju laughed dismissively. 'Tell you what, why don't we have a picture of the three of us with the mouseion in the background?'

That should ensure that the couple spread the photo far and wide, thought Minju. She gave a self-deprecating smile and wave into the hologram.

Thanking the couple for the honour of their time, she continued on to the hospital. She had never considered her public persona before. At work, she was happy to be ruthless and terrifying in her execution of her duties, but publicly no one knew who she was. Well, now that had to change and she was going for self-effacing grandmother. And in truth, she knew what her society needed, and she was going to deliver it. It was a strong elder who knew how to look after their family, and a wise child that did as it was told.

Minju entered the building and headed towards the reception. 'Good morning, I'm here to visit Neith Salah.'

The receptionist smiled and said he would ask Doctor Bitsoi to escort her. No one could visit Neith without supervision, but usually a junior physician would attend. The receptionist had decided that no one less than the

Head of the Facility was a suitable choice for Adviser Chen.

As Koda Bitsoi walked towards her, Chen stood up from where she had been waiting.

'I am so sorry to disturb you. I said it was completely unnecessary,' she said.

'My pleasure.' He gave a small bow of the head which pleased Chen, and the pair of them headed down the corridors to the secure wing, her small stature dwarfed by his height.

'I believe you haven't seen her since your first visit?'

'I didn't want to intrude.'

'If only everyone was so courteous.' He smiled back at her. 'So, I have to warn you she is not much improved. We've been keeping details of her recovery private, as her progress is distressing.'

'I thought she was conscious?' Chen knew exactly Neith's current state. People still talked, and she still listened. Remaining silent and unobserved had served Minju for years, and she had quickly fallen back into her pattern of whispers.

'She is, more's the pity. I'm afraid the neurological damage is extensive. Her language acquisition has been severely damaged. Worse than that, though, is how she is processing information. We can't communicate with her and she doesn't appear to understand her surroundings.'

'Is she in pain?' Minju sounded concerned, but in truth she was curious.

'Her brain waves suggest she is pain-free, but she sometimes falls into an extreme state of distress. At which point we have to sedate her. If we can't make progress soon, I am going to recommend full sedation and suspension until our technologies advance enough to treat her properly.'

'She's that bad?'

The director turned and took a deep breath. 'If I were to express myself as a regular citizen, she's about as bad as it gets.'

They approached a door where an armed custodian stood in a red uniform.

'Who do you think is coming for Salah?' asked Minju in open astonishment.

'He's posted there in case she tries to escape.'

'Your doors aren't biometrically locked?'

'They are, but this is Neith Salah and I will not underestimate her ability to escape. Even in her current state.'

Minju paused, looking at the custodian, then turning anxiously to the director.

'Koda, just how dangerous is she? Will I be safe?'

He placed a reassuring hand on Minju's arm and she struggled not to shake it off.

'Completely. She is restrained most of the time. If her rages last longer than five minutes, we sedate her.'

'You let her suffer that long?' That surprised her. It seemed an unusual approach.

Koda scratched the side of his chin before replying. 'If it were down to me, I would have sedated her immediately. But Curator Strathclyde suggested we let her rage.'

'What on earth for? I thought she was his friend.'

'His reasoning is that she needs to build resistance, or get used to new networks or some such.'

'The very notion!'

Minju tutted in concern, but inwardly she laughed. She really admired Julius, but he was like lightning. You had no idea where he would strike. His thoughts were so fresh and challenging and twice he had nearly undone her entire enterprises as he stumbled about in the dark. He was entertaining, intelligent, and excellent company. But he was also unpredictable and for that reason, he might have to go. He certainly couldn't be allowed to carry on in partnership with Neith. The two of them combined were lethal.

As she frowned, Koda nodded in agreement and continued. 'That was how we all felt, but he was so distressed that we humoured him.'

'And you are still humouring him? Even whilst he's away?'

Minju's voice was critical, and Koda had to remember he was addressing his equal, not some concerned well-wisher whom he would have happily dismissed.

He removed his hand. 'We are not humouring him. It turned out that there was some merit to his suggestion.

We have been monitoring her brain activity when she rages. We can see an area that is engaging that we wouldn't expect to be associated with emotional outbursts.'

'And?'

'And we are due to operate on her this afternoon to see if we can repair the damaged tissue in that area. It is our hope that it might resolve some of her issues.'

'Might?'

'Brain medicine is still in its infancy, but yes, we think this part of her brain might actually be part of Strathclyde's brain, following their splice. If that is the case, her body could be trying to reject it, literally tearing her brain in half.'

'But why now?'

'It was probably caused by the bullet in her head.'

Minju checked for any sense of sarcasm, but, seeing none, she nodded. There was no point in antagonising him. She needed to see Neith and reassure herself that Anansi's trick had extended to Neith. So far, everyone believed she had hunkered down in the archives, protecting her artefacts since the glyphs first appeared. In reality, only a few people knew she was actively involved and now they were either dead, reformed, or simply didn't remember her involvement. She had looked Luisa Githumbi, Head of the Red Custodians, in the eye and the woman had done no more than smile. Minju sensed a state of scorn for her apparent cowardice. The entire uprising was blamed on Grimaldi and now Chen was seen as the epitome of Alpha virtues. Staying safe, protecting what was hers to protect, and not fighting. The custodians naturally had a different take on fighting to most of Alpha, and Githumbi had failed to mask her disapproval.

Minju had disappeared from all recordings. It was as if she had never been there. The last person who might have a memory of her was lying in a hospital bed, and now Minju wanted reassurance that Anansi's manipulation had been total.

'Are you ready?' asked Koda.

The custodian stood to one side as Koda opened the door, and the pair of them walked in. The room was empty except for a wall of monitors and a hospital bed.

'No chairs?'

'Neith broke one, used it as a weapon, then threw the others at the monitors. We had to refurbish all the equipment after that incident.'

One of the monitors chimed, and Koda walked forward, advising Minju to stay where she was. 'She's waking up. No doubt she's registered our voices.'

'So, does she understand what's going on?'

'We think so, but it's only partial.'

He stepped towards the bed and laid his hand gently on top of Neith's, saying hello to her before taking a step back.

As Minju watched from the corner of the room, Neith's eyes opened. She looked blankly up at Koda, muttered something illegible, then turned her head to look out the window.

'Neith, I have a visitor for you.'

Neith continued to lie still, watching the birds rise from the lake. Koda turned and beckoned Minju forward, and gestured for her to speak.

'Hello, Neith. I'm Minju Chen. Do you remember me?'

Neith exploded from the bed. In an instant she jerked up into a crouch and launched herself off her bed, her feet pushing away from the white sheets. Minju had barely time to recognise the fury in Neith's face as she flew at her. The alarms were all screaming.

Minju braced for impact and deflection, just as Koda intercepted Neith. Tackling her around her waist, he threw her to the floor. Koda's knee was on her back, pinning her down as she screamed at Minju. Her words were unintelligible, but their intent was clear. Neith looked at Minju with undisguised savagery, spittle bunching up at the sides of her mouth. Over the sound of the alarm, the automated translator was having a hard time keeping up with Neith's torrent of abuse.

'Twll tyn. Die. Die. Crumpets. Pass the fucking elephants. That isn't how you fold socks!'

The custodian, along with two nurses, rushed into the room, shoving Minju into a corner. As the custodian protected Minju, the nurses turned and stabbed needles into Neith's thigh.

69

Koda removed his knee from Neith's back, and she sprang up again. Both hands were restrained as Neith scrambled to shake off the medics. Inch by inch, she pulled herself and the medics towards Minju.

Minju cowered in the corner, making sure everyone could see how terrified she was. It was only partly an act.

Within seconds, Neith collapsed, the drugs kicking in.

'You can put the gun away, Custodian Jones,' Koda panted. 'Help me get her into bed.'

Neith was already drifting away. She laughed and said something that the automated voice translated as, 'Liar. The spiders are eating the truth. Fools.' Then she fell silent.

Minju looked at the custodian and medics, and was surprised by how calmly they were taking this explosion of rage. Minju knew exactly what Neith was trying to say.

'Please, let's go to my office,' said Koda in a reassuring voice. Asking the medics to monitor Neith, he steered Minju towards his office where he poured her a cup of tea. She took the cup, making sure it rattled as she placed it on its saucer.

'I'm so sorry. We haven't had an episode like that in a while.'

'But why does she hate me?'

Koda looked instantly contrite. 'It's not you! Oh, you mustn't think that. She's like that with anything. There seems to be no rhyme or reason.'

'But she looked at me as if she knew me?' Minju was genuinely rattled. It seemed that Neith did remember what had happened, but the doctor was acting as though this was normal.

'It's impossible to say. All we can be certain of is her irrationality. If it helps, she also attacked Julius.'

'Really?'

'Yes. As I said, there is no explanation. I mean it's not as if she has any reason to attack you, does she?' He laughed and offered Minju a mint cake.

'And you think this operation will stop these attacks?'

'Possibly, but after that outburst, we are going to have to wait a few days for her to recalibrate her neural pathways. I'll need to check her charts later, but from what I briefly glimpsed just now, that was a major event.'

'Are you sure surgery won't make things worse? Maybe instant suspension would be better for her?' Minju's voice shook. 'She must suffer terribly.'

Koda exhaled deeply. 'Honestly, I agree with you. I feel heartbroken that we can't do more for her. Hopefully, Masoud and Strathclyde will furnish us with enough language data that we can repair her linguistic pathways. Maybe if she can communicate with us... Maybe that will help.'

Minju nodded and changed the topic of conversation on to next month's University Summit. After what felt like an appropriate time, she apologised for causing such a disturbance and for ruining his day. The doctor was at

71

pains to stress that she mustn't blame herself, but nonetheless she left the building with her head bowed and her face wet with tears. She made sure everyone noticed her distress and went to great lengths to keep surreptitiously wiping her eyes.

Only when she was back in her archives, did she allow her expression to change. She pursed her lips. Was it possible that, out of an entire planet, only Neith Salah remembered the truth? She had been technically dead when Anansi had erased Minju's actions from everyone's memory. Did that mean she alone now remembered the truth of the situation? Neith's comment about spiders swallowing the truth was loud and clear, but was that a buried memory? On recovery, would she remember or forget? Neith's survival depended on it. Minju admired Neith, but if she was going to get in her way, Minju would have her permanently removed.

Minju called the pharaoh and invited her for lunch. She'd been working on the pharaoh for months, and found her wonderfully pliable. A woman elected beyond her talents, she was ripe for manipulation, and Minju was happy to steer Pharaoh Cleeve in a direction that suited Minju's goals.

Chapter 10 - Julius

Having disabled the override of the library's music systems, we made our way to our desks. Clio had cheered up immeasurably, and I was furious. Her prank may have jeopardised the mission, and yet she was behaving like it was a wheeze.

'Okay?' Clio looked across the table at me. Now she was all readiness. The plan was ludicrously simple and utterly boring. We would open our laptops and log into the library wi-fi. So far, so normal. Then, boosted by the braces, the laptops would establish a secure and high-speed wi-fi network. Once established, we would download the entire digital network on the Welsh language, including every lecture given, book scanned and essay written. Even with the enhanced Alpha technology, it was going to take a while.

We set our equipment up and, after a quick scan, our braces estimated the download would take about an hour spread across the two units.

I pulled out a notepad and pen and began writing letters. Clio retrieved a novel and started to read.

We were halfway through ignoring each other when the fire alarm went off.

'Dammit, Julius, what have you done now?'

I looked across at Clio in exasperation and put my pen down.

'I have been sitting here the whole time. More likely this is connected to your music prank.'

No doubt, following the earlier glitch, some bright spark had decided to test the whole system. It was the right thing to do, but incredibly irritating.

'Well, do you have any bright ideas?' she said as she looked around the tables.

The problem was that we couldn't leave our laptops, as the braces were powering the downloads and compiling the information.

'We have to remove our braces.'

I looked at Clio, gauging her reaction. It was an irregular suggestion. In fact, it was utterly forbidden and I doubted any two other curators would even contemplate it, but it made sense. However, before we did, I was going to suggest sitting tight. Sometimes drills were so lackadaisical that a quiet student tucked away in a corner could be totally overlooked. I could see we weren't going to be that lucky, as an oaf of a man started lumbering towards us. His shirt buttons were strained over his waist and his belt was slung below his belly. His very walk was belligerent.

'Come on, you two. Everybody out.'

The guard looked like he was born to sneer at students and tourists alike, and before he and Clio exchanged views, I simply nodded in agreement with her plan. We left with the rest of the crowd as our braces and laptops silently continued to download a copy of everything, undetected.

Outside, the students and visitors milled around as the bells continued to ring out. Fags were lit and vape clouds obscured the view.

'Alright, Shitfly,' said Clio, very much taking charge of the situation. 'I suggest we find a side door and go back in. We accelerate the fire and nab some of the older unscanned books. They can be accounted lost in the flames.' She stopped talking as she took in my expression. 'What? Why are you staring at me like that?'

'Are you insane? Are you actually proposing we set fire to a library?' I grabbed her arm and pulled her away from the crowds.

She followed me, then stopped. Her strength matched my own, and I was once again reminded of her superior skills. She looked at me in contempt. 'Are you one of those "can't burn books" sorts?' She snorted. 'Of course you are. We'll manage the fire. Only books that have duplicates will get destroyed and we'll remove the others.'

I didn't know where to begin. 'That's theft, Psycho. Remember, you Alphas are all about not actually stealing or breaking the timeline. I'm pretty sure you swore an oath or something. Whatever the hell that means, as far as you're concerned. Oh yes. It means sod all. Your word isn't worth spit.' I was on a roll now. I was so incensed by the idea of someone purposefully burning books to hide the theft of other books. It was wrong from every angle.

'Besides which, there isn't an actual fire, stupid. This is a drill. You wouldn't be accelerating anything. You'd be starting one.'

She glared at me as she realised her plan would not work.

'I can't wait for the authorities to watch this footage back home and realise that you are still exactly the same old Clio.'

She laughed. 'Now who's being stupid? We don't have our braces on. The connection to our contacts is currently offline. I could break your neck right now and jump back full of sorrow at your regrettable accident.'

Her smile was thin and cold and contained far too many teeth. I felt a moment of fear, then brushed it off. 'You think they'd believe you? And who would be left to help Neith recover? Remember, it's my brain that spliced with Neith. I imagine the engineers still have subroutines they want to run on me to see if they can map her language paths. That's going to be pretty hard if my body is on Beta.'

She glared at me, then stalked off towards a bench, and I watched her go. I had no desire to be any closer to her, but I wasn't going to let her out of my sight. The bells stopped the moment she sat down, and I had the juvenile pleasure of watching her immediately spring back up as she hastened towards me. As we walked in, she cleared her throat.

'New plan. You and I will work together. We have a shared goal, and that's Neith. Sod the quantum facility, Neith is all I care about, and they are not locking her away while I have any breath in my body. Agreed?'

I shrugged. Of course I agreed, but working in partnership with Clio was proving to be a nightmare. However, Rami's belief that I was safe with Clio had borne out, and when it came to Neith, we were united. No matter how wrong that felt.

'Julius. Do we have a deal?'

I nodded. I was too petty to shake her outstretched hand, but I could certainly work with her for Neith's sake.

When we got back to the table, the guard from earlier was looking at our laptops.

'Can I help you with anything?' Clio had moved to the guard's side and was now towering over him. She was also standing too close. He took a quick step back.

'I thought I heard it buzzing.'

'And?'

'And I thought it might be—'

'What? A bomb?' Clio laughed loudly and a few students looked our way. She held the laptop aloft and waved it around. 'This man here thinks the latest iMac is a bomb.'

'This, mate,' she said, addressing the guard again and pulling a proper London accent, 'is state of the art. The only things it's going to explode is your brain!'

There were some laughs now from the crowd and I guessed that this guard was not popular.

'You're creating a disturbance,' said the guard, trying to regain control. 'The rules state—'

'I think you'll find, mate, that the rules say that this library has a policy of non-discrimination on all grounds including,' she paused and smiled sweetly at him, 'race and gender.'

And he collapsed. In the face of Clio's provocation he knew she had moved him into a perilous position.

'I was checking if the laptop was safe,' he stammered, then, deciding he wanted no more of this, he quickly left the room. An hour later, we did the same. I prayed this was the last time I had to work with Clio.

Chapter 11 - Julius

Back in the step room, we handed over our braces and headed off to the infirmary. It had been a textbook step, but we still needed to wait onsite as a safety measure after the implementation of new technology. In my opinion the engineers were being overcautious. It had been the smoothest step I had ever experienced, but the engineers were being cautious. Still, what did I know? I headed for the canteen. Clio had asked if she could spend her time in the contemplation gardens on her own. Which was fine with me. There were a lot of familiar faces when I arrived. I knew everyone was excited that soon, they could also step. I sat down next to Sabrina, and was about to tell her about the step, when Ludo came over and offered me beer. It was a bit early in the day, but it had been a successful jump, and was worth celebrating. Hopefully, the linguists now had everything they needed to recalibrate Neith's language cortex.

Pulling up a chair, Ludo sat down and took a swig out of the bottle.

'Julius, can we ask you a few questions?'

I looked around and noticed that a few other people beyond him had gone quiet. Exactly how many was "we?" I smiled. No doubt they wanted to know how the new step felt.

'Fire away.'

'It's about the gods.'

I put my beer down carefully and scanned the room. Pretty much everyone was listening to what I was going to say next. Either explicitly, their faces poised and attentive, or surreptitiously, their backs to me as they ate and drank at a different table, heads slightly turned my way. Had this been a lecture back in Cambridge, I would be in my element. I would engage, throw questions out, challenge preconceptions. Shake things up a bit in the more rigid minds, try to guide the more frenetic ones into a more rigorous approach. But here? With these individuals and now, after I had witnessed the terrifying reality of the gods, I didn't know what to say. Theirs wasn't the only reality torn to shreds.

'What do you want to know?' This was going to be tricky. I had gone from expert to novice in a matter of hours. 'And remember, the beings we encountered have been classified as G.O. Dimensional Subjects.'

Ludo brushed the acronym aside. 'Who come from your Earth.'

'No.' I cleared my throat. That may have come out too sharply, given how five people recoiled. 'In our culture, we certainly refer to them, but no one has ever actually seen them. They don't live on our Earth. We know of them, but given recent events here on Alpha it's obvious they aren't ours. I suspect, like this Earth, they once visited my Earth, maybe staying for a while, given their length of influence on early societies.'

'But you still have gods today?' Ludo looked confused.

'Yes,' I said slowly. I was moving into territory that I now felt desperately uncomfortable with. I had been quite complacent in my agnostic stance. It felt a good place to stand in the absence of evidence, but now I had evidence and felt at sea.

'So no one believes in gods anymore?'

'No. Millions of people believe the Abrahamic faith system, it's the largest in the world. Plus, there are many other belief systems.'

'And have you ever seen those gods?'

'Well, it's a system based on a single God with angels, prophets and trinities, rather than a plethora of gods.'

'And if people don't see them, then how do they talk to them?'

'They pray.'

There was a moment of silence whilst I offered up my own silent prayer that we could stop talking about gods. I felt like a charlatan. My entire academic career was built on a granite bedrock that had turned into sand.

'So,' said Ludo carefully. 'There's a lot of praying and there are no god visitations?'

I nodded. I wasn't sure where he was going with this, but the crowd was beginning to smile. I really didn't want to have a discussion on the power of invocation.

'I understand.' Ludo was smiling now. 'In order to keep these gods away, we need to pray to them.'

The room broke into an excited little hubbub of conversations as small groups started discussing the merits of this idea and seemed to agree with it. What the hell had I started?

'Um, guys, I don't think it works like that.' What did I know? But using prayer to repel gods seemed counterintuitive. 'During the battle, we noticed that paying attention to the subjects actually helped them gain strength, like you were feeding them when you thought about them.'

Some chap at the back of the room actually slapped his hands over his head, pushed back his chair, and quickly left by the side door. A blast of warm air filled the air-conditioned room, and the looks on the faces in the crowd went from excitement to fear in seconds.

'They aren't coming back.' I had to raise my voice over the panicked murmurs. 'Firenze made that very clear. She is more powerful than them, and she said this Earth was off-limits.'

'Firenze is a most powerful god.'

'She's not a god.' In my head, I heard Terry Jones squawking about messiahs and laughed. My audience looked at me in disappointment.

'This isn't funny, Julius,' said Sabrina. 'You may have grown up with this, but we are still trying to understand what has happened, and what it means to us and our society.'

'You're right. I apologise and I wasn't laughing at this situation. I was laughing at an old memory that jumped into my head.' I looked around the room. 'I'm sure you've all had that happen?'

There were some nods, and their positions seemed to relax. Everyone was now looking at me. There was no pretence of carrying on with private conversations.

'The thing is, Firenze was born just like you and me. Then, through a series of cybernetic and genetic modifications, her brain and body were altered, using technology that none of us understand. But she is sort of human, like any of us. Just with some extra modifications.'

'She turned into a flock of swallows and destroyed a god.'

'Okay, some *incredible* modifications. And she understands quantum reality in a way our engineers are only scratching at. But she is not a god.'

'Can we trust her?' asked Sabrina.

Another voice called out from the back. 'Can we trust the gods to stay away?'

I shook my head. 'I don't know, but for what it's worth, I doubt the gods will come back. Not when there are so many other Earths to visit.'

'But now that they've found us?'

'And are the other Earths as good as this one? I think not.'

I didn't catch who spoke, but it was pure Alpha pomposity. 'Honestly guys, they've moved on. They left my Earth, and I believe they have left this Earth as well.'

'So, if it wasn't prayer that got rid of them, what was it?' asked Ludo. 'Did Firenze visit your Earth?'

I shrugged. I really wasn't bringing anything helpful to this conversation.

'I have no idea. They just sort of died out. There are plenty of papers written about the decline of faith, but now, given that they appear to be real, I think some other factors must be at play.'

A voice piped up from the side of the room, but I couldn't see the individual. 'It was the Romans.' His words fell into a sense of awed silence.

The room fell quiet. The young voice piped up again as some people turned to look his way. I saw a young archivist. He seemed the quiet, unassuming sort, but I knew a fox when it was sitting in the henhouse.

'It stands to reason,' he continued. 'Wherever the Romans went, they assimilated the existing gods into their own. Slowly, their gods, and all gods, died out. And who else but the Romans were powerful enough to obliterate the gods? Maybe we've been looking at Romans the wrong way all these years? Maybe we should have been more grateful.'

I stared in astonishment as the room erupted into excited chatter. In the space of fifteen minutes we had gone from prayers to keep gods at bay, to the Romans had vanquished them. It wasn't even lunch, and I appeared to have witnessed the birth of a new philosophy.

'That's not what happened.' I tried to shout over the hubbub, but no one wanted to hear me. They were too caught up on the idea that the terrors of their childhood may be the saviours of their adult nightmare. I tapped Sabrina on the shoulder as Ludo was engaged in a frenetic conversation, detailing the Roman's merits and detractions.

'The Romans did not kill the gods.'

She smiled. 'If you say so, I will agree with you, Julius. You understand this better than any, but look at their faces.'

The excitement was palpable. 'For the first time in ages, these people have something they can hope with.'

'But they beat them. It was custodians and curators and everyday citizens that fought and won. Not Romans.'

'I know that, and soon they'll remember that and calm down. This is just people letting off steam. Don't worry. The idea that Romans will save the day is silly, and by the afternoon that's what everyone else will say too.'

After a quick hug, I left the canteen and called Minju. Given how busy she was, I was always flattered that she answered straightaway. I made sure to only call her at work if I felt it was urgent.

'Julius.' I could hear her smiling down the line. 'How can I help you?'

'It's the new entertainment feeds. I think they are being interpreted the wrong way.'

'How so?'

I explained what had just happened and was relieved when Minju started laughing.

'Oh my, Julius. You know I am the Romans' number one fan. But god killers? That's a step too far, even for me.' She chuckled some more, and I began to feel a tad foolish.

'Trust me. People are looking for answers. By the afternoon, they'll be onto something else. Dragons, maybe?'

Now we both laughed, and I apologised for wasting her time and promised to call in for tea.

In the meantime, I had a book I wanted to finish and was heading out with some of the guys for drinks later. As I walked back to my apartment, I was in a great mood. Disaster was staring me straight in the face and I was humming *In the Jungle*.

Chapter 12 - Julius

The following day, I headed over to Minju's office. Despite her new offices in the central administration buildings, she still preferred the archives, tucked down in the basement. I liked it down in the tunnels, away from the unrelenting heat and sharp sunlight.

We had got into the habit of weekly lunches and would chat about world history. My version of it. It was fascinating to compare how the two worlds divided, and I loved playing the What If game with live data. She adored my empires. I was fascinated with her academics.

I knocked on the door and entered the room to the smell of steamed fish and a citrus. That was the other reason I loved coming here. Her cooking was fabulous, and she never offered me insects.

'I've been thinking about what you said last week,' said Minju, pouring me a cup of green tea.

This was what I admired about her. Straight into debate. She had such a stimulating mind.

'I said a lot of things last week.'

I sank down and looked around a room that was now almost as familiar as my own apartment. Lots of artefacts on the shelves that should clearly have been in boxes, labelled and filed. Minju had decorated her space with them instead. And why not? Her own tiny gallery, safe and secure.

'You said it's remarkable that a society brought up on academic principles, full of curiosity and wonder, should be so blinkered. And it got me thinking. What did you mean?'

I shrugged. This was at the heart of this brilliant, kind, caring society. They had somehow allowed their critical reasoning facilities to stagnate. I cleared my throat. 'The engineers. They clearly manipulated scientific discourse for centuries, but why were they never challenged? Where were the dissenters, the rabble rousers? Where are your free thinkers? Is it possible that because you haven't faced adversity, you became complacent?'

'I don't think that's a fair assessment,' said Minju as she placed the fish in the steamer. 'Maybe we took our eye off the ball...'

'Even now, people are coming to bizarre conclusions. I was in the canteen yesterday... Well, you know what I told you. Who in their right mind would think the Romans got rid of the gods?'

'It makes sense to me.'

I looked at her in astonishment.

'That is to say, I can understand the reasoning. This society has no experience of the Roman Empire. It fizzled out before it became an empire. They also had no experience of gods, until they did. And now they understand them to be real. So you can forgive them for thinking Beta Earth saw them as real as well.'

I put my cup down. I was waving my arms around and I didn't want to splash anything. 'But the rise of the Catholic Church was long after the Romans. In fact, you could class it as another empire.'

'Indeed, but you have the benefit of growing up with your knowledge base. We haven't.' Minju put her knife down. 'We are seeing the Romans in a new light. At the same time, we are exercising our critical minds, that you accuse us of not using, and we are questioning everything. Don't judge us harshly if we make mistakes along the way.'

I slumped back on the sofa. 'I'm not judging, I'm—'

'Judging. Yes, you are. And who can blame you? We have lost our way, but I feel the tide is changing. The engineers held society in their thrall for a long time. Now that grip has gone, and we are trying to find a new path.'

I scratched my chin. 'A tidal surge can be a dangerous thing.'

'Not if you know it's coming, and you know where it's going.' She grinned at me as she served the fish.

'No one knows the future,' I said as my mouth began to water. 'You guys specialise in the past. Who knew a year ago that a coup was on the cards? Or that the gods were quantum beings?'

I walked over to the table and poured us both another cup of tea. The teapot was made of glass with exquisite silver threads running through it. Easily five hundred years old, I had no idea how it was made. Little things like this were a daily reminder of how evolved their society was and yet sometimes they acted like naïve fools.

Minju placed a plate in front of me. The fragrance of lemon, limes and sea bass caressed my senses, and I exhaled contentedly. Beautiful objects, stimulating conversation, and delicious food.

She returned my smile. 'Yes, the gods were certainly unplanned for. But sometimes we can see the direction of travel and plan for it.' Minju sat down opposite me, but didn't pick up her fork. 'Which is why I need to draw your attention to an issue that is ongoing, and may not be travelling in a direction you desire.'

I was about to place my fork in my mouth, but I didn't like the sound of this.

'It regards Neith,' she said. 'As you know, her recovery is slow and her mental and physical state is chaotic. I know you've been visiting her, trying to get the doctors to prolong her waking time. But they are concerned, as am I.'

I placed my fork on the table. 'I think it's good for Neith. It gives her time to stabilise. No wonder she is unhinged when she first wakes up. Her agitation is also understandable.'

Minju held her hand up. 'Did you hear that she attacked me yesterday?'

I hadn't heard that, and I ate a forkful in silence, trying to process the information. I thought Neith's violent protests were behind her. If they were still ongoing, maybe I was fooling myself that she was on the mend.

'Were you hurt?' The idea of Neith, a curator, attacking an elderly lady, was appalling.

'It was nothing. Koda Bitsoi was able to intervene, and then the medics and custodians rushed in. But I was shocked. I had heard she was improving. Bitsoi tells me this might now be her long-term state of mind.'

I resumed eating, but now the food was tasteless. Just something to chew. The conversation was becoming uncomfortable. It was hardly Minju's fault that she was the bearer of bad news, but I felt churlish and resentful. If I didn't engage, maybe she would stop talking.

'The thing is, my dear, that if the language fix doesn't work, the consensus is that Neith will be placed into a long-sleep. Her attack yesterday made the physicians' minds up. I tried to argue for her because I know how much she means to you, but I wonder if I'm not working in her best interests.'

I leant across the table and gripped her hand.

'You must. You must keep fighting for her. I am amazed that you would after she attacked you, but trust me, this language patch will work. It just has to.'

***

Minju watched as Julius left the room. It hadn't been as enjoyable as usual. Normally, conversation was fast and

91

furious as they laughed back and forth, debating and second-guessing random events in each Earth's histories. Today, though, had to be done. Picking up the plates, she ran them under the hot water. Julius and Neith were a dangerous partnership. They had proved time and time again that they worked together efficiently, and could back up each other's instinctive leaps. Minju needed them split up permanently. She had reviewed his step with Clio, and it had been all she could have hoped for. They set each other on edge, both making poor choices to assert dominance, constantly needling the other. They would never be the team that Julius and Neith were. Too often, they had destroyed her plans. Now she had to eliminate their threat before she made her move on this society.

She had been so close, but Grimaldi and the quantum beings had screwed it all up. But now she had more quantum technology at her fingertips, and knew exactly how to use it. She just had to make sure no one got in the way.

Julius and Neith combined were a threat, but if she could remove just one, that should be okay. Julius was the easier target to remove, but she was fond of him. Neith, on the other hand, was almost disposed of anyway. Why push water uphill? Send Neith to long-sleep and Minju could continue her lunches with Julius. Who knows? She might even be able to involve him. A Beta individual understood the power of a military empire and the need for it. She flicked on the air-dry switch and left the dishes to dry as she pottered around the room, straightening it up. As she whistled to herself, she realised she was happy. Either Neith or Julius would have to go and it looked like it was going to be Neith.

Chapter 13 - Julius

That evening I had drinks with Rami, Jack and Sabrina. I assured them that Clio had been a model citizen, although an unreformed one. I didn't mention her suggestion that we burn down the library, but I pointed out that she was simply acting contrite. I had discussed it with Rami earlier and he suggested for I keep that little gem to myself. There was no point in scaring the curators. Burning libraries was something of a sore point in Alexandria.

'But how is that even possible?' asked Sabrina. 'You can't fake those results.'

'The methods only work if you really want them to,' said Jack, and Rami agreed. Jack got up from the table and collected our drinks from the server. As he returned, I noticed he re-positioned himself and was now sitting next to Sabrina. She thanked him and held his eye a fraction longer than was necessary, then turned and continued talking to Rami.

'Not everyone survives the Bokbok method, though?'

'Not everyone is Clio,' said Jack. 'She has travelled further than any of us and spent a year in the company of a quantum dweller, namely Anansi, the trickster god. Who knows what she learnt?'

Sabrina nodded intently, paying attention to Jack's words. They would make a good couple, similar age, and I thought they would bring out the best in each other.

Sabrina was overcautious. Jack was all over the place. Plus, they were both kids. They needed some fun in their lives.

'Back home, the best sort of lie is the truth, or the one you believe,' I said. 'I reckon Clio is more than capable of just going along with the tests. Then later shrugging off the re-conditioning.'

'That would be very hard work,' said Sabrina dubiously.

'I don't think anyone in their right mind could accuse Clio Formerly-Masoud of laziness,' said Rami. 'I worked with her for years, and she is brilliant. It's easy to assume if you are bad, you must be stupid.'

I thought about what he said. I didn't think that at all, and I doubt any Beta individual would either. It was just the Alphas that had this weird notion of good equalling clever.

As I headed home, the sun had set, and the cicadas were busy chittering away on the warm breeze. I nodded to a few people I recognised and smiled to myself. I was finally fitting in, or at least, people had finally stopped pointing at me and nudging. Well, mostly.

'Julius!'

I turned around and was delighted to see Shorbagy heading towards me with another custodian dressed in yellow. Shorbagy had been one of the first people I got to know when I arrived and, given my daily transgressions, we soon became regular acquaintances. When I finally understood all their tiny misdemeanours and learnt to behave like a model citizen, I saw less of him, but by then, we had become friends. Shorbagy still watched me carefully, but I think we both saw the humour in our interactions. I certainly enjoyed his company.

His companion was looking less approachable. She appeared to be in her mid-twenties with straight black hair, cut into a short bob that fell just below her ears. To match the severe cut, she sported a serious expression. The white sash over her uniform told me she was a probationary. I had seen a lot of those in the past few months. Losses had been high for both curators and custodians. Take-up in recruits was higher for the custodians, though.

'Greetings to your house,' said Shorbagy, uttering the standard greeting. 'How lovely to see you.'

Greetings to your house was just a phrase, but it always made me smile. Maybe it was the newness of the saying in my ears. I liked it every time someone wished me blessings to my heart and home. Whereas for them it was almost a throw away sentence.

'Hello.' said Shorbagy. 'You are drifting.'

I laughed. 'Yes, I was. My apologies. I was just thinking how beautiful words can be.'

'They are indeed.' He turned to his companion. 'Florence Nanzala, this is Julius Strathclyde, Curator and Scholar.'

I smiled at her. 'Although, most people call me Blue.'

'I am not afraid of your name, Julius.'

I have to confess, I gave a small double take and raised my eyebrows at Shorbagy, who simply shrugged.

'Well, good for you.' Thinking about it, fewer people were calling me Blue these days, but I hadn't really noticed it until she put it so bluntly. I tried to think what to say. I couldn't fall back on the weather. Isn't the weather hot and sunny? Yes, and what about yesterday? Hot and sunny. Have you heard the forecast? Hot and sunny. You don't say. That really was the smallest of small talk. Instead, I went for the obvious.

'So, are you enjoying the job?'

She considered the question, then nodded. 'Yes. I had never thought to be a custodian. I was a gardener, then after the coup I got involved in the Adaptation Department, and from there I realised I wanted to get more engaged in my society.'

'You had no interest in being a curator?'
She looked directly at me. Her forehead was furrowed, and her intensity was slightly overwhelming. 'No. When they come again, I will fight them here.'

'I'm sorry, who do you mean by they?' I couldn't think who she was thinking of. Was she expecting another coup?

'Betas. If I went to Beta, how could I not want to take action?'

Well, that was alarming.

'You do know that during the battle, the enemy forces comprised of your own citizens and quantum beings?

97

Neither of whom came from Beta.' I tried to sound reasonable, but my tone may have been a tad sharp as she quickly responded.

'Loki, Anansi, Thor, Athena. These are your gods.'

'They used to be yours, as well,' I said, trying to count to ten. 'Have you been to the Valley of the Kings? You have statues of Anubis and all the others.'

Well, not now they didn't, or fewer anyway. In the battle's aftermath, many of the statues were destroyed by mobs fearful that stone could somehow animate itself.

'The battle had absolutely nothing to do with Beta Earth,' I said. 'It was purely an Alpha engagement.'

She took a step back from me and gave a small bow as she bit her lip. 'I have offended you.'

'Not in the least. I was just setting the record straight.'

'You are correct and I was foolish.' Before I could reply, she turned to Shorbagy. 'There are some tourists over there. May I greet them and offer assistance?'

Shorbagy nodded, and as Nanzala left, he exhaled deeply. 'Sorry about that. She can get somewhat fervent at times. Her heart's in the right place, but sometimes her head isn't. She lost a few family members in the battle, and feels guilty that she wasn't able to protect them.'

'Poor kid.'

'Indeed. I suspect that soon she's going to apply for Red.'

That didn't seem wise to me. The reds were the military branch of the custodians. The yellows, like

Shorbagy, took care of civil day-to-day engagement. Reds got involved when it went wrong, which until recently was rare.

'Will they take her? She seems quite fervent.'

'Absolutely. There have been calls to increase the original number of reds. Yellow numbers are already almost back to what they were, so, if she wants to go, they will welcome her with open arms.'

'I'm glad you are nearly back to full strength,' I said, happy that at least some sectors were recovering. 'We are still woefully understaffed.'

We walked slowly along the concourse in the direction of the harbour.

'Well, you are much more specialised. The training is longer, plus the whole quantum thing has now taken on a new hue. So to speak. In the minds of the public, curators have gone back to being a very high-risk occupation that is now even scarier.'

'But we don't have gods flying around at home.'

'But you do have wars. And now people have direct experience of what that means.'

For a society built on peace and culture, the previous conflict had been brutal. Until then, they had enjoyed their thrills vicariously via the Beta media sources. Bullets and laser blasts were thrilling when safely contained within a screen or projection. Reality sucked.

Florence Nanzala rejoined us, scowling. 'Ghouls. They wanted to see any evidence of the battle. I sent them to the memorial and reminded them of how many had died.'

Battlefield tourism. Was there nothing new under the sun?

'Were you friendly?' asked Shorbagy, his tone was stern. Clearly, they had been through this before.

'Yes. They even offered me a commendation for my helpfulness.' She proffered her brace to Shorbagy, where it displayed her gratitude chip.

'Well done. Now we had best get on.'

With a small nod of his head, they set off and I continued on my way. I understood battlefield tourism, but had never indulged. Except for research. I chided myself for being superior and decided to change into my running kit and get some exercise. An evening run along the boardwalk would be perfect. The past few days had left me unsettled. Alpha citizens were out of sorts, shaken from their unchallenged lifestyle, and looking to Beta as the source of their discomfort. I didn't like where this was going. Suddenly, I had an overwhelming desire to call for a dog to run alongside me. Things must have been bad if I was missing Shuck, the devil's dog that would steal your soul away. Or take up too much of the bed, depending on his mood.

Chapter 14 - Minju

Minju knocked on the heavy cedar doors and waited for a response. The pharaoh loved to make people wait, and Minju knew how to work this to her advantage. Eventually, she heard Nolyny Cleeve call out that she could enter. She pushed the doors open. Nolyny looked up and leapt to her feet, rushing around the side of the desk.

'Minju, please, you don't need to wait. How rude you must think me.' The pharaoh was flustered and waved Minju towards the cane benches, strewn with embroidered cushions and throws. Minju waited until Nolyny had arranged the cups and tore some leaves for the pot.

'Oh, tea?' Minju picked at the tassels on the cushion. 'Yes, well, why not then?'

The pharaoh looked at her askance. 'You don't want tea?'

'I'm sure that will be perfect.'

Nolyny relaxed and placed the kettle under the hot waterspout. Holding the teapot carefully as the boiling water hit the mint leaves. The room filled with their fragrance.

'I just thought we could have something a bit stronger, it being the end of the day. But a tea will be perfect,' said Minju, her tone light and dismissive.

Nolyny put the teapot on the tray and quickly moved it away. 'What a good idea. What would you like? Wine, beer, saki? Something stronger? Cocktails? Oh, cocktails would be fun, wouldn't they?'

The pharaoh was now in a state of mild anxiety, which suited Minju perfectly. Over the past six months, Minju had managed to get Nolyny to rely on her for all her major decisions, and consult her on every piece of policy. Minju was very careful to play her role down amongst her colleagues, but always made sure that the public saw them together at every possible occasion.

'Maybe not late enough for cocktails. How about some red wine? Do you still have that Ribera?'

Minju hid her smile as Nolyny visibly sagged in relief that she had successfully offered her guest a drink.

'Actually, I'm glad you called by. I've just had the reports from the linguists regarding the Welsh language module.'

And why do you think I'm here? thought Minju.

'Good news, I hope?'

Nolyny poured the red wine into a glass and held it out. 'Not exactly.'

Minju tasted her wine, focusing on the flavours of the Spanish grapes. This was the best possible news, but she would never let that show.

'Damn. What's gone wrong?'

'It's the age of Neith's Welsh. She seems to have acquired large sections that are far older than anything the library had digitised. The linguists are very excited that we may touch on old-Welsh as well as—' She flicked up a holo-screen and scrolled through the document. '—proto-Celtic.' She flicked the screen away. 'They are very excited about that.'

Minju sipped her drink and looked thoughtful. 'But this sounds like good news?'

'It would be, if Tiresias could map it, but it seems the curators failed to get enough material.'

Minju went still, then placed her glass back on the table. 'I believed they retrieved all that was available?'

Nolyny rushed to excuse herself. 'I meant no criticism. I simply meant there isn't enough source material to help re-programme Neith's brain.'

'Oh dear. Well, thank the stars we can keep her in long-sleep until we are better able to help her.'

Minju leant back on the couch and relaxed. With Neith out of the way, she could crack on with her plans.

'Only, the engineers have a suggestion,' said the pharaoh, 'and the Chancellor seems to think it will work.'

Sam Nymens had been promoted to Chancellor of Alexandrian Mouseion. It had been a huge step up from Captain of the Curators, but no one could say he hadn't deserved it, and he did the job splendidly. It grated Minju that she hadn't been able to get a candidate of her choosing in place, but matters had moved so swiftly that she wasn't ready. Had she known that Sam would be appointed, she would have worked harder. The man was

103

as incorruptible as they came, and he thought the society was perfect as it was. She was working on Githumbi and Giovanetti. Both ladies knew trouble was in the air. They had opposed her in the coup, and recognised how narrowly they had won. They would be alert to any future disturbances.

The silence dragged on, and Minju realised Nolyny was waiting for her to speak.

'Wouldn't it be best to discuss it with them? I'm honoured that you would discuss it with me, but am I the right person?' She took another sip of wine and noticed that Nolyny had already refilled her own glass. 'I don't want to overstep the mark.'

Nolyny shook her head vehemently. 'Of course you wouldn't. You are so careful, but it really helps to have a friend to confide in.' She looked at Minju hopefully.

'Then if it's just in the name of friendship...' She smiled at Nolyny warmly. 'What's their idea and what's the problem? We all want Neith fully recovered, don't we?'

'Well, the curators have suggested going back to one of the early medieval libraries and borrowing some of their scrolls. The engineers have said that the new stepper technology is at ninety-five per cent efficiency, and that it is feasible.'

She looked hopefully at Minju, who gulped her wine in annoyance. Re-filling her glass, Minju paused and tried to look thoughtful.

'So, what they are saying is on the one hand, we can put Neith safely into long-sleep and wait for technological improvements. Or on the other hand, we prolong her suffering whilst we send two more curators off, using equipment that isn't fully stabilised, in order to help the linguists with an experiment?'

Nolyny's eyes were wide with alarm. 'Bast! When you put it like that - the engineers didn't make it sound so dreadful.'

Minju laughed softly and refilled Nolyny's glass. 'And I'm sure they are right. They have always had society's best interests at heart.' She paused and made a show of thinking something through. 'I just wonder if sometimes they forget the individuals?'

Nolyny nodded emphatically. 'I know! What about hiding the existence of other Earths from us for so long? Even that Julius Strathclyde, a Beta, knew more than us.'

Minju nodded her head as the pharaoh waffled on about how dreadful the engineers were, until Minju had had enough.

'Well, it's your decision, and I'm sure the engineers and the curators know what they are doing.'

The bottle of wine was empty and Nolyny was about to open a second when Minju stood up.

Nolyny jumped up and leant closely towards Minju. 'I'm sure they do, too. But is it the right thing? That is the question. They send me these long-winded reports and hope that I'll be bounced into simply agreeing with them. But oh no, not with my good friend Minju, by my side.'

Minju turned back from the door. This was too much. She couldn't have anyone thinking that she was steering the democratically elected pharaoh.

'You mistake me. I think the engineers are right, we must try to save Neith. But if you disagree, I am certain that will be the correct decision. After all, you are the pharaoh and you have led us magnificently these past six months. A beacon in the night.'

Nolyny smiled soppily, and Minju left quickly before she laughed in her face.. The dice were loaded, now all Minju could do was wait to see which way the pharaoh rolled them.

The easiest option would be to shut Neith away. But if Julius and Clio failed to return from the mission, Minju would miss them. Both had talents she would love to make use of. If only she could get them to see things her way.

She was certain she could never turn Neith. Clio she could never trust, and Julius was a loose cannon. Well, now she just had to wait and see if the mission went ahead and if it did, if it was a success.

Chapter 15 - Julius

A week later, we were all back in the briefing room. There were so few of us that we were now all briefed on the same shift. An engineer began with a report on how our step had gone, which was terminally dull. I had hoped to see Jack, but he was far too busy to give briefings. That kid's rise had been meteoric.

'In conclusion. Live steps are as stable and safe as they are going to be within an acceptable margin of error.' I loved those caveats. He continued. 'Steps back in time to a geospatial point of our choosing have a greater range of error, but so far those have also been within a corresponding margin of error. In addition to which, accuracy has been increased to excellent levels.'

He went on to explain that steps were now ninety per cent pinpoint accurate, five per cent were within an acceptable margin of error, and the last five per cent were batshit crazy. They were working around the clock to reduce those odds, but the technology was new and occasionally threw a curveball.

'Excuse me.' Sabrina had her hand raised. 'Please, can you elaborate what the acceptable margin of error is for the five per cent?'

There was something about the way she asked that suggested she already knew the answer, but wanted to make sure everyone else did as well.

Sabrina and Jack must have the most fascinating pillow talk. I glanced over to the engineer, who seemed annoyed by Sabrina's intervention. He tapped on the screen in front of him then looked out at us.

'An acceptable margin of error is up to a month prior to the event, and up to three hundred miles from your destination.'

We looked at each other. We could live with those parameters. Not pleasant, but similar to what we had already encountered on previous steps.

The engineer continued. 'All of your braces have been calibrated, and you are instructed to return immediately if you fall outside of these safe parameters. If within them, it will be your call whether you wish to proceed. Obviously, the ninety per cent window is the optimal setting and the engineers are working every day to increase this percentage.'

Rami cleared his throat and stepped forward. 'Thank you, Engineer 365-Brown.' He winced as Rami used his new title. One of the new First Engineer's directives had been to make the engineers more approachable. This included removing their numerals and returning their names. Some engineers were finding the adjustment tricky.

'Now, if I can just remind everyone, regardless of the margin of error, if you need to return, do so immediately. Gone are the days of staying in dangerous scenarios because we might not get another opportunity. Now we can simply step home and try again. There is no need to unnecessarily risk our lives. Especially as there are so few of us.'

'The energy involved in a step is quite significant,' said the engineer in a frosty manner.

Rami's look was equally glacial. 'And how much energy is involved in replacing a human?'

Seeing that the engineer was actually about to start calculating, Rami shook his head and turned back to us.

'Right. Three live steps this week.' There was a general grumble in the room. 'I know you all want to head back in time, but for now, except for one pair, that will have to wait. The odds aren't there yet.'

The engineer stepped forward, frowning. 'Statistically speaking—'

'Yes, yes,' Rami cut him off, 'very low risk. But unless it's an ironclad guarantee of one hundred per cent, I'm not risking my curators. And even then I wouldn't send them, because I don't trust ironclad guarantees. One hundred per cent is never one hundred per cent.'

I smiled, watching the engineer flinch.

Rami rattled through the list for the live steps. 'Finally, Sabrina Mulweather and Ben Wakandi are going to step across and retrieve all Beta entertainment streams for the last six months.'

He smiled over at me. 'Seems like the powers that be are as anxious as I am to find out how some of those series ended.'

'Well done, Blue,' called out Ludo. 'Any recommendations? I don't think I can watch another rerun of *Downton Abbey*.'

The room burst into laughter.

'It depends what makes it onto the streams, but you are going to love *The Mummy*. Or maybe not.' I joined in the laughter. 'You might have had enough of ancient Egyptian curses and the like.'

'Mummy! Mummy! Mummy!' chanted Ludo as the others joined in. Nothing fazed the curators. Thinking of mummies, I suddenly thought of *Doctor Who* and realised they had some great viewing ahead of them. So far, only dribs and drabs had been released.

'Alright, calm down,' shouted Rami over the top of the chants, but he was smiling as well. We were getting back to normal, and that felt good. 'Now. I have news about Neith's language issues.'

I jerked in my chair and looked over to Clio. She was leaning forward, her eyes locked on Rami. For the past week neither of us had been allowed into the hospital, and every time I asked after Neith's health, I was told everything was in hand.

'Following the data retrieval from the Strathclyde-Formerly-Masoud Step, the linguistics department are very excited by the improvements that have been made in medieval Welsh language. They have been feeding the data sets into Tiresias, and developed an extensive model of language developments.'

110

'What about Neith?' snapped Clio. 'Have they fixed her?'

I leant forward and watched as Rami considered his next words. I knew it was bad news.

'There have been improvements, but no. Neith's language is still erratic and unintelligible.'

Clio jumped up, pushing her chair back noisily, as all eyes turned on her.

'Camel shit. I brought back the entire digital catalogue. That should have been enough.'

Any sense of Clio as a demure model citizen went out the window. Here was the Clio we all knew of old. I looked up at the ceiling, tempted to remind her that we *both* brought the archives back, but what was the point?

'Clio. I know this is disappointing—'

'It's not disappointing, it's fucking ridiculous.'

'Can it, Clio. If you let me finish. The authorities have been discussing this for a few days and decided to undertake a historical step back to the early twelve hundreds in Wales. The brief will be to borrow a number of ancient Welsh manuscripts and see if that works. But first, we needed to find out if you were willing. The technology is not quite at the stability levels—'

'When do I go?' snapped Clio as she grabbed her chair and sat down again.

I didn't care that she claimed the credit for retrieving the books from the National Library of Wales. I didn't care if she claimed all the credit, but she was not going alone.

'We go.' Now everyone looked back at me. 'She doesn't go alone. I'll be making the step as well, okay Rami?'

Sabrina raised her hand.

'Yes Sabrina?' Rami looked across at the young curator.

'Sir, you just said that type of step isn't safe yet?'

The engineer replied before Rami had a chance. 'Of course it is safe. The stepper is incredibly safe. We have tested and calibrated and—'

'I meant, is it safe for Julius and Clio? We have always been taught that a rest is required after submitting our brains to the quantum field. Surely, with this new technology, there are new risks following frequent exposure.'

The engineer replied again. 'They are perfectly safe. We engineers have been going back and forth daily for months now.'

'Yes,' muttered Sabrina, 'and you are the very pinnacle of normality.' Her sass was met with claps and whistles, and Rami had to settle the room down.

Clio had been sitting on the other side of the room, and now she spoke clearly. 'We are expendable. A renegade curator and a Beta. Who cares if we don't return?' She looked around the room and shrugged. Then, catching my eye, she winked. It was a bold statement, but she wasn't wrong and it made me uncomfortable.

'That's rubbish,' said Ludo. 'We are all curators together. It doesn't matter who you are, what you've done, or where you come from. If you are in this room, you are one of us. We are curators. We preserve!'

Hands slammed on tables, and the curators on either side of me were quick to reassure me they would grieve my loss deeply. I even believed them. I also believed that they would equally grieve Clio, although for the life of me I couldn't see why. Despite all their genuine protestations, I couldn't help wondering if Clio had the truth of it. Beyond these four walls, who would cry if we were gone?

'You are not disposable, Clio,' said Rami sharply. He then turned to Sabrina. 'Sabrina. They are perfectly safe. I wouldn't send them if they weren't. If anything, there is some speculation that their recent visit may establish a level of affinity.'

'Guinea pigs, then?' drawled Clio.

'If you like. But in a beneficial manner, and I know how much you want to serve and support your society, Clio.' Rami spoke calmly, but Clio heard the challenge in it and remembered to present a more docile version of herself.

'As you say. We preserve, and I serve, and am grateful to society for giving me the opportunity to make myself useful in any way that I can.'

Sabrina looked at Clio carefully, then shook her head. 'But are you certain? I am happy to volunteer in Julius's place.'

Good old Sabrina. I smiled across at her and mouthed a thank you, but Rami was adamant.

'He'll be fine. Besides, he and Clio seem to work well together. Let's leave it at that.'

Chapter 16 - Julius

Clio and I were standing side by side again in the step chamber. We'd been fully tested. The Beta time map up on the balcony hadn't flickered an iota during our last mission. Although, as we had stepped in real time, no flicker was expected. No one knew what the future held, so how could we disrupt it? Although, of course, we did our best to act as if we weren't there.

We were stepping back in time again, and to a time frame that had been decided by the engineers and curators, not allotted from the quantum algorithm. In theory, humanity was in command, not machine. I wasn't entirely comfortable with that. But again, this had been tested rigorously over the past six months, and Jack had laughed at me last night as he tried to reassure me that the maths was solid.

'Okay, positions, please,' an engineer called out from the gantry. Clio and I picked up our hessian sacks and lifted our hoods onto our heads. We were off to the thirteenth century and had a range of provisions in case the accuracy of the step location was off.

'You are calibrated for August 1205, Carmarthen Priory. Countdown proceeding.'

Clio and I hadn't spoken since yesterday's briefing. What was there to say? We would discuss strategies when we arrived. Anything beyond that was of no interest to either of us. All we had in common was disdain and distrust.

'Step through.'

I walked into the wall.

The rain was phenomenal and bitterly cold. I pulled my cloak even tighter around me and checked where Clio was. Again, she was standing beside me. Now though, she looked like a cat that had been dunked in an icy river. I smiled and checked my brace.

'Bloody engineers. When the hell are we?'

I wiped the rain off my face and shouted over the wind. 'Pinpoint accurate. August 1205, Carmarthen Priory.'

'It's bloody freezing. This can't be summer,' said Clio, shivering.

I grinned at her. 'Welcome to Wales.'

With a look that made me take a step back, she turned around and strode off in the direction of the priory. The foul weather meant no one else was around and, once we were in the shadow of a large oak, we could work out what to do next. All we had to do was make our way to the scriptorium, borrow a couple of books that were not on our list of known titles, and return home. This was stealing. There was no way to gild the lily, but it was for Neith, and we would return them once our boffins had scanned them.

The fact of the matter was that two hundred years later, the collection of books here at Carmarthen would be trashed by Owain Glyn Dwr in 1403.

'I don't know why we don't just jump to 1403,' I said, thinking about it. 'Then we can save and keep the books and it wouldn't be stealing.'

We were currently sheltering in the lee of the oak, and I was glad for the shade from my hood so Clio couldn't see me wince. It had been a stupid observation on my part, and confirmed her low opinion of me. We were after ancient texts. In another two hundred years they may have already deteriorated or been lost. Now was a golden age, when manuscripts were fresh and being duplicated at an astonishing rate across the monasteries of Europe.

'Sorry, that was stupid of me. Right, how do you suggest we get in?'

I wasn't sure what Clio was thinking, but she dismissed my apology and carried on.

'As planned. You are a visiting scribe from Cîteaux Abbey. It's a great honour that you would travel all the way from France to copy the Welsh manuscripts, yada yada yada. I will be your faithful companion.'

'Faithful and silent,' I stressed.

With her tall, athletic build, I suppose a blind man might mistake Clio for a man. However, they were likely to be too busy looking at the colour of her skin to pay any attention to what the skin enclosed. If they were to ask, I would say fists and venom.

'Faithful and silent,' she drawled. 'Well, let's get on with it. After you, oh noble one.'

We left the protection of the tree and made our way around to the front of the building. It was stone built and constructed for defence as much as shelter. Inside the walls there would no doubt be allotments and areas for livestock to roam, but out here it was just a wall of imposing stone. At one corner, I could see the rising tower of the priory church. The wind tugged at our cloaks, but their linings ensured we stayed nice and dry. Bless those little nanobots. There wasn't much to be done about our hair and faces though, unless we went to full shield. And I could just see the raised eyebrows reading the report if we explained why we went to full deployment: "It was wet."

I pulled the cloak around my sack manoeuvring the heavy load inside. Happily, the sack was imbedded with the same technology as our cloaks, but it didn't make the load any lighter. I would be happy to get shot of them as soon as possible.

'Are the books too heavy?' said Clio. 'Would you like me to carry them?'

Ignoring her, I strode towards the entrance.

The first set of guards standing hunched against the rain took one look at our monks' robes and waved us across the bridge. I looked down at the steep grass ditch surrounding the priory and thought how difficult it would be to storm this place. Happily, I was just going to rely on words. The next set of guards were less obliging than the first, but when I explained I had come from the illustrious Abbey of Cîteaux, and was here to visit the scriptorium, a runner was dispatched and soon the abbot appeared. I judged him to be newly appointed, as his robes were too long and whilst the hem of the cassock had been stitched up, his sleeves were still overlong and had a comical effect as they flapped in the wind. He was a dumpy little man with an amiable smile and a bald head. He clearly made up for this lack by sporting a magnificent long, red beard.

'Greetings, traveller. I am William of Monmouth, Abbot of Carmarthen Priory.'

We were still standing in the portico and, whilst not warm, we were at least no longer buffeted by the wind and rain. I pushed the hood back from my head and smiled at our host.

'Bless you and bless this house. My name is Brother Julius, and my companion is Brother Michael.'

I stopped abruptly as William stared into my face with unconcealed fascination.

'My eyes?'

The man nodded, and I recovered quickly. For some reason, my contacts were in, but not working.

'A blessing from God. When I was born, my mother, a noble woman from the house of Alvili, took me to Rome and presented me to our Holy Father. She asked if I was cursed, and he told her I was a gift. That through my face, man could see all of God's colours and hold all in balance.'

The abbot stared at me in wonder. Clio thankfully kept her head bowed.

'You met the pope himself?'

'Well, in truth, I was but a babe in swaddling cloth, but I fancy when I feel weak, I can still feel the touch of his hand as he anointed me with holy oil, and I am strengthened.'

The abbot looked at my forehead in wonder, as if he too could see the mark. Clio gave a little shudder, shaking her cloak, and he remembered himself.

'It is an honour to meet you, Brother Julius. How may we help you?'

A quick exchange established that we were here to copy some books and that, unfortunately, the scriptorium was currently out of bounds following a recent vow of abstinence. It seemed the monks had deemed themselves too proud and had chosen to spend a week in reflection on their sin of pride. As the scriptorium was the source of their pride, none were permitted inside until they had properly atoned.

This could have been viewed as bad luck, but I saw it as a blessing. I still hadn't worked out how I was going to convince a room full of monks to leave their beloved books and quit the joint. I myself hated to leave a great library and knew it would have been a struggle. Now all I had to do was get in. I was preparing to soft soap the man when Clio decided she had had enough. Pushing her hood off her face, she stared at the abbot.

'Are we to be turned away? As our Lord Jesus was.'

She had lowered her voice, and her beautiful tones had become rougher. The disdain was familiar.

The abbot stepped back in alarm.

'An infidel.'

Chapter 17 - Julius

The two men-at-arms quickly came to attention, and the harmonics of the gathering changed completely. Clio closed the gap between the two of them and stared down at him. His shortened stature was no match for her six feet.

'Do I look like an infidel?' she said.

It was all I could do not to laugh. Poor William, looking up at this terrifying spectre, could do nothing but shake his head slowly. I could see he was trying to find a way out of this, and I was worried that he might decide that the quickest way would be to hurl us off the drawbridge.

'Brother Michael. Please.'

Clio returned to my side. Her expression was almost blank as she looked around the portico. The barest curl of her lip was speaking volumes.

I smiled at William, pretending I hadn't even heard him say infidel. 'We have arrived unannounced, I see. A letter should have arrived by courier, but we appear to have outstripped it. Yesterday we woke up in a dreadful inn. We were not two miles away when we were set upon by bandits who stole our horses. We have been on foot ever since, and unforgivably out of temper.'

'Did you come via Abertawe?'

I nodded.

'Fearful reputation there. The lord is a scoundrel and is incapable of running his lands properly. You should have come straight up the river.'

I gave a gallic shrug, my palms raised in universal entreaty.

'We were blown off course. Our boat landed at Abertawe and we have been travelling ever since in joyful expectation of reaching Carmarthen Priory. Its reputation extends far past the borders of this land, and is spoken of in the highest terms from Cîteaux to Rome itself.'

I was waxing lyrical, trying to put everyone at ease after Clio's outburst. Not that I was exaggerating. Carmarthen held a magnificent collection of books during this period. The Black Book itself was said to have been written here. It was why we were here, after all. I continued to gently push.

'It is known for the warmth of its hospitality and the excellence of its scriptorium. We did not know that on reaching land we would have to pass through barbarians.'

The tension had calmed down. The men were flattered by my description. Now, if Clio would just keep her mouth shut, I could land this.

'Abertawe is in shocking repair. I will tell the Lord of Carmarthen of your difficulties on his return. Can we at least offer you hospitality for this evening?'

'You can, of course, and I accept most humbly. As you can see, we have no horse or belongings for you to accommodate.' I laughed. 'In the morning, we shall set off to the scriptorium at St David's or Tintern. Which do you think would be the more worthy recipient of this treasure?'

Now I played my ace. I gingerly placed my sack on the floor and retrieved a large leather-bound volume. Standing up, I held it in my palms and instructed Clio to open it and turn the pages. Our artificers had done a wonderful job, and I had rarely seen a more beautiful, illustrated manuscript. It was a Book of Days, burnished in gold leaf and painted with vivid reds and blues, paintings of daily life and celestial scenes. In this dull wet stone building with rain dripping off the grey edges, and muddy puddles forming at our feet, this book shone. As each page turned, there was another gasp of wonder and awe from William and the guards. I nodded to Clio and she closed the book as I placed it carefully back in my sack. Standing up again, I shook my head sadly.

'It truly is a thing of beauty, but I'll be honest with you.' I leant forward, lowering my voice so only he could hear me. 'It's damned heavy!'

He laughed as I grinned at him. 'I have three more here, though not so fine. All copied from the scriptorium of Cîteaux as a gift to yourself in exchange for copying some of your own fine books.'

Now Clio spoke. 'I will carry them. When the load becomes too heavy, Brother Julius. No matter how stony the road, it will be my honour. I have heard great things about St David's scriptorium. We should go there and stop trespassing on the hospitality of Carmarthen.'

Realising that he was about to lose a great treasure, as well as insult someone who had met the pope, whilst simultaneously enriching St David's, the poor man panicked.

'Please, you would be most welcome here. I will arrange to replace your losses, and quarters for you.'

I shook my head sorrowfully. 'I regret I cannot be idle in the service of my Lord. If I can't start working in your library immediately, at least I can be on the path towards St David's. My every day must be spent in honest endeavour. Waiting for your vow of abstinence to pass would be a sinful idleness on my behalf.'

Now the abbot was almost visibly back-pedalling as he wrung his hands together and smiled obsequiously. Unclasping his hands, he pulled on his beard, then came to a decision. 'In which case, I shall open the library for you today that you may start work immediately. We have vellum, inks and pens here that you may use, and by the time either man returns, you will have started work and be able to show them the fruits of your labour.'

'And offer them my gift from Cîteaux?' I asked, allowing a hopeful tremor to enter my voice.

'Indeed!'

Now everyone was smiling and as Clio and I followed William towards the scriptorium, I noticed she was whistling *The Queen of Sheba*.

'Aren't you worried about your little anachronisms being recorded?' I hissed and she turned back and smiled at me. The smile with all the teeth.

'The live monitoring isn't working. No error message, but not recording either. The engineers will have mud on their face when we get back. Two equipment failures!'

She turned back and caught up with the abbot, whilst I wondered about my personal safety. If the brace was acting up we might be in trouble.

We entered the castle proper and climbed a stone spiral staircase until we came on to a wooden corridor lit with torches. We were obviously in the main habitation wing. We walked along another corridor, up another staircase no less claustrophobic than the last, the cold seeping out of the stones. At the top was a single door and, as the abbot unlocked it, we all stepped into a room that made my heart sing with wonder. I was standing in a medieval scriptorium in all its glory, and I'm not ashamed to admit tears sprung to my eyes. I had been a scholar in Cambridge my whole academic career, and I had seen nothing so wondrous.

The flame from his torch sent shadows dancing around the bookshelves. Passing the torch tentatively to Clio, he headed over to the windows and removed the wooden boards. Fresh air and daylight swept into the room through the narrow slits in the wall, and the books sighed in enjoyment of the light, muted as it was.

'Thank you,' said Clio abruptly. 'You may leave now. We don't wish you to dishonour your vow of abstinence any further by remaining. If someone can call for us when food is served? Until then, we shall start working.'

'Can I show you—'

Clio cut him off. 'This scriptorium is a wonder and keeps to the same rules as our own at home. I can already see all that we need. Perhaps you could post someone at the foot of the staircase. Then, if we have need of anything, we can approach them?'

That was a good idea. It also allowed the abbot to monitor us without making it look like he was doing just that. Always helps to let the other side think they have the upper hand. It relaxes them.

As he closed the door I glared at Clio.

'Are you mad?' I challenged Clio. 'What part of *silent* did you not understand?'

'It was taking too long. They needed to be thrown off balance so you could offer them a way back and gain the upper hand.'

I narrowed my eyes. 'You did that deliberately?'

'Yes, of course. I can see you are good at flattery. Maybe you learnt it from Neith. Either way, we regularly did this.' Clio looked over her shoulder at me as she examined the shelves. 'I would unbalance them, then Neith would steer them back. Only this time, it would be to the position that we wanted, and they would think that they had come to the position of their own volition.'

127

'Good cop, bad cop?'

'All our custodians are good.'

'You know what I mean.'

'Yes, I do. And Neith has trained you well, I'll give her that.'

I fumed. 'I am quite capable of speaking. No one has to teach me how to be polite.'

'It's a waste of time. All that chatter.'

'Not all strength comes from your fists, you know.'

She looked at me and scoffed. 'Bast, now you even sound like Neith.'

'Shame she couldn't teach you a few more lessons. I don't know what your agenda is, but I'm here to save Neith.'

'What would you know?' Clio snarled. 'I'd do anything for that girl. I don't care who tries to stop me. Not that she appreciates it.' Clio smiled indulgently. 'She broke my sodding leg. Ended up in hospital overnight, then had to endure a week of therapy about how—'

I cut her off. '*We are all just a petal in a flower?*' It was the standard therapy they used when you are hurt by someone unaware of their actions.

'Seriously?' Clio looked at me afresh. 'Sweet Bast! What did you do to get to endure that tripe?'

'Tried to free Neith.'

Clio roared with laughter. 'What did Neith do?'

'Broke my wrist.'

Clio looked at me smugly. 'She shattered my femur in three places. She clearly knows which of us was the greater impediment to her escape.'

'That, or she likes me more,' I snapped back.

Clio's smirk turned back into a scowl. 'Whatever. Grab some books and let's get out of here.'

We split up and started at either end of the room. Removing books and opening each to see the contents. As we weren't as skilled in text as we were in speech, we were relying on our braces and our contact lenses to read the text and recognise anything in Welsh as opposed to Latin. What we really needed was a Welsh book that the brace couldn't properly translate, then we would know we were on the track to a missing linguistic link.

'Is your contact scanning properly?'

I nodded until she asked again.

'I don't have eyes in the back of my head. Do you think you could use your words, Shitfly?'

'Give it a rest, Psycho.'

I carried on scanning the books. My lens was working fine, thankfully. I had no idea why the colour filter had failed, and I wondered if I had picked up the wrong pair. I continued to open book after precious book. Each one I opened was in a form of vulgate Latin, with no rhyme or reason as to the subject matter. This meant the books were filed according to language rather than subject. No doubt the monks broke it down into subject matter within the language. Or maybe not. I had been in libraries where books were shelved according to size, some by colour, some by date of publication. Many old libraries had their own systems and often only the librarians themselves understood these systems.

'Found something!' said Clio.

I hurried over to join her, annoyed that she located them first. Standing at the same set of shelves, I picked up a book at random and the brace informed me this was indeed Welsh. I looked up and down the shelf and carefully removed a book that lay on its side. There were several, all similarly shelved. It was no bigger than the Lindisfarne Bible but looked tired and worn. Gently opening the limp leather casing, I could see the pages inside were vellum and written on in black gall ink. There were no illustrations, and whilst the writing was meticulous, the translation was almost gibberish.

'Bingo. The brace can only pick out twenty per cent of these Welsh words.'

We quickly looked through a few more and found what we guessed were a diary, a ledger, and a bible. Clio placed them in her artefacts case, whilst I tidied up the shelf to hide the gaps. I then placed our gifts on the lectern.

Within a year, the ink from these gifts would decay and all that would be left would be the vellum and leather.

'Time to go.' It was with relief that I realised my partnership with Clio was at an end. When we returned to

Alpha, I would request a new partner, and I was confident Rami would understand.

We returned to the wail of sirens.

Chapter 18 - Julius

As soon as we re-emerged in the step room, we could see the timeline up on the gantry showed a small time-splinter. A siren was wailing and staff were running around, tapping keyboards and shouting back and forth at each other. It wasn't a big splinter and it seemed to dwindle after a few hundred years, but it made that section of time extremely unstable. No one would be able to revisit that period of history. Given that included the Renaissance, arguably the rise of some of the world's greatest artistic movement, that was not a period of time we wanted in quarantine.

'Cat's teeth' swore Clio.

I looked across at her. She was already handing her brace and storage box to the waiting ground crew, swearing as she did so. Her eyes constantly watched the timeline. I handed my brace over as well, just as Rami burst through the door and told us to report to him immediately.

'When you say immediately, you want us to go through the bio scans first. Yes?' asked Clio.

Poor Rami. I could see his indecision. Fix the timeline as fast as possible, or make sure we were fit and healthy.

'Bio first, then my office.'

We headed towards the bio scans with Clio in a foul mood, barking at the staff to hurry up.

'It's not their fault, you know,' I called over to her from behind my body scanner. My blood had been pricked, I'd been squirted with nano-bacteria, and now I was feeling tingly all over. It was probably wrong to enjoy a medical procedure, but I always felt lovely and fresh after a bacteria shower. As unappealing as that sounded.

'What are you talking about?' snapped Clio.

'The staff, stop taking it out on them. They're working as fast as they can.'

'Nubi's balls, Shitfly. Stop sucking up to everyone. I don't give two spits for these people. We need to get back and fix your mess.'

'*My mess?*'

By the time we got back to Rami's office, we were sniping at each other like some married couple shortly before the axe incident. In the office I was disheartened to see not only Rami, but Sam and First Engineer. We really had screwed up.

'Okay,' said Sam, taking charge. 'Your braces are being processed as we speak, and the books are being scanned. Have you any idea what might have happened?'

'Micro-fracture, sir,' said Clio, now cold and efficient. 'The books we left behind could have triggered a conversation that triggered an action. The books we took could have been missed. This again could have resulted in a conversation-slash-action that we can't determine. Our appearance and subsequent disappearance may have created a ripple.'

The three leaders nodded their heads, but I felt I had to confess.

'It could have been me.'

Damn, I didn't like the way the First Engineer looked at me.

'Why am I not surprised?' She raised an eyebrow and languidly waved her hand at me. 'Continue.'

I spoke to Rami, ignoring her gaze. 'When I arrived, it looked like the colour filter on my contact failed. The abbot was startled by my eyes, and I had to make up a story about visiting the pope and being blessed by God.' I trailed off. It sounded insanely stupid, spoken out loud.

'It wasn't that,' said Clio. 'Curator Strathclyde dealt with a difficult situation quickly and chose a suitable story to explain himself. In fact, his story helped us gain quicker entrance into the priory.'

Well, that surprised me, but I knew when to stay silent. Sam turned to First.

'So they were dropped outside the priory, rather than inside, and suffered an equipment failure.'

'None of which should have caused a micro-fracture!'

Rami cleared his throat. A turf war wasn't required. 'No one said the step was foolproof, and equipment failures happen. We also have no evidence that the curators did anything wrong. Best thing is to send them back the minute the books have been scanned. Remove the books we left behind and replace the ones we took.'

'What about the abbot and the guards?' asked Clio.

'Memory tap. Everyone if possible, but the abbot especially.'

I had never done a time repair before and only knew the drill from lectures. I seemed to remember a lot more emphasis on doom and gloom, and woe betide the curator that had to go back and clear their mess.

'And we'll be safe during all this, will we?'

I swear I could hear Clio's eyes roll.

First addressed me directly. 'No, Curator Strathclyde, you will not be *safe*. You are returning to your own timeline.' She paused, possibly sympathetic to my appalled expression. 'But, we shall spend the next hour calibrating your braces and the stepper so we drop you into the room exactly five minutes after you left. You will not meet yourself. If this fails, it will be our fault, not yours. And engineers never fail.'

Several tense hours had passed, and Clio and I were once again standing side by side in front of the step wall. Given that she had supported me in the briefing, I felt the need to make a bridge.

'That was reassuring, wasn't it?'

Clio stared at me.

'When First said engineers don't fail.'

She sighed, and I realised I had once again confirmed her opinion of me.

'Engineers don't fail,' she spoke slowly, 'they just find a thousand ways that don't work before they find the one that does.'

I gulped. The most troublesome thing in my life used to be whether to mark a student down for their improper use of citations. And, honestly, the coffee maker could be tricky as well. Now I was stepping through a quantum portal to fix a rent in time and space, whilst ensuring that I didn't bump into myself and thereby destroy myself or the universe. Furthermore, I was travelling with a woman who thought I was less than dirt. If I was on fire, she would save me. But if it was a choice between a bucket of water or a bucket of urine to put out the flames, she'd take the piss every time.

'Positions.' The voice rang out from the gantry. 'Strathclyde, control your heart rate.'

I took a deep breath. Clio looked across at me and smiled warmly. I was so shocked that when the countdown came, I stepped into the wall with no hesitation.

The room was dark. I could smell stone dust and polished wood, but beyond that I had no clue.

'Sweet Bast,' murmured Clio. 'Julius, check your brace, see if it agrees with mine.'

I checked quickly and swore. 'Tower of London, 1483.'

'Balls.'

'What do we do?'

We had landed well beyond the margin of error. We were two hundred years and many miles away from our destination. On top of that, we were in the most fortified building in England. The place would be bristling with civilians and soldiers.

Without discussing it, we both instantly switched on our perception filters and used the infrared to look around the room. We seemed to be in a residential apartment. There was a dining table and chairs. The fire was burning low, which made me wonder if anyone was about. There were also two doors. One presumably led to a corridor, the other to a sleeping chamber.

'Right, let's head to the library,' said Clio. 'Leave the books—we are still within the timeline fracture—then get out of here.'

'Shouldn't we just head back and try again?' I was looking around. As fascinating as being in the Tower of London was, I wanted out.

'No. That many jumps in close succession may affect our brains. And we need yours intact.'

That sounded as comforting as it was meant. If she could have kept my brain in a specimen jar, with blood and oxygen running to it, she'd be happy. So long as the splice with Neith was safe and intact, Clio was happy.

I didn't see it quite the same way. 'Have you been here before? Is there a library?'

'I've been here a few times, 1220, 1642 and 1812. Of course there's a library. This is England's royal seat of power. What about you?'

'2005. School trip. Gift shop, no library.'

Clio laughed. 'Fair enough. I'll lead, then. You check that door, I'll check this.'

I headed over to the heavy oak door. Clio was becoming slightly bearable, and that made it less stressful to work with her. I checked the door and found it locked. Grabbing my tools, I moved the heavy bolts and carefully opened the door.

'Nice and quiet,' whispered Clio as she rejoined me. 'There are people sleeping next door. Let's not wake them.'

We slipped out into the corridor. Clio took the lead as we walked along the quiet passages. It was three in the morning, a perfect time for wandering around a medieval stronghold. We were finally blessed by a bit of good fortune as we passed no guards and made it to the library. Clio clearly knew her way around, I needed to spend more time in the holo-suites.

Slipping into the library, Clio removed the books from her satchel. They had been fully scanned. Now it was up to Tiresias to process all the texts and find a proto-Welsh language stem. Once that was established, they could fix the mess in Neith's neurolinguistic pathways.

Clio placed them on a shelf in plain view, then turned back to me. 'Right. Let's see if that fixes it. If it doesn't, they'll have to send another pair.'

I frowned.

'What?'

'Nothing.' I shook my head. 'I just don't like other people cleaning up my mess.'

She looked at me for a full count of five before she nodded. 'I agree. But, for now, we have to make the best of a bad situation. Hopefully, this is the end of it. Let's go.'

I didn't want to smile at her. I didn't even like her. But the fact that we agreed was momentarily surprising. She appeared to be looking at me with something akin to recognition.

I tapped my brace and we stepped back. Fingers crossed, we had fixed the anomaly and all would be well.

Chapter 19 - Julius

I blinked. Instead of the white room of the quantum stepper, I was standing outside in daylight. I was on a patch of grass beside a dirt track. The air smelt sweet, with roses and lavender. A couple were in the middle of row about the price of a pig. The pig was happily rooting through the dirt, oblivious to its impending future. Another voice was shouting about his fresh bread. He didn't need to shout, it smelled incredible. A woman was pushing a cart shouting over the top of him that her breads were cheaper. From a distance I could hear men's voices calling out. There's a distinct sound voices have when travelling over large bodies of water The way their voices sounded, I guessed they were on a large river.

There was a small stream in front of me, and a cart pulled by an ox trundled past me, heading towards a wooden bridge. The cart was laden with sacks, and a few dead chickens hung from poles. Someone was off to market. The man driving the cart spat at a few urchins that jumped around in front of the cart. As they did so, a third child ran towards the back of the cart and liberated a chicken. As he ran off, the other children joined him.

'Very smooth. I don't think the trader even noticed.'

I turned and looked at Clio standing beside me. Like me, she was still in the monk's robes and I wondered what had just happened.

140

'When are we? Where is this?' I groaned. 'What has gone wrong?'

I was about to interrogate my brace when Clio held up her hand. 'Wait. Neith and I used to play this game. We had to guess when and where we were just by using our senses. Whoever was closer was the winner, and the other had to buy the drinks for the evening.'

I looked around. This was clearly a medieval scene. Across the stream and grassed area were buildings and, as I looked behind, I saw we were standing in the shadow of an enormous stone wall. In front lay a medieval city. There were properties made of thin red bricks, wattle and daub houses, pantile roofs in a higgle of slopes and angles. From every roof, a chimney billowed out smoke into the afternoon sky, as meals were being prepared, homes kept warm. I could see little lanes weaving away from the green in front of us and into the mass of buildings. There was no sense of order, this city had bloomed as each individual saw fit. I knew I was biased, but I felt certain this was England and said as much. Clio snorted, so I tried again.

'A city, given the size of the settlement, and early second millennium.'

Clio snorted. 'You don't get a prize for that.' She was standing a few feet away and looking over my shoulder. 'Tell you what, come over here and see if you can spot any other clues.'

I walked over to her and looked backwards.

Towering over the boundary wall was the unmistakable outline of Westminster Abbey. Its huge circular window on the south transept shone in the sunlight. Without all the other customary buildings that I was used to seeing surrounding the abbey, it was awe-inspiring. Even St Margaret's, Westminster's parish church, was small and only peeped over the wall from this angle. The cathedral rose in splendid isolation and, for a moment, I stood breathless, bathing in its beauty. This was what the medieval builders had been aiming for. A glorious offering to God, and a reminder to the populace that the Church was more powerful than the Crown. In the sunlight, its white stone walls were blinding. Time and the industrial revolution had yet to mar the masonry, and I was speechless.

'Give up?'

'No. Give me a moment.'

Shaking myself out of my wonder, I looked around. Behind us ran a lane of wattle and daub buildings, with a few brick buildings here and there. Over to my left, I could see the Thames and a few boats docking at a small wharf.

'First half of the second millennia,' I began, and Clio laughed again, 'and London, obviously.'

'If you don't want to be buying drinks all evening you're going to have to do better than that.'

I glared at her. 'Look, this is silly. Shouldn't we be trying to get home? Not wasting time playing *Where's Wally.*'

'Wally's right in front of me.' She kicked away some sheep droppings and sat down on the grass. 'We can't jump anywhere for a bit whilst our bodies adjust. I have no idea why the brace didn't snap us home, but that's a problem we can't solve right now. So relax. When are we?'

So far, we hadn't attracted any attention, even though by now the perception field had worn off and we were fully visible. Two monks hanging around outside Westminster Abbey seemed perfectly reasonable in the minds of the local Londoners.

As I watched, there seemed to be a mix of what could only be described as peasants going about their daily business, herding geese, carrying sacks of grain. Children were barefoot, running back and forth earning themselves a cuff around the ear if they got in anyone's way. Dotted amongst the labourers were well-dressed individuals on horseback, and others walking in and out of the abbey gatehouse. Scribes, lawyers, priests. Honestly, there wasn't much in the way of clues, or rather, the scene was littered with them. I just didn't know how to read them with any level of accuracy. I gave it a stab.

'Given the clothing of the men on horseback, I would say between the twelve and fifteen hundreds.'

Clio beckoned to one of the children who had been hanging around, no doubt deciding if we were worth robbing. He peeled away from where he had been skulking and swaggered over. An arrogant urchin, ready to rob the world.

'Bring me some apples.'

The kid looked at her. His hair had been cut back to the scalp and was growing out in random tufts. He had a broken nose, snot was caked to his filthy face, and he had a big grin. 'It'll cost.'

Clio stared at him. 'No, it won't. Two apples, now. Otherwise I'm going to break your arm, then call the city guard and tell them you stole a chicken, then tried to rob two monks.'

The boy's smile slid away. Now he just looked like any other child trying to survive in a world that was brutal and uncaring.

'Clio—'

She ignored me and looked at the boy. At least, I thought it was a boy. They hadn't hit puberty yet.

'Well, why are you still here? Two apples. Now.'

The child ran off and, I hoped, legged it home to their mother where a bowl of warm food was waiting, and a nice story at bedtime. Sometimes my hopes got away from me. Best that child could hope for was somewhere dry to sleep, and no one giving them a kicking.

'I'm sure you're only trying to blend in, but can we not add to the general misery of that child's life?'

Clio scoffed as she looked around. No doubt scanning the environment for threats.

'That girl needs to learn who is not a safe target. And she needs to learn quickly. There are few trades for girls beyond their back. I'm helping her by giving her a lesson.'

I scratched my chin and wondered when I could get a shave.

'Why do you think she's a girl?'

I was getting used to Clio looking at me as if I was a fool and this was no exception. But honestly, the child was prepubescent, how could Clio tell?

'It's obvious. She's trying too hard to look a mess. In this era, boys are almost as likely to be abused as girls but she's playing the odds. Female prostitution is more common and of course pregnancy is every unmarried woman's downfall. So she's pretending to be a boy.'

I felt well and truly schooled. I could learn a lot from Clio if I could just bring myself to come to terms with her. And I couldn't see that happening.

'So,' continued Clio, 'have we got a better date for when we are?'

'My audible implant recognised her using Middle English before the great vowel shift, so I'm narrowing it down to between 1100 and 1400.'

'Any closer than that?'

'No, that's it. What about you?'

Clio laced her fingers and cracked her knuckles, then pointed over to the cathedral. 'After 1269. Look, the north transept is finished, but the old nave is still attached. That isn't replaced until 1376.'

I was impressed and said as much.

She smirked. 'I haven't finished. As the nave is still standing, we are therefore at the early side of the time frame, rather than the end. Those men on horses were wearing hoods as well as chaperons, meaning that the fashion is on the change. By the 1400s, chaperons are all the rage. No one of status would be seen wearing a hood. So my guess is we are early 1300s.'

'Well, go on then. Let's see what the brace says.'

'Hang on,' said Clio. I looked behind me and saw the kid running towards us. She stood in front of Clio and threw two apples at her.

Clio looked across at me and took a bite, then waved the apple at me. 'Early summer. These are last year's crop.'

Before I could respond, a guttural shout rang out, and a second later two men came lumbering around the corner of the wall. Swords hung from their belts and they were wearing grubby, padded jackets and metal helmets. They struck me a woefully unsuited to the job of guarding. They paused looking left and right, then spotting the urchin, lurched towards us.

'Julius, throw a whizz bang in front of us. Memory setting. Kid, sit down here beside me. Quickly.'

The kid looked between us and the guards. Her eyes darting left and right. She was bouncing on the spot, ready to bolt. Then Clio did something utterly unexpected. She pushed back her hood and smiled at the girl, placing her finger on her lips.

'Trust me, this is going to be fun. Come here.' Clio patted the grass beside her. 'You're safe with me.'

Clio's words were calm and reassuring, despite her earlier threats. The urchin dashed forwards and sat down by the wall between us. As she squeezed herself by Clio's side, I could see that she was shaking in fear at being caught but prepared to trust this intimidating stranger.

I threw the small ampoule out onto the grass, just as the guards changed direction and started running towards us. They were about twenty feet away when they paused and came to a halt. They had run through the little nano cloud that now gently drifted around their heads.

'Why have they stopped?' whispered the girl, looking up at Clio.

'Magic.'

The little girl looked stunned, and Clio giggled. She actually giggled.

'Not really, but my friend and I are good at getting rid of people.'

We watched as the two guards looked around them, seemingly perplexed, then walked back from where they had come, arguing as they went.

'They didn't even see us,' she said in amazement. 'I mean, they did, then they seemed to forget what they were doing.' She made to get up.

'Where are you going?' asked Clio.

'To see what he threw,' she said, cocking her head in my direction.

147

'So you can also forget?' asked Clio. The urchin's eyes opened wide and she sat back down again.

'You know, that wouldn't be a bad idea,' I said. We were supposed to be covert. Hell, we weren't even supposed to be here.

'Chill. I think it will be useful to have a little bit of local help.' She tossed the second apple to me and handed the remains of her apple to the girl.

'I don't follow.' Any minute now, we were heading out of here. Why would we need local knowledge?

'Have a look at your brace. I think I know why we ended up here.'

I pushed up my sleeve and tapped the face of my brace. Westminster Abbey, London. June 1303. My eyes widened in shock. That was a date every curator knew. This was one of the big ones. Clio was grinning at me.

'I think our braces got messed up for some reason, then got yanked here like a gravitational pull. We returned the books. Tried to head home and, maybe because of that small splinter, the braces went astray and brought us here.'

'Are you kidding?' I had a dreadful feeling that I knew what was on her mind.

'Nope. I say we stay a while. What do you say?'

'I say you are insane.'

'Just think. How fabulous would it be if we were successful? It would be the haul of the decade.'

'Clio, we are not going to steal the crown jewels.'

'Course we're not,' she said, smiling at me broadly. 'We're going to save them.'

Chapter 20 - Julius

'Well. Shall we do this? We're here, we're curators. Time is waiting for us.'

She smiled, and I felt the pull of her idea. It couldn't hurt and, as she said, we had all the time in the world.

'You're on, but if we are staying, I want food. Then we need a plan of attack.'

Clio punched me on the arm and I tried not to wince. 'That's the spirit, there's hope for you yet, Shit—'

I held up my hand. 'That stops right now. It's Julius, or Strathclyde, or Curator. Hell, you can even call me Blue, if Julius is too unnerving. But no more Shitfly. Is that clear?'

God knows if I was stuck in her company for this, the least she could do was stop using that nickname. I couldn't give a rat's arse what she thought of me, but I was sick of hearing it out loud.

'Very well, Julius.' She smirked, then turned to the child, who had been listening agog. I suspect we shouldn't have mentioned the crown jewels in front of a thief, no matter how young. 'Now, child. We need your help. If you are willing, we will feed you and we may even pay you. What do you say?'

'How much?'

'More than you can imagine.'

'I can imagine the crown jewels.' She cocked her head and grinned up at Clio. 'Is it as much as that?'

I laughed. 'Not remotely, but we will see you right. Now, what do we call you?'

'Alys, sir.'

'Very well, Alys. First of all, swallow this.' I had been rummaging in my sack, and now pulled out a small self-care capsule.

'Julius!'

'What? We have plenty.'

'That's not the point. You know the rules. We don't fix or interfere with the local population.'

'You just got her to steal two apples for us, then had to confound the guards. All I'm going to do is fix that broken nose. Imagine what her life is like with snot constantly running down her face. She'll be dead of a lung infection if that doesn't get sorted.'

'And maybe that's exactly what her path is.'

'And maybe you scared her into becoming an apple thief, and that was her path ruined.'

At some point, our argument had moved from angry to jocular. I knew Clio had no real objection to helping her. Indeed, as we had been talking, the little girl had swallowed the pill, releasing tiny nanobots into her system. She promptly fell asleep.

'Ah, damn,' I said.

'I would have suggested waiting until we have accommodation.' Clio sighed. 'Wait here. I'll go and find somewhere. The nanobots won't take too long fixing her, but they probably have a lot to sort out. They won't stop at the broken nose once they detect rickets, scurvy and who knows what else.'

Clio walked off. The child was sleeping by my side, the sun was shining, and I was just going to simply watch history trundle along in front of me.

Within the next few days, the most audacious jewel robbery in medieval history was about to take place. Back in 1303, the crown jewels were kept in the cloisters in Westminster Abbey. More specifically, they were held in the pyx, a secure underground vault that could only be accessed via the cloisters, and only then if you were a monk. I had to laugh at the coincidence of our attire. As if it was meant to be.

Beside me, the little girl whimpered and I noticed her nose looked properly aligned. The snot remained, but we'd get her cleaned up in a bit. For now, she remained asleep. No doubt the bots were healing other sections before deactivating. I tried to remember if they would go dormant or disintegrate. If dormant, our little thief would never catch the plague, or any one of a myriad of other ailments, and would die of old age. This was a complete no-no, but I got the impression from Clio that this wasn't the first time she had intervened in Beta lives. I could certainly believe that Neith would help along the way with tiny acts of kindness. I suspected Clio only did it for self-interest, but the way she had smiled at the little girl, maybe she sensed a kindred spirit.

'Right, I have found accommodation and some clothes for her.' Clio's return startled me out of my speculations. 'No inn will permit her looking like that. She's also going to need to wash. When she wakes up, throw her in the Tyburn.'

I peered at the small river in front of us. 'This is the Tyburn?'

'Lovely, isn't it? Once upon a time the London rivers flowed fresh and sweet. Neith and I would drink from them, bathe in them. Now they are full of tallow and piss. In a few more centuries you choke them and fill them with sewage, then bury them under your filth and greed.'

I glared at her. She liked to blame all of Beta's flaws on me, as though I were personally responsible. I noticed that she never praised me for all the art we made, that they were desperate to save.

'Bloody hell, I'm starving!' Alys stood up and grinned at us. 'You said there'd be food.'

'Soon as you've washed and put on new clothes,' chided Clio. 'From now on, you're going to be our oblate. Do you know what that is?'

Alys waggled her head and sneered at Clio, pulling a stupid face. 'Someone too young to be a novice. I'm not stupid, you know. But you are. I can't be an oblate, I'm a girl.'

Clio laughed and leant forward, whispering, 'So am I!'

153

We both laughed as she stared at Clio in horror. 'Won't God strike you down?'

'He'll have to catch me first,' said Clio, winking. 'Now, get clean and think of a boy's name. I use the name Michael and this is Julius.'

'Is he a girl as well?'

I gave a mock growl and with a little shriek she ran towards the river, stripping off her rags as she went. Her nudity attracted zero attention. I noticed that downstream a woman was washing out some rags. Further along, two lads were washing some dung off their feet. Others were drawing buckets from the river and returning to the houses. It was a timely reminder to only drink beer and that Clio might have a point about how Londoners treated their rivers.

Alys returned, and I looked away as she shuffled into a clean tunic that Clio had found whilst finding accommodation. I wondered if even now some child was being shouted at by their mother for losing their clothes. Taking out a blade, Clio cut the rest of Alys's hair to an even stubble.

'Why does my nose feel funny?'

'Because he fixed it,' said Clio, pointing to me. 'No more snot face for you. Plus, you'll find you can breathe easier now. Maybe you can also smell better?'

'Is this witchcraft, or a miracle?' She squinted at us, her face screwed up in a suspicious scowl.

'What do you want it to be?'

She looked hopeful. 'A miracle? Please.'

I smiled at her. 'A miracle it is, then. But it's also a secret. If anyone ever asks, say you fell over and broke it straight. Agreed?'

She looked serious and thought it through as she ran her hands over her face and new haircut.

'Like the time Blind Tom fell over and grew back his leg?'

Clio and I looked at each other. Poor Tom, he must have cursed that stumble.

'Sort of. Now what's your name going to be?'

'What about Arthur?'

'No!' Clio and I shouted together.

Alys took a step back. We were on Arthur's home turf, and the last thing I wanted to do was draw his attention.

'Sorry Alys, pick something else.'

'Odel?'

I nodded. 'Now then, Odel, what say we get some food? Brother Michael, lead the way.'

Chapter 21 - Julius

An hour later, Alys was burping happily, having stuffed herself on a bowl of stew and a hunk of bread, heavy with seeds and a good crusty loaf to mop up the juices. We were sitting in the corner of a tavern a few streets away from Thorny Island, the land mass that the abbey sat on.

'Did the innkeeper not think it odd that we were sleeping here rather than in the cloisters?' I asked.

It was imperative that we didn't draw undue attention to ourselves. Especially considering what was happening this week. We needed to keep out of the history books.

'Perfectly standard, apparently, for visiting monks to stay in places other than the cloisters. I think it's a power-play thing. Which suits us.'

Clio nibbled on a drumstick, scowling as she did so. We had to appear wealthy, and wealthy patrons ate meat. I, for one, was enjoying it and found myself burping. Happily, greedy wealthy monks appeared to be something that the local population was used to.

Raised voices were coming from the bar. A well-dressed man was arguing with the alewife and pointing in our direction but she was having none of it. His shoes were leather, rather than wooden clogs. His hose had clearly been made to fit him rather than handed down but were dirty around their hem. The same was true of his doublet, a rich blue velvet, but some of the seams had frayed and had been poorly resewn. A wealthy man, once upon a time. Now he was down on his luck. Getting nowhere with the woman, he sidled towards us, a wet smile on his face. The transformation from belligerent accuser to sycophantic patron was astonishing and I marked him as someone who lived by dint of manipulation and cunning. I suspected he didn't have an honest bone in his body and I immediately took against him.

Clio kept her hood raised and lowered her face as she carried on chewing her drumstick. To the untrained eye, she was the personification of disinterest.

'Greetings, Brothers.'

His tone wavered between confident and belligerent. He was certain that we would accede to his wishes where the innkeeper wouldn't. I looked over at her, but she had already moved on to serve a group of travellers who had just walked in, mud on the hems of their cloaks.

I looked back at the trader and bowed my head. 'Greetings.' I took a swig as I raised my eyebrows. Clio drained her pint then belched loudly and called for ale. Whilst she waited she returned to her food ignoring the man who hovered uncomfortably. His smile was forced and he kept clearing his throat, tugging at his collar. There was an air of desperation about him that stank of foolish choices.

'I find I need to avail myself of your charity.'

I took another swig. Whatever he wanted, we couldn't get involved. Our brief, as always, was to lie low. I hoped my disinterest would dissuade him from continuing, but his need overrode my polite dismissal.

'I have been staying here these past few weeks, and quit this morning, but I appear to have left some items behind.' He seemed blustery, and I wondered what the problem was. 'It appears you have now taken my rooms—'

He paused as the alewife brought Clio's drink over to her muttering about the laziness of the clergy and headed back to the bar where even more patrons were waiting. Clio scraped her tankard across the table towards her. Her face was still lowered, but just the grip of her fingers and hunched shoulders suggested someone ready to start a fight. And I clearly wasn't the only one to think so. Our petitioner began to stammer.

'—not my rooms, obviously. The alewife's. And now they are in your rooms. Of course they are. A silly slip of the tongue. They were once my rooms and now...' He broke off for a weak chuckle. 'They are yours.'

I sighed. Why did Clio always have to unnerve people? I decided that in this partnership, I would always be the good cop.

'And you would like to get your stuff back?'

He let out a great sigh and slumped onto the bench opposite us. 'Exactly. If you can just give me your key—'

Clio's tankard slammed on the table as she stabbed at her food.

'Well, I'm afraid that won't be possible,' I said in a friendly tone. 'Without meaning to give offence, we don't know you from Adam, and now all our things are in there. Tell you what. Tell me what you are missing, and my companion can retrieve them.'

I didn't think he'd want to spend any time on his own with her, but even my company seemed to alarm him as he quickly recoiled.

'No! Sorry. I must retrieve them. I must because...' He spluttered, failing to think of a reason why he didn't want us to see what he had forgotten to pack. No doubt some nefarious activity.

'I think you can trust us?'

'Yes, of course I can.' He was sweating now. 'Are you part of the abbey?' His voice was hopeful, and he looked crushed when I shook my head.

'Merely visitors. Brother Michael and I are on pilgrimage.'

'Very good, very good.' He sat and fidgeted, rearranging his jerkin and collar. 'But please, you can trust me. I would never dream of stealing from holy men such as yourselves. I am an honest trader. Richard de Podelicote at your service.'

Sitting across the table was the man who was going to break into the pyx chamber and steal the crown jewels. If he checked out this morning, tonight he would be sleeping in the crypt. Over the next few nights, he would smuggle items out to waiting accomplices through a high window.

He stuck out his hand, and I shook it numbly.

Now Clio stirred. 'Odel!'

Alys was sitting by the fire, playing with the pub's dog. A huge hound that dwarfed the small girl, but relished having its tummy rubbed. Clio picked up a lamb bone and threw it at her, shouting her name again.

Alys jumped up with a start. She caught the incoming bone, passed it to the dog and ran over to our table. 'Yes, Brother Michael?'

'This gentleman has left some of his items in our room. Accompany him, then return to us with the key.'

She turned and glared at de Podelicote. 'I take it you have no issue with a child of God accompanying you?'

Although framed as a question, he knew there was only one answer that would get him anywhere. As the two made it to the staircase, Clio called for Alys again, and she ran back.

'I want to know what he took, but don't alarm him. If he tries anything funny, just shout. We'll be with you instantly.'

She ran back with the key and headed up the staircase with de Podelicote following.

Clio turned to me with a smug grin. 'Well, aren't you worried about leaving a young child with a known villain? Don't you want to rush to protect her?'

I shrugged. I knew something that she didn't know. My reaction was not what she was expecting, but she carried on.

'The thing is, I placed a bug on her sleeve just now. So if she shouts, we really will hear.' There was that smug grin again. It really was most tiresome.

'Did you also put a tracker on her, in case he knocks her out?'

Clio's face twitched. 'A listening bug will be fine.'

I nodded. 'Of course it will.' I took another drink of beer. It helped cut through the fat of the stew. 'Besides which, I put a tracker and bug on de Podelicote when I shook his hand, so we're covered.'

I grinned at her, and she scowled back, but there was definitely a twitch to her lips. An acknowledgement that I wasn't quite as useless as she thought.

'Right then, smart arse,' said Clio. 'It would appear the break-in starts tonight.'

'Possibly. It would help if the braces were properly reading the timeline. What do you think the problem is?'

Both of us were probably sharing the same thought. Our last step hadn't taken us home. What if our way home was broken? Since we had arrived, I had been checking my brace. There was a connection, but it hadn't stabilised yet. Readings flicked on and off, and whilst the link to our suits and each other was working perfectly, the link to Alpha was far from perfect.

Clio drank her beer and smiled. The brew wasn't that bad, almost Egyptian in quality.

'I suspect it has something to do with the new technology. No doubt your friend Jack will bore us all about it when we get home. In the meantime, we'll just wait until it's time to go, and worry about it then.'

Alys returned to the table and handed Clio the key.

'Report,' said Clio, but her tone was friendly. Alys sat on the bench and leant towards us, her legs swinging beneath her.

'He grabbed a heavy bag from under the bedstead. It was long, and sounded like there was metal inside. Tools or maybe swords?'

She grinned at me and pinched a turnip from my bowl. I was impressed by her reasoning and said as much.

'So, what do we do now?' My eyes slid significantly over to Alys. There was no way I was getting her involved in the most notorious heist in her lifetime.

'Odel, go ask the innkeeper if she has any chores. Say it's part of your training to offer good deeds.'

I suspected from her sigh that Alys wanted to go back to the fire and play with the dog, or follow de Podelicote through the streets. Pot washing held little appeal. We watched as she dragged herself over to the bar and spoke to the woman leaning over the bar. The alewife looked across at us suspiciously, but when we nodded, she told the child to come around.

I returned to my brace. de Podelicote was now around the back of the abbey. Forgetting his tools for the last stage of the break-in felt about right for a heist run by the Keystone Cops and the villagers of *Whisky Galore*.

I took another drink and happy that Alys was engaged, I began to lay out what we needed to do next.

'Here's the plan.' Clio raised her eyebrow, but I continued. 'We wait until dark, then we explore the location.'

The cloisters where the theft was going to take place were surrounded by walls. Access was via the Thames, or via a gate house and across a small stream. We wouldn't be able to get in during daylight without drawing attention to ourselves. Better to arrive in the dark and see what was going on. We knew from the records that this theft took place over three nights.

'Call that a plan? How about we wait on the banks of the Thames? We might find access easier?' said Clio.

I don't think she was being contrary, just examining other options, but this was one that I had already dismissed.

'No go. It will be high tide. There'll be no bank, and we'll just get wet.'

'You're connected to Tiresias?' She tapped her brace in relief.

'No. I just know my tides. I used to go sailing out near Ipswich. Knowing the state of the tides is pretty essential around there. And from what I remember, the Thames is a much more violent river in this time frame. I don't want to be wandering its shores in the dark. Especially with no moon.'

Clio rapped her fingertips on the tabletop. 'No moon?'

'High tides at lunch, so high tides at midnight, which also means either full moon or new moon.'

'So it could be a full moon,' said Clio with no shortage of sneer in her tone.

'Could be,' I paused, 'but if I was going to steal the crown jewels, I'd probably pick a dark night?' I smiled sweetly. 'Wouldn't you?'

I received an unnecessary amount of pleasure as she glared at me. She really brought out the worst in me. Needling a colleague was beneath me but I just couldn't help myself. I would give anything for Neith to be here right now. We'd be in sync and having a good time. Instead, Clio and I were disagreeing over every aspect of the mission and I was fed up. I scratched my chin and grimaced. We needed to get home, or I'd be forced to shave with a knife.

'Relax, pretty boy,' said Clio, 'no one cares what you look like.'

And with that, she stabbed my remaining turnip and ate in silence. My punishment for outsmarting her.

Chapter 22 - Jack

Jack stared at the monitor and groaned. At eighteen, he had never expected people to think he was a genius. He had grown up knowing he was bright and had performed well at the quantum academy. It wasn't until he had met da Vinci and Firenze that his brain had woken up. As Firenze transported them home, she and Jack had paused to chat and, as they did, universes unveiled themselves to him. The maths sang in his mind, and he could see through the veils of the world he thought he understood.

He returned to his Earth, fizzing with ideas and suggestions. Within days, he had understood what was wrong with the stepper, the limits built into the equations. And, over the past six months, he had delighted in unpicking them and designing new technology. Much still eluded him, but he could feel the shape of ideas in his head, and it was wonderful.

Today, though, he had bigger things on his mind. This evening, he and Sabrina were off on a date, and she had asked him to surprise her. Now the smartest person in Alexandria was stumped. It was all well and good asking for him to surprise her, but when it came to girls, he was clueless. A knitathon? Surely she'd find that too dull. A basketball match could be a laugh, but knowing her, she'd probably want to join in. Maybe one of the lakeside dances? That way, he'd also have an excuse to hold her.

The more he thought about it, the better the idea became, and he pushed away from his desk, grinning.

Today was going to be a good one. He could feel it in his bones. Which, of course, was when all the alarms went off. He had never heard the temporal bells outside the step room before. That was reserved for a cataclysmic failure. He was out the door and running across the plaza as the full enormity of what this meant sank in. Only Julius and Clio were out in the field. What had they done?

Slamming through the doors, red lights flashing along the corridors, he ran up the stairs two at a time. Bursting into the stepper control centre, he tried to take it all in. From the gantry, he looked down onto the step floor to see it unoccupied. The same four blank walls, although now red lights were flashing against the white surfaces.

'What's happening? Where are the curators?'

Jack had to yell twice before anyone heard him, then he was mobbed by engineers all shouting at him. Despite being the youngest in the room, he had devised half the equations in use today. If something had gone wrong, and it clearly had, hopefully he should know how to fix it.

'Report!'

Behind him, Hypatia came crashing into the room, panting, her breath wheezy. The minute she entered the room everyone knew. Jack was young and untested. Hypatia was the head of the engineers and an absolute legend. If anyone could fix it, she could.

An engineer came running over, and Jack curled his lip in distaste. Timon was an oaf of a man. Clever enough, but lacking imagination. He seemed to know everything there was to know, but was incapable of finding a new idea in an egg cup.

'First.' He strode towards her, and Jack grinned internally to see Hypatia frown. She had asked the engineers to not call her by her old title and, of course, Timon was incapable of taking on something as radical as a name change.

He pointed to the timeline board. 'We have suffered a significant time-splinter in 1483.'

'That wasn't the year we sent the curators to.'

'No, they were sent to 1205. Carmarthen.'

'And is that where they arrived?' asked Jack.

Now Timon looked at Jack, his face defensive. 'The readings were unclear.'

'Unclear?' said Jack in amazement. 'Why the bloody hell didn't you call for me? You told me the jump was going perfectly.'

'It *was* going perfectly,' snapped Timon, angry that he was having to explain himself to a younger colleague. 'Need I remind you we don't always know what's going on with the curators when they jump?'

Jack was about to explode when Hypatia stepped in. 'And need I remind you that this is new technology, and we have been able to see exactly when and where people have landed in the test jumps? The minute that aberration was noticed, I should have been notified. And I presume, since this is the first I heard of it, that you failed to notify me?'

Timon nodded, sweat beading on his brow.

'Right.' Hypatia turned her back on him and studied the timelines. Across the screen, new lines were radiating from various fracture points. From the initial fracture, new blooms were radiating all across Europe.

'London, 1483. Tail end of the War of the Roses. Sweet Anubis, this could be catastrophic. Jack, pull the curators back immediately. Let's see what they have done and start fixing it as soon as possible.'

'We just tried that,' stammered Timon. 'Nothing happened. It looks like a serious failure in technology.'

Jack couldn't help but notice that in all the chaos, the engineer found time to give a sour smirk in his direction. How had the technology failed? Julius and Clio had been untraceable after their step. Now a time-splinter, scrap that, a time explosion was manifesting and they had no way to pull them back.

'Hypatia, we need to send another pair to see what occurred and report back.'

'But the technology is unstable,' protested Timon. 'We could lose another pair of curators, we could make things worse.'

'If we don't, we are going to lose Beta Earth irrevocably,' said Jack. 'Our link will not survive such a massive alteration. Beta is transforming into a totally different Earth. And it's our fault.'

'Maybe the link will survive?' stammered Timon hopefully.

'And what of our duty of care to all the residents of Beta Earth that are currently dying out, never being born? Nations never rising, new civilisations emerging. New wars, nuclear wars, chemical annihilation. Who knows where this timeline ends? All because of something we did.'

'The current timeline is heading that way anyway,' said Timon, sulky.

'Then that is their choice, not ours,' snapped Hypatia. 'Jack, get me Sabrina Mulweather and Ben Wakandi. The oldest and youngest. Hopefully, they can fix it.'

'First. I protest,' said Timon. 'We risk throwing away two curators. And maybe making the situation worse.'

Hypatia looked him up and down. 'Noted. Now leave the room. I have no time for malcontents.'

'We've hit 1533,' shouted an engineer, and everyone turned towards the screen as the timelines blossomed like fireworks. 'What the hell was that?'

'Best guess. No Tudors, so I think England hasn't broken with Rome. Tiresias is struggling to keep up with the changing data streams. The information is coming in lumps. The closer to the fracture, the more garbled the information.'

'But he's certain the Tudors are gone?'

'Looks that way. Or maybe one of Catherine's boys survives?'

The speculations were running thick and fast. If Henry the Eighth never divorced Catherine of Aragon for failing to give him a male heir, where would history go? Jack had remained quiet during this exchange. Sending a pair of curators made sense until one of them was going to be Sabrina. Now the risks seemed too high.

'Jack, are you listening?' Jerking himself back to attention and away from the memory of Sabrina laughing at the camel races, he shook his head as Hypatia continued. 'Look at the readouts. See if you can find out why the automatic recall isn't working. Also, try and get a lock on where, by Anubis's balls, they are!' She paused, collecting herself and gave him a saccharine smile. 'Maybe if we can get them back, we won't need to send your Sabrina.'

Jack flushed. He hadn't realised his feelings towards the curator were well known, but then Hypatia didn't miss a thing.

She shouted to another group of engineers. 'How are their vital signs?'

'Strong. No sense of overstimulation from their readouts. I would say they are wide awake, but not stressed. It's been five minutes since the splinter. I suspect they are not even aware of their actions, given their readings.'

Jack was half-listening as he started running through the digital readouts from the initial step. That Clio's heartbeat hadn't changed meant less than nothing. She could face a volcano and yawn. Julius, on the other hand, might flinch, or just become wildly excited. Jack enjoyed Julius' company, if only for the weird way he looked at the world. Now Jack was processing the figures and an idea came to him.

'Hypatia. I think I can see what went wrong. I have a suggestion. We could try a Firenze Fold.'

First Engineer paused and gave Jack her full attention. 'It's too risky.'

'It is, but it would flatten out all the timelines in the infected area.'

'Not would, could. This theory of yours has failed more often than it succeeded in trials. Added to which, it could wipe out Clio and Julius.'

'But it might work, and it might spare Sabrina and Ben?'

At that moment, Sabrina ran into the gantry, followed by Ben. 'What's happening?' She stared at the timeline in horror as tiny little fractures continued to creep across the screen. 'It looks like ice on a pond.'

'Yes, and Beta Earth is about to drown,' said Hypatia. 'I need you two ready to jump.'

'Hypatia,' begged Jack. 'The Firenze Fold, if it works, will be quicker than two curators.'

'1580. Balls! Look at China.' All heads turned to look at the wall, as a new blossom of cracks radiated on the Asian timeline.

'Jack. Firenze Fold, now!'

Jack was already moving to a screen where he tapped into an isolated Tiresias feed. The fold, when it worked, undid everything that had happened on the jump. Including the arrival of the curators. The idea being that as they stepped, the stepper would shut down. The engineers would be alerted to the fact that a fold had taken place, but not why, as, in theory, nothing had happened.

That was when it worked. When it didn't work, sometimes nothing happened. Sometimes it worked, but left bits of history outside the fold. This meant that the curators effectively jumped and were then wiped out of existence. The Beta timeline continued to splinter, but only a little bit. And sometimes those little splinters were just as bad as the one the fold had tried to fix. A perfect fold currently had a sixty per cent success rate.

He might lose Julius, but he'd spare Sabrina. As he and Tiresias ran through the drills, he realised Sabrina meant more to him than losing the whole of Beta Earth. Did that make him a bad engineer?

'Jack,' said Hypatia. 'are you ready?'

Sabrina and Ben were arguing with Hypatia, saying the risk was too high and they were ready to step. The sirens wailed as the cracks in the screens continued to spread, when another alarm rang. Not the wailing sirens, but the simple bell of an incoming step.

Jack jumped up. 'Hypatia, they're returning!'

'I have ears.' She took a deep breath. 'Yes, Jack. Let's see what they know.' Raising her voice over the sirens and bells, she called out to the entire gantry. 'Be ready. The minute they arrive, we need full calibrations from the braces. Get a team together. I need Clio and Julius fully prepared to step back.'

As people ran to get everything in place, the air started to fizz. Everyone turned to look down into the step room when the wall shimmered.

Chapter 23 - Julius

Having left Alys asleep on a pallet in our room, we headed out onto the street. The innkeeper had offered us torches, but as soon as we were out of sight, we ditched them and activated our infrared contacts. Just before we set off, Clio had had a word with the alewife.

'Just making sure *Odel* doesn't sneak down to the stables.'

Alys hadn't stopped talking about the horses in the livery. She had spent the afternoon brushing their coats and cleaning out the stables under the eye of a grateful groom. They were short staffed, following one of their apprentices deciding to go off on crusade. Clio continued.

'Apparently, our alewife has strong views on fools that go traipsing across Europe, and she doesn't care who knows.'

As we snuffed our torches, the darkness was all-encompassing, compounded by a heavy fog rolling in off the river. We headed along the streets towards the abbey and heard the odd shout or laugh from the houses. Otherwise the doors were closed, the windows shuttered, and nothing moved on the lanes except for the rats. The silence was muffled, and the air was wet. Clio shivered and pulled her cassock closer around her. Our soft leather shoes made no sound as we walked along the cobbles.

The ground beneath our feet turned to impacted mud as we got closer to the abbey grounds. I tapped Clio on the shoulder, and we both crept around the cloister walls. Peering through the fog, my contacts could just about make out the looming shape of the abbey high above us, but that was it. The fog smothered everything, and without my lenses I would have barely seen a hand in front of my face.

A bat flittered past, and as I jumped I might have made a small sound.

'If you are going to scream at every ghostie, do you think you can warn me first?' asked Clio.

'I didn't scream.'

'No? I imagine the bards are at this very moment writing tales of the weird shriek that plagues the abbey's hallowed grounds.'

We came around the corner. The gate was open, and two people were standing outside it. As we watched, one man handed a sack to the other. The bag clinked and the two men muttered something, then the second man grabbed the bag tightly to himself as he turned and shot off across the bridge. Without my contacts, I wouldn't have even seen the bridge, let alone the thief as he slipped into the cramped lanes leading away from the cloisters.

'Quick,' whispered Clio. 'Let's see if we can slip in before the gates close.'

Checking behind us, I followed Clio as she ran lightly towards the gate, then came to a sudden halt as a voice called out from inside the wall. For a moment, I had thought someone was following us, but just as I was about to investigate, the disembodied voice addressed us.

'Brother Michael, is that you?'

The coincidence was strong, but that was all it was. However, the conspirators, whilst mostly monks themselves, might remember that their Brother Michael wasn't Black. I hurried in front of Clio and spoke up.

'We're over here. Keep your voice down.'

I walked forward, my hood low over my face, and Clio in the darkness behind me.

I was facing the fattest monk I had seen outside of a Disney film. I assumed he wasn't involved in the actual hauling out of the treasure. He was just the lookout. I also realised, as he peered at me, that he could barely see me in the fog.

'This fog's a stroke of luck, isn't it?' I said with an excited laugh.

'It's a bloody nuisance, is what it is.' He turned, picked up a sack from his feet, and handed it to me. 'Now, see this gets to John the Taps, on Fleet Street. He knows what to do next. When you've dropped it off, get back here. There'll be another lot shortly.'

He could barely lift the heavy sack, and it clanked loudly as the sides pulled together.

'Why not just blow a horn?' I muttered and carefully placed the sack over my shoulder. Jerking my head to Clio, we headed towards the bridge only to see three monks were heading over the stream in our direction. Our lenses had given us the upper hand. Without speaking, we crossed in unison to one side, eager to avoid a close encounter. As they passed, I felt I could have reached out and tugged at their hoods, so dense was the fog. Clio and I grinned at each other in silence, an unexpected moment of camaraderie then we continued to creep towards the bridge. We had just got to the bridge when the monk at the gate challenged the newcomers, his voice breaking the silence.

'It's me, Brother Michael, you fool. Hand us the sack. I'm sick of this sodding fog.'

Clio and I looked at each other. 'Run!'

No sooner had we legged it, than a holler rose from the gatehouse. Hitching our robes up into our arms, we sprinted onto the bridge. The bag clanked in the fog and something whistled past my head.

Clio turned and shouted back at them. 'Oi! Stop chucking them sodding axes!'

I sprinted back and grabbed her by the shoulder. 'Time and place. Neither is now.' Yanking her forward, we ran across the bridge as the three men came lumbering towards us. From this distance, their accuracy with the axe was less pertinent. We legged it into the lanes and, as we did so, a childish voice shouted through the fog.

'Hey, Dog face. You a nun? You smell like one!'

Clio swore, then laughed to herself, as Alys continued shouting insults. Then she addressed an imaginary group.

177

'Head for the front of the abbey. Dog Face won't be able to run that far.'

We stood still, as the monks, believing our accomplice had inadvertently told them our direction, followed the sound of her voice.

'We have to get Alys,' I whispered, placing the treasure sack on the floor as quietly as possible.

'Absolutely not,' said Clio. 'She knows what she's doing. I bet the minute they have followed her enough, she will slip back into the darkness and head home. Remember, she's grown up here. She knows this place blindfolded.'

I looked at Clio in concern. 'Did you tell her to do this?'

'Of course I didn't. She obviously followed us. Which in this fog took skill. Now, let's take advantage of her diversion. Let's see what's in the sack.'

As the treasures tumbled onto the floor, silver goblets and sapphire necklaces spilt out over each other. There was a crown tangled up in a gold chain belt, as well as coins of every shape and size.

'Scan them and see if any of these items are on Tiresias's missing inventory.'

Moments later, we had separated the two piles, including our star treasure, Prince Llewellyn's Crown. There was also a very elaborate necklace, and a stunning ruby and pearl brooch. We left the cups and coins in the other pile. Whilst unmarked, they were also not important enough to save.

'I told you it was a bloody ruse.' The voice snarled across the night air.

'Well this has been fun,' whispered Clio, 'but now we need to go.'

'But Alys—'

'Alys is taken care of. I've left a letter with the alewife. If we fail to return, she's going to offer Alys a job.'

'Our kit—'

'Also taken care of. Payment for Alys's care until she earns her own keep.'

We hunkered down on the street. The sound of the three monks grew closer as they made their way towards the lanes. With no light to guide them and the fog from the Thames, they were relying on their torches and moving slowly. They weren't exactly stealthy.

'How are we supposed to carry all this stuff?' said Clio.

I placed the crown on my head.

Clio grinned, strapping the sword and belt around her waist. In a frantic scramble, we adorned our bodies in jewels and regalia. Trying not to laugh at each other, we looked back down the street where we could just about see the flame of a torch heading our way.

My heart was racing and as Clio and I played in silence I wondered how I could joke around with her. She had killed Charlie and yet working with her I was beginning to see another side of her. She cared about Alys. She was

179

prepared to do anything to save Neith. Christ, she even had my back. It was an uncomfortable feeling. I was beginning to trust her and yet I was certain that she would betray me in an instant if it suited her. Like I said, uncomfortable. She was currently tucking a dagger down her vest. I placed a signet ring on my finger and waved at her. The guards were almost upon us.

I could imagine them getting here and finding all the treasures on the cobbles. Hopefully, they would assume we panicked and ran. It was not as if they knew what was in the bags, and so they wouldn't know some things were missing.

'And you're sure about Alys?' I whispered.

'Absolutely. Now, are you ready? I can't wait to see their faces when we step back, covered in the crown jewels.'

'If the brace works this time,' I said sourly. God knows where we might end up.

'Live a little, Julius. This is fun!'

We hit our braces, and the last the monks heard as they crept towards us was a belly laugh from Clio, echoing across the fog.

Chapter 24 - Julius

This time, it wasn't just sirens.

Bells were ringing, lights were flashing, technicians were running from machine to machine up in the gantry. Behind them, the temporal anomalies field that tracked the smooth progress of time looked like it had been attacked by a squad of drunken paintballers. Fractures were radiating out from multiple splats of colour all across the planet.

The door flung open, and two technicians ripped the braces off our wrists and sprinted out again.

Clio stared at me in horror. 'What did you do?'

I recoiled and blinked at her.. 'What did *I* do? Nothing. It must have been you.'

Rami and Sam ran into the room.

'What happened?' roared Sam.

At least now Clio and I had a shared purpose, as we both turned and shouted 'Nothing!' at the same time. I looked at Clio, utterly baffled. She shared my expression until a flash of something crossed her face. Now, looking horrified, she spun away from me.

'Sam, we have to send Julius back. We have to get him out of here!'

Sam and Rami looked at me, each face drawing pale as they drew the same conclusion that Clio had.

'When?' asked Rami.

'Before the Carmarthen visit. Anything before 1205.' Sam turned and shouted up to the gantry. 'Reset the stepper to England 1200. Anywhere quiet.'

'Cancel that instruction,' roared First, who had just run into the room. Technicians were stripping our treasures from us in a mad fumbling of hands. Alphas don't flap. At the moment, this lot looked like a flock of geese trying to get airborne.

'Julius.' First walked directly in front of me. 'Tell me about Gloriana.'

I looked at her, confused. Was she asking about a hymn? If so, it was one I was unfamiliar with.

'What about the Tudor dynasty?'

That rang a bell, but I was getting a headache.

'Tell me about the 1500s.'

'Which bit?' I was confused. Something was wrong, but I couldn't put my finger on it.

'Highlights.'

'Well, I guess we'd need to mention the rise of the Irish Empire and Henry's break with Rome.'

'Who is Henry?'

I looked at them, baffled. 'The Eighth. Henry Tudor.' I paused. 'No, hang on, that's not right. I think I've misremembered that. How embarrassing, I think that was a film I watched. The Irish Empire, however...' I stopped. For some reason, I couldn't quite recall that either. My head was now pounding. I felt sweaty and wondered if I was about to faint.

'We can't risk him,' pleaded Clio. 'Send him back to a safe spot.'

'No,' said First abruptly. 'He's okay for now. The splinters have only reached the 1600s. We have a short amount of time to save him and Beta. If we lose Strathclyde, Masoud will have to go back on her own.'

I was beginning to feel groggy, and I leant against Clio. Bizarrely, I felt comforted as she placed her arm around my waist and supported me.

'What the hell is going on?' I tried to sound crisp and calm, but my head hurt so much, my speech was slurred.

'Strathclyde, concentrate,' said First. 'Something catastrophic happened. Time is altering rapidly on Beta Earth. You two did something that damaged the timeline, and we need to work out what it was. Then you need to go back and undo it.'

'And if we don't?' I was struggling to keep up.

'You may cease to exist. Beta's history will be utterly altered, and our link with it may be permanently broken.' She turned back to Clio. 'Report.'

Clio took a deep breath then she spoke clearly and precisely.

'Instead of returning us to Carmarthen in 1205, as expected, the step malfunctioned, and we arrived at the Tower of London in 1483. We had landed in a residential room. We walked down a corridor, opened a door to the library, returned the books, then left. We spoke to no one and we interacted with two doors. And that was that. The books. That's all it can be. However, when we jumped to return, we were yanked off course and ended up at Westminster Abbey in 1303. Hence the jewels. But looking at the fracture, it seems that the harm didn't happen then. It must have been at the Tower.'

The four of them nodded, but I shook my head.

'Three doors.'

They looked at me. I stepped away from Clio's support and looked at her. 'Remember you opened a door to a bed chamber? You said there were people asleep in there. While I was unlocking the door.'

'The door was locked?' asked Clio.

I nodded. I was having trouble trying to remember which film I had seen Henry Tentpole in. Even his name sounded wrong. I was also trying to concentrate on what was going on, and felt my mind throb. Any second now, I was going to hurl.

'I didn't know that,' she said carefully.

'Did you lock it when you left?' asked Sam, looking at me.

'No. I was in the corridor. Clio closed it, and I just assumed. Damn, could that be it?'

It seemed so unlikely.

'Who was in the room?' asked Rami quickly. 'Describe the people who had been locked in.'

Clio shook her head. 'It was just two children.'

I looked at her in astonishment.

'Two children, locked in the Tower of London in 1483.'

'Oh shit!' Sam looked at First. 'The Two Princes.'

'But they escape,' I said, even more confused. 'Everyone knows this story. How they fled the Tower, and Edward was crowned king, securing the line of York for the following hundred years. And then...'

I trailed off. I really was going to be sick, the pain in my head was so severe.

'Stop!' Now Jack ran into the room. Really, we'd need name tags at this rate. He hurtled past the others. His hair was a mess. He was sweaty and out of breath. He bundled into me and gave me a massive hug.

'Julius. What did you have last night in the pub?'

I tried to remember. 'A shake. We were stepping in the morning and I—'

'Forget the step. What did I order?'

'A snake eyes.'

'What about Ludo?'

As Jack took me through the round of drinks, my headache calmed down.

Jack kept nodding encouragingly until I got to the end of the round.

'Okay, listen to me. This is some bad shit, but we can fix it. For now, you have only one thing to do, and that is remember every single detail of the past week, but not the steps. Just focus on the last seven days here in Egypt, every tiny little detail. Avoid thinking about your home or past at all costs.'

I nodded. My headache was still buzzing, but it made sense. If the timelines were changing, I needed not to think about them. My brain was not built to allow two co-existing realities. There may even get to a point where, in another reality, I didn't exist at all. I winced.

'What was playing on the karaoke?' demanded Jack again.

'*The Wandering Caribou.*'

'Good, try to recite the words.'

As I did, the others moved away from me and began talking urgently. Two technicians came into the room carrying two heavy travel sacks whilst I concentrated on how the caribou got stuck in the tar.

A voice from the loudspeaker called down from the gantry. 'First, we have reached the 1800s. The effects are now global.'

Ah yes, I thought. The great Chinese-European war fought on American soil. So many deaths, but the rise of a new empire.

I threw up.

Clio came over and helped support me, walking me away from the vomit. I was so weak, I couldn't have pushed her away even if I wanted.

'How do we walk to the sea front from here? Do we turn left or right when we exit the Sinai Entrance?'

'Left.'

186

'Then?'

People were rushing in, jabbing Clio and me with booster shots, and fixing our braces back on our wrists. I could feel the hum of the wall start up, and I tried desperately to remember how to get to the sea front.

'Clear the room,' called a voice from the gantry. Everyone quickly exited, running up the stairs to observe from a safe position.

'Julius,' said Clio. She gave me a quick shake and I tried to focus on her. She was Clio. She was... Who was she? 'Can you make it through on your own? I can't be touching you.'

She looked up behind her.

'We're losing him!'

I didn't know who she was talking about. A moment later, I felt a strong pair of hands shove me from behind. They were trying to push me towards a wall. I struggled. Was this a mugging? What was happening? There was a second shove, this time much stronger, and I hit the wall. Except I didn't.

Chapter 25 - Julius

I was on my hands and knees. The grass was damp, and I threw up again. Clio was a few metres away, also vomiting. I rolled over on my back, looked up at the blue sky, and felt an incredible rush of euphoria. My head felt cool, the pain was gone, and all my memories were intact. Even those from the previous ten minutes.

Clio staggered over. Stepping over the vomit, she sat down on my other side.

'Are you okay?'

'Yes. All safely back online. What the hell happened during the step? Was it me, or was that a tad bumpy?'

Clio laughed weakly. 'A tad bumpy? I think I vomited my eyeballs out through my ears. I think with the timeline in such a flux, it was going to be rough. Jack and First did say it might be difficult. I shall tell them it was, in fact, *a tad bumpy.*'

She laughed again, then laid back in the grass alongside me.

'Who is Gloriana?'

'Queen Elizabeth the First.'

'The Asian-European wars?'

'Never happened.'

She sat up. 'Good. Let's crack on and fix the future. Now let's pray to all your gods that we are in the right location.'

I continued to lie on my back and smelled the air. A silly grin plastered over my face. Whenever we were, we were in England. Damp grass and warm soil would always smell like this. Sitting out on the slips, waiting with Charlie as the wickets fell, and it was our turn to bat. I could hear her tapping on her brace as I lay still, enjoying the sunshine on my eyelids and the memories.

'Okay. It's ten miles to London, we've got our walking staffs, it's sunny and our contacts are working. Hit it.' She grinned at me. 'Did I get that right?'

Holy cow. Was Clio trying to be nice? Was she trying to build a bridge? I might have just forgotten who Henry the Eighth was, but I would never forget that Clio was Charlie's killer.

'Do you think a joke makes it all alright?'

'Now what's wrong with you?' She got up and brushed the grass off her monk's robes.

'You know what? Forget it. Get up and let's get to work. We have to get to the Tower, hide from ourselves, the minute our previous selves leave we are to close that door. Then we go home and I put in a request to work with someone else.'

I nodded along as I looked through my kitbag. It had been chaotic in the step room, and I hadn't been able to process what was going on around me.

'Are you paying attention? I said that our braces have been hard timed to return one minute before the fracture occurs. We need to shut the door, then hide and wait. I

189

can't ever remember a fracture this calamitous, and there you are right in the middle.'

I stood up, slinging my bag over my shoulder. 'I heard what you said. And trust me, I won't shed any tears about losing you as a partner. You killed my best friend. If it hadn't been for Neith, I wouldn't be working with you at all.' I glared at Clio. 'You were standing right beside me, remember? This chaos is as much your fault as it is mine. Now, enough of this nonsense. We have a job to do.'

I looked around. There wasn't a soul in sight. Nor were there any buildings. I was standing in a meadow, in a rolling landscape of grass with a wood in the distance. I checked my brace. Ah, Peckham, you had never smelled so sweet. We were also twenty-four hours early. Plenty of time to get in place. It would have been better to be dropped directly into the Tower and hour before, but given recent steps, I was grateful to be close enough.

This was the tail end of the War of the Roses. A dynastic fight that had simmered and festered for several generations and exploded into outrageous violence over the past twenty years. From the decline of a weak king into infirmity, a desperate and ruthless Queen, unloved by the people. And a fierce warrior with a good heart and a strong claim to the throne, but not the stomach to take it.

Now all three were dead. The warrior's son had become king and had also died, leaving his two sons as heirs, their uncle as protector. In the wings, Henry Tudor was getting ready to wipe them all from the throne. So fell

190

the House of Lancaster to York, and soon York would fall to Tudor. All in the space of twenty-five years.

Most historians had watched *Game of Thrones* and commented on how tame it was. The War of the Roses was Britain's greatest bloodbath, and here we sat in the middle of it. It was hard not to feel a sense of excitement. However, I had a job to do. It was about time that I took control of the situation. We were still wearing our monks' robes, so we would have to work with that.

'Right, we should be able to get to London before sundown. If anyone asks, we are men of God and have no say in royal disputes. If pressed, we are for...' I paused, trying to remember how Richard was currently styling himself. 'For the Lord Protector. I don't think there are any problems at the moment. No marauding armies this year.'

Clio barely nodded and set off towards the trees. I couldn't tell if she was sulking or just angry. Or just being Clio. God knows why Neith had regarded her as such a good friend. Watching her stride away, I thought even the most desperate churl would think twice about approaching her, even if she was dressed as a holy man. Nothing about her deportment suggested she'd be an easy target.

I sighed and followed her. I doubt I cast as threatening a figure. Maybe I could bore them to death with the minutiae of translations between calligraphic interpretations.

As she reached the woods, she paused, waiting for me, and pushed the hood off her head. The wood wasn't particularly dense. In the distance, I could hear a river. I wondered if this wood was used for hunting.

'I take it you know the way?' I called after her, adjusting my sack.

She turned and frowned at me. 'How should I know? The brace doesn't have a detailed map for this area. I was going to head to the river, then follow it to the Thames. Unless you have a better idea?'

I thought about it, then smiled, asking the brace to show me the local Roman roads.

'There it is,' I said, pointing in the direction of the trees. 'The A3, or, as it's currently known, Stane Street, is just over to our west. We can cut through these woods, follow the road into Southwark, and cross the Thames at London Bridge. Then we turn right.'

I tilted my head. 'Or would you rather fight your way along the undergrowth the entire way to London, then struggle to find a crossing?'

She didn't reply, but headed off alongside me and, I noticed, slightly ahead of me. I had no argument. She was the better fighter, and if something happened to her, I would get over it. She wasn't moving particularly quickly, though, which felt like a mistake. This seemed the perfect place for desperate men to live. If we were going to fight, I would rather be in the open with room to move. I stepped over some brambles. There were no proper footpaths in here, and I was likely to trip in an attack.

'Do you think you could pick up the speed?'

She looked over her shoulder and raised an eyebrow and I carried on.

'It's just you were in one hell of a hurry back in the step room. Running around telling everyone I needed saving.'

She stopped and turned. I wondered if she was about to punch me, then her expression relaxed and she shook her head. 'Well, yes. I suppose I was overreacting. Neith always says I'm a rubbish Shah player. I would rush in with all my pieces, trying a full-on assault on the king, losing my pawns and rooks in a bloodbath of speed and force.' She shrugged. 'Anansi was brilliant at it, and he kept trying to improve my game.'

As I watched her, I couldn't interpret her expression, but I suddenly felt uncomfortable. There was something in her face that looked haunted.

'It wasn't to help me improve,' she continued. 'I just think he was bored playing with someone so poor.'

'Your time with Anansi, what was—'

She cut me off. 'It's like Neith said. I need to think ahead.'

I followed her lead and stepped away from any mention of the trickster god.

'So, what are you saying? That I wasn't at any real risk?'

She started walking again and laughed bitterly. 'Oh no, you were definitely at risk. Your brain was getting close to a full-on embolism. Lots of grey matter going splat inside your skull. But as it turns out, it wouldn't have mattered.'

I have to confess, I felt it did matter, at least on a personal level.

'In what way was my brain exploding not an issue? I thought you were so concerned about my brain being preserved for the splice link I share with Neith?'

She whistled, forcing me to repeat myself. Looking over her shoulder, she smirked at me. 'Do what Neith always tells me to do. Think it through.'

I quite like chess, or Shah, as she called it, and would play with Charlie. He came from the Clio camp of tactics. Full-on assault. Whereas I liked to sit back and look at the bigger picture. I didn't know Neith played, and looked forward to getting back and challenging her to a game.

Now, as I trudged through the fallen branches and ferns, I tried to look at the whole scene. My brain had been suffering because I was trying to hold two separate timelines in my head at the same time. Nature might abhor a vacuum, but it really would not tolerate two realities within the same space and time, either. As the time fractures had raced towards the modern day, I was getting worse. There would be a moment when my brain would, as Clio had so charmingly expressed it, splat against my skull. At least figuratively. And then what? Take me out of the equation. I would be dead. And useless, as my brain would no longer have a viable set of pathways, full of tiny embolisms. And there would be nothing for Neith's doctors to study in repairing her own splice. Oh, hang on… I groaned.

'Worked it out?' asked Clio cheerfully.

'If the other timeline played itself out, the chances of my existence would be reduced. As would the chances of me ever getting in your way during the hunt for the Fabergé Egg. Hell, even Fabergé might never exist.'

'Exactly. And if Neith never met you, she could never save you, and never jeopardise her own health. Had the timeline run on, Neith would have been cured.' This time, her laugh was sour. 'Everything would have changed.'

We walked in silence as I thought about how many things would be different for all of us.

'Sorry.' It seemed strange to apologise for my own existence, and I knew it was none of my fault. Everyone made their own choices and played the hand they were dealt, but I knew Clio cared for Neith deeply. It was, in fact, her only redeeming feature and for that alone, I could feel sorry for her.

'Not your fault,' she said. 'I should have thought things through and let you die.'

Sort of sorry for her.

'But we're here now. And Neith would want this mission to go ahead. So that's what I'm doing. Even if I don't care if we succeed.'

We walked on in silence. There was the occasional call of birds, and the river continued to flow to our right. My heart felt heavy, and I wished I could find the source of my pain. It had nothing to do with the headache. This was a sense of deepening unease with every step that took us towards the Tower. I had been excited when we first arrived, but Clio's talk of the mission reminded me of what we were here to do. Setting the timeline right was all well and good, but it meant that I had to ensure the two princes died.

Clio's fist shot up, and I stopped abruptly. In my introspection, I had failed to hear something big making its way through the undergrowth towards us. I turned towards the sound just as an enormous boar burst out of the bushes.

Clio swung her walking staff into position and fired a laser shot at the animal.

It roared, only momentarily slowed, as it continued to tear towards us.

It's funny how time can slow down. In my state of heightened awareness, I could see arrow shafts dug into its flank. One of its tusks was broken and blood poured from a slashed jaw. Dogs were baying, and I could hear the sound of hooves approaching. But they wouldn't get here in time. Our weapons were calibrated to stun a human only. It wouldn't take much to adjust them to kill an enraged boar, but it would take more time than we had.

Clio must have come to the same conclusion, screaming at me to get to the river. Yanking up our cassocks, we sprinted towards the water.

Everything was becoming loud. The sound of dogs barking in excitement, the breath of the boar, my pounding heart and with every stride the river got closer, not some small stream but something loud and monstrous in its own right.

I had got within sight of the engorged river when a bramble snagged my sleeve and jerked me off my feet. I could feel the weight of the boar's charge as it thundered down on me, the damp earth under my hands, vibrating with its approach.

Then Clio was by my side, swinging her staff down and smashing it against the side of the boar's head. I scrambled to my feet as the boar turned with ferocious speed, its broken tusk catching Clio's arm. Flinging her sideways, I saw her brace wrench loose, falling into the brambles.

A dog burst out of the undergrowth, launching itself at the boar's flank. As the pig turned to attack the dog, I ran over to Clio and grabbed her, pulling her towards the river. We would have to come back for the brace. For now, we needed to get to safety.

'Get to the trunk.' Clio's face was pale, blood gushing down her arm. Without her brace her suit hadn't activated and she was bleeding freely. If we could just climb onto the tree trunk that had fallen across the river, we should be safe. Over time, people had removed branches and fashioned it into a somewhat perilous bridge.

The river below ran deep and fast, eddies tugging at the surface then racing on downstream, where the water was white as it crashed over rocks and plunged downhill. I pushed Clio ahead of me, as she shuffled onto the trunk crouching down on all fours. We edged our way out above the torrent. I looked behind, where the boar was fighting three dogs. Several men on horseback slowly approached the animal, spreading out into a circle, their spears all pointing towards it.

One shouted over to me to stay where I was, and I had enough time to wonder if he thought I was an idiot, when Clio shrieked in alarm. She jumped up, trying to brush something off her hand. In her haste she slipped as her arm gave way under her. She looked at me in sheer terror, her eyes wide, then fell into the river.

Chapter 26 - Julius

The weight of Clio's cassock dragged her straight under the water. She didn't re-surface and, without her brace, I realised her second skin would only offer her basic assistance. She might not get bruised, but she would surely drown.

I stripped off my cassock and jumped off the trunk. Almost immediately, a hand closed around my foot. Pulling her towards me, I dragged her head above the surface as we rushed towards the rocks.

'Swim for the shore!'

Ahead, two men stood in a section of shallow water. There was a small beach ahead of the cataract. They were shouting at us to move to the side of the river. If I could just get us to their side, they might be able to grab at us. My arm was straining, trying to pull through the water as I held onto Clio. She was also kicking, and I was suddenly reminded of the time I saw a cat fall into a canal. The look of fury on its face reminded me of Clio, and I found myself laughing.

I felt the riverbed with my foot and, bracing myself, I hurled the pair of us off to the right. The men grabbed at us, then dragged us out of the river.

Panting, I pulled myself up onto my hands and knees, then sat on my calves and looked around. Clio was leaning on one arm and still coughing out river water. Blood was running down her other arm, but I knew she'd be okay. I sat back and laughed again.

'Are they hurt?'

A rider had joined the others and swung down from his saddle. The two men turned, ignoring us, and nodded as he walked towards us. He threw one of the men his gloves and waited for their report.

'They are, my lord. But this one may be a holy fool, and I've no idea about that one.' He pointed towards Clio as she continued to cough.

I sat up. 'He's Nubian. That's all, and I'm not a fool, just grateful to our Lord that he should test us, then send us rescue. He is indeed all-powerful.' I made the sign of the cross and the men followed me.

The newcomer nodded to the men as one of them took the reins of the horse. He was a tall man in his fifties, grey haired and clean shaven with a scar pulling on his chin. His embroidered jacket was trimmed in fur and the long sleeves, moved in the breeze. Once a man of action now he seemed relaxed in finer robes.

'Fetch this man's robes and bag.' He lent me his hand and pulled me up. The skin of his palm was rough so maybe he was still a fighter. In this time period he was getting on in age, but the War of the Roses had been turbulent. Relax and you were likely to find yourself on the wrong side and dangling from a nose or a sword.

'We'll get a change of clothes for your companion and dress that wound as well. My apologies. We wouldn't have

200

driven that hog towards you, had I but known you were there. In fact,' he paused and shrugged off his jacket, 'have mine. The Lady Anne always makes me wear this dreadful jacket. She believes it will impress the beasts of the field. I think they are simply overcome with laughter.'

He seemed comfortable in his position of authority and generous in the way he treated those around him. I suspect if we weren't dressed as monks, he might have had a greater issue with us being in his woods.

'Brother Masoud is fine. It's just a scratch. And the clothes will soon dry.'

I wanted to get away from these men as soon as possible, retrieve Clio's brace, and continue on our way.

'Nonsense. You will accept my hospitality for the night and tell me what the two of you are doing here. I have to say, you're not the sort of monk I'm used to.'

He looked me up and down, and I realised I probably looked odd. I was tanned, tall and, if not muscular, I was certainly stronger looking than when I had just been a college professor. You don't get to be a curator without being fit.

And as for Clio. Well, she really needed to keep her wet clothes on. She might not be the curvy sort, but standing in just her skin, her sex would be instantly obvious. I needed to think of a cover story, and fast. I passed her the jacket and tried to hide a smile as I watched her examine the fancy trim in barely disguised horror.

'We're travelling from Burgundy. We are on a pilgrimage and wish to pray at the tomb of Henry the Fifth.'

I thought mentioning their warrior king who had beaten the French might go down well and, given the way our lord was smiling, I had judged it correctly.

'You've come a long way.'

'Yes. Some monks are good at reading and writing. Some monks are better at walking.'

'Some monks are quite good at drowning as well!'

He laughed at his joke and I joined in.

'Very good, my Lord.'

I knew I'd get a kicking from Clio for that later, so I doubled down. 'Brother Masoud has been complaining since we arrived on your shores. Your climate doesn't suit him, but God loves to challenge us.'

The man made the sign of the cross again and I thought we would probably be okay. Even if we had to stay the night at his manor, it would mean a warm bed and some food. We needed to be at the Tower tomorrow evening, so this wouldn't delay us.

'Come on, Masoud, the Lord has provided shelter for the night. Don't just sit there dripping.'

Clio gave me daggers, but got up quickly, leaning on her other arm. Her robe was clinging to her frame, and I walked over to her quickly.

'Flap your robes. The fabric is shaping your body.'

'You flap your robes,' she hissed, but pulled the fabric away from her skin. 'I need my sodding brace to activate my second skin. I'm going to die of pneumonia.'

I laughed loudly, slapping her on the back, then strode off to join the lord. 'We are honoured to accept your invitation.'

As we returned to the clearing, some men were already tying the dead boar onto poles. A man jogged towards us and handed me my robe, which I gratefully put back on. My second skin looked like a cotton loin cloth, but I didn't want anyone to inspect it too closely. My bag was intact, but I couldn't see my staff. As the lord wandered off to let me change, I activated my brace and told it to locate our missing items. Within a few minutes, I had Clio's brace, but my staff was down river beyond the rocks, sweeping away on the current. I swore. That was my only form of weapon.

When I returned to the clearing, one of the servants was treating Clio's arm. The look of disgust on her face was priceless.

She spoke quickly in Arabic. 'Julius, these bloody fools are going to give me blood poisoning. Look at this shit.' She thrust her arm out at me to reveal a sticky brown paste with bits of leaves in it.

The man who had been treating her stepped away in alarm. He couldn't understand her words, but her tone was crystal clear.

I smiled at him reassuringly. 'Brother Masoud is telling me how impressed he is with your poultice, and wonders what might be in it. He also says thank you. Their language can sound deceptively harsh, but he really is terribly grateful.'

Clio all but growled at me as the poor servant muttered about comfrey leaves and juniper berries. When he mentioned the urine of a virgin, I nearly wet myself, but managed to turn it into a cough. Clio simply stood and fumed, allowing the man to bandage her arm.

He moved away rapidly, and I stepped closer to Clio, shielding her from view as I handed over her brace. As soon as it was on, it disappeared from view.

Clio smiled. No doubt her second skin, now activated, had slid over her limbs and was starting to warm her up.

'Don't make it heal your arm totally. They may want to re-dress it later. Miracle cures lead to accusations of witchcraft and burning around here.'

She glared. 'I take it you have no issue with me instructing the brace to prevent any of the gunk from entering my bloodstream?'

'None at all.' As I walked off, I whistled *For She's a Jolly Good Fellow* to myself, and took the horse that was offered to me.

'Father Julius, my men tell me you have lost your walking staff?' said the lord as he rode over to me. 'I will arrange a replacement for you back at the manor.'

I gave a small bow from my saddle. 'I thank you, and again, you have the advantage over me. I don't know who it is I am thanking, but surely you must be a very important lord.'

Flattered, the nobleman pretended to brush off my words, but then informed me he was the Baron Hugh Monteville. 'We are living through good times,' he demurred. 'I am just lucky.'

I felt that was a rather optimistic view of the War of the Roses and said as much.

'That was all in the past. The trouble was, we were under the yoke of a French woman. What country can prosper like that?'

I nodded an agreement. 'And now?' My ignorance could be easily explained as a traveller from Burgundy. Besides, I was keen to know what people thought of Richard.

'Now we are settled. King Edward died too soon, God rest his soul, but he left two bonny heirs.'

'The idea of a regency doesn't cause alarm?'

'With Richard steering the ship?' He laughed, amused at the notion. 'I have never met a better soldier, but he's no king. He loves his nephews. When you think the pain that man endured losing his only son, I'd warrant he looks on those boys with a paternal love. He will protect them as young Edward reaches his majority.'

'Good times, indeed.'

Monteville looked over his shoulder at the convoy riding behind us, then looked back at me.

'Your companion is steaming.'

I shrugged. 'He's a good sort, but I think being dunked in the water dampened his spirits. He'll be better company when he is warm again.'

None of that was true. Clio was a bad-tempered, snide individual, but I couldn't help remembering that look of fear before she fell in the water. She had been stripped raw and her terror was wrenching.

'No, I mean actually steaming. Look.'

I tuned in my saddle and saw Clio bringing up the rear of the horse riders. Steam gently rose from her cloak. With the falling sunlight, she appeared bathed in a personal glowing cloud. Some of the men walking behind were making the sign of the cross.

'Maybe the holy spirit is moving in him,' I said, cautiously.

'I suspect it's more likely his cloak drying out and the sun emphasising the effect,' said the lord, kindly.

My lips twitched. That had been pretty ignorant of me to assume that my companion didn't have the wits of his own eyes.

'Still,' he said, 'it is causing a bit of a stir amongst my men.'

He removed his cloak and handed it to me. It was a sturdy garment made from worsted and perfect for a day out riding.

'Give him this and let's see if we can dampen down that effect before I'm forced to recognise you as messengers from God.'

I trotted back and pulled up alongside Clio, handing her the cloak.

'Put this on. Your under-skins are being too efficient. You're currently surrounded by a holy nimbus.'

'Are you kidding me?' she grumbled. 'That cloak will slow the drying time. This is killing me.'

'Stop whining. You're a curator.'

With the challenge thrown down, she wrapped the cloak around herself, and the steam and mist instantly dissipated.

'What are you waiting for? Me to thank you?'

'Lord Monteville suggested the cloak, not me.'

'No, I meant for thinking you saved me. You didn't, you know. I was already busy saving myself. I wasn't drowning.'

'Really? It felt to me, as I struggled to pull you to the surface, that you were busy sinking. You know, given your lack of brace meant you couldn't activate the second skin, and the heavy hessian robes were holding you down at the bottom of the riverbed.'

'I was fine.'

Our horses clopped along, their hooves the only noise. We were an island of silence amongst the celebrations of the hunt. For two pins, I would have given up. What was the point? She was the worst of companions and yet, that look in her eyes.

'When we were on the tree trunk, something seemed to alarm you. Cause you to lose your balance and fall.'

'There was a spider. I disturbed a spider's nest. Hundreds of them swarmed over my hand.'

Her voice trailed off and we rode in silence for a minute. Anansi's preferred form was that of a spider. God knows I had my opinion of Clio, but I had never thought what it must have been like to spend a year living at the whim of an all-powerful and somewhat deranged trickster god. I had assumed they were kindred spirits, but maybe the price of her travels had been higher than I had cared to consider.

'What, no clever comeback?' she said. 'No snide observation? Maybe, arachnophobia is irrational. Or, I'm a thousand times bigger than them.'

I shook my head. 'No. You slipped on wet leaves and fell in the water. The report needs no further elaboration as far as I'm concerned.'

We rode in silence again.

'I didn't actually kill him, you know.'

I looked at her, confused.

'Your friend. Charlie. He died because of my actions, but I didn't kill him.'

I couldn't speak.

'I just didn't pay him any attention, and through my neglect, I am guilty of his death. When I told the local

208

crew to get him out of the way, I forgot how that could be interpreted on a world where life is so cheap.'

A flock of small brown birds flittered past us and, as we came closer to the manor, the hounds ran ahead of us towards the stables. I still couldn't think of a word to say.

'You want me to forgive you?' My voice was harsh.

'No. I don't want your forgiveness,' spat Clio. 'What do I care about your opinion of me? I just wanted to set the record straight and, for what it's worth, I am sorry for his loss of life.'

She dug her heels into the horse's flank and rode forward to speak to our host for the evening. I was so angry that, right then, I didn't care if she completely screwed up the timeline. I didn't want to spend another second in her company.

The following morning, we rose with the servants and headed off. By breakfast we were walking through Southwark, ready to allow two children to die and save the world. I felt sick.

Chapter 27 - Julius

We had been hiding in a dark corner under a stone staircase, running through various micro-stretches to ward off cramp. From time to time, the brace warned us of nearby activity and we stayed as quiet as we could. Starting a fight in the Tower of London was not high on my list of life goals. I couldn't say the same for Clio, but I knew she wanted this mission to go without a hitch.

A wave of nausea overwhelmed me and I slumped down the cold wall. Beside me, Clio uttered a small moan and placed her hand over her mouth.

'I guess the other us have arrived,' I whispered.

The plan was to wait until our first incarnation appeared, then wait until we/they had left the room and the corridor. We would then sneak along, lock the door, and instantly head home at the exact same time our previous selves headed home. The braces had been synced to automatically retrieve us, so there would be no error. The theory was that our two timelines would "merge" in the quantum stream, and all would be well.

'I don't like this bit about merging.'

'No, really?' said Clio. 'You haven't mentioned it much.'

'I'm just saying. What if instead of merging, we cancel ourselves out?'

'First assured me that wouldn't happen.'

'So it occurred to you, too?' I said.

'Of course it did. I'm not a bloody fool. Shh.'

I didn't need her to tell me I had already heard bolts sliding, followed by a whispered conversation. I sounded weird, but then one always does when one hears oneself. Clio sounded perfectly the same.

'Okay, give it a minute,' said Clio. 'We didn't hear footsteps last time, so let's make sure that we/they, don't this time.'

'I still don't feel good about this,' I said.

I couldn't see Clio's face, but I knew she had turned towards me as her voice projected in my direction.

'Need I remind you, you're a curator.' She said, chucking my own words back at me. 'We need to fix the mess we created and save this stupid Earth's timeline. Bast knows I would be happier if it all fell down around your ears, and Neith was restored to her former glory. But no, we have to fix this and continue to experience the joy that is Julius Strathclyde.'

'All I'm saying is—'

'Sweet Bast!' Clio cut me off and shuffled out from under the steps, straightening as she emerged into the corridor. In front of her stood two young boys in long white nightgowns.

'What are you doing out of your bed?' said Clio.

The boys stared at her in horror. The flames from the sconces flickered, and I saw the face of the older boy glare at her in defiance. His little brother gripped his hand. Their bid for freedom had failed at the first corridor.

211

'Come on, back inside. Quickly.'

I stood next to Clio, and the look I received was no less hostile.

'I am the King of England.'

'I don't care who you are. It's past your bedtime,' declared Clio firmly. 'Now do as you're told.'

My misgivings about this mission were now running amok as we herded them back into their chambers. They were so small. All that bravery collapsed in the face of two adults.

'I can't do this.'

Clio glared at me, her face as furious as the young king's.

'Yes, you can.'

'But the boys will mention us.'

'Yes, we will,' piped up Edward. 'We will tell everyone.'

'So what?' Clio ignored the boy and spoke to me. 'Who'll believe them? They will call it night terrors. What does it matter anyway? They won't be around much longer.'

'Clio!'

She had the grace to look abashed as she realised the impact of her words on the two children.

'I'm sorry, Julius. And honestly, I agree. This sucks, but all we are doing is restoring history.'

I noticed she couldn't bring herself to look at the two brothers as they stood side by side, shivering in their flimsy gowns. Richard rubbed his pale white feet, one over the other, as they stood on the matting. Edward squeezed his little brother and continued to stare at us. With his mop of blond hair and his good-looking countenance, he was probably the spit of his father. As he stood bravely protecting his little brother, it was clear he would probably make for a righteous king. Yet here I was, ensuring he died.

'No. I can't.'

'Julius.' Clio sounded alarmingly desperate now.

'They are children, for God's sake.'

'Are you here to kill us?' asked the smaller boy. His voice wobbled, and Clio winced.

She continued to ignore him. 'Julius, they disappear. That is the fixed point. We can't let them escape.'

Her words exploded in my head as I stared at her in wonder. 'They disappear!' I shouted, hope overwhelming me. 'Just like we are about to.' I waited for her to catch up.

She looked at me blankly.

'*They disappear.*' I stressed her words.

'Are you insane?' She had caught up. I don't know why this hadn't occurred to me before, but it was the perfect solution.

'Why not?'

'We can't take Beta individuals back to Alpha. It's strictly forbidden.'

'Except for angels.'

'Except for them.'

'And me.'

'You were an accident. And look what's happened to my society ever since you arrived.'

'A catalyst is not to blame for a situation just waiting to ignite.' I shot back as we argued back and forth.

'But we can't.' Now Clio was pleading with me. 'That's not what happened.'

'How do you know? No one knows what happened to them. Not even when they disappeared. Maybe this *is* what happened.'

I was whispering so intently now it felt like I was shouting. I knew my suggestion was foolish and dangerous, but if it meant I didn't have to be a party to their murder, then it was a risk I was happy to run with.

'We don't have spare braces.'

I exhaled in relief. She was considering it. 'We don't need them. I'll just hold the boys.'

Time was running out, the brace had flashed. In sixty seconds we would be automatically pulled back to Alpha.

'It's too dangerous. What if you splice?'

'That's rare, these days. Jack says they have been working on that side effect recently. It's apparently an almost negligible risk factor.'

'No. Not a chance.' Clio hissed. 'We're doing this partly to keep your brain intact for Neith.'

'Sod that. What do you think Neith would do right now?'

FIVE

The brace began to count down, and I ran towards the boys.

FOUR

Clio threw herself at me, and I punched her in the face.

THREE

The two boys ran to the door. I sprinted towards them. If I could just grab their arms...

TWO

I felt a sudden crack on my flank. Clio had shot me with her staff, and I flew sideways in the air away from the boys.

ONE

I hadn't even landed when I felt the world around me turn inside out, as the brace yanked me back to Alpha.

Chapter 28 - Julius

I landed in a heap on the floor of the step room. Slamming my hands down, I pushed myself up, spinning around to attack Clio. She was looking around her, blinking as she patted her arms and legs, wiggling her fingers and twisting her neck. Beside her sat two very alarmed little boys.

I lurched towards her and gave her the biggest hug I had ever given anyone. Then the four of us fainted.

I woke up in the curators' triage wing. Clio was beside me, groaning, and everyone was looking furious as various doctors poked and prodded us.

'Where are the boys?' My voice sounded tinny, and I could taste fish in my mouth.

'They're fine, Julius,' said Sam, looking as angry as I had ever seen him. 'They've been sedated and taken to angel quarantine.'

I relaxed, but the enormity of what I had done was beginning to dawn on me.

'How could you be so stupid?' roared the pharaoh as she strode into the room. She turned to Sam. 'Is it true? Have we actually extracted two of Beta's principal characters?'

Sam nodded, and I tried to explain myself. I felt dreadful, both physically and mentally.

'It's not his fault,' said Clio, her voice slurring, then she fainted.

I tried to sit up and then I fainted as well.

The next time I woke up, I was in a hospital bed. Clio was lying in the bed alongside me. We both had pads on our foreheads, quantum scanners measuring our brainwaves.

Clio's eyes were open, and she was staring at the ceiling.

'Are you okay?' I said.

She remained motionless. I tried again, but there was no response. I pulled myself up as the door opened and Dr Bitsoi walked in.

'Ah good, you're awake.'

'Yes, I'm fine,' I said and it was true. I was feeling a lot better. 'But I'm worried about Clio. She's unresponsive.'

Bitsoi looked across at Clio and checked his monitor. 'Clio, are you alright?'

'Perfectly fine, thank you.'

He nodded. 'And did you hear Julius speak to you a moment ago?'

'Yes, doctor.'

'And the reason you didn't reply?'

'Because he is a Shitfly of the highest magnitude, and I was ignoring him.'

Bitsoi looked a little embarrassed, then looked back at me as he scratched the side of his face.

'Well, there we are, Julius. She seems like Clio Masoud to me.'

I shook my head. 'Yep. Situation absolutely normal. Can you tell me how the princes are?'

'Sod the princes,' said Clio. 'Why do we keep fainting?'

Bitsoi pulled over a chair and sat down between our two beds.

'The princes are fine. They remain under sedation. They are in perfect health, so we haven't had to do any interventions, but we have tweaked their immune systems for the twenty-first century. We don't want the poor boys to die of a cold. We've decided to keep them sedated until the council decides what to do with them. It's being discussed at the moment.'

He turned and smiled at Clio. 'As for you two, we think you are suffering from the mother of all quantum hangovers. This also explains any strange tastes you are experiencing. The engineers are running the data from your braces and comparing it to the data that was removed the first time you jumped back from that timeline.' He grinned to himself. 'They really are very excited.'

'And the mission itself?' I asked.

'I understand it was a success, but you'll need to ask Chancellor Nymens.'

There was a knock on the door and Rami poked his head around. 'Are these two well enough for me to speak to them?'

'Yes, I'm here to discharge them anyway.' He turned to us. 'You'll need to keep the medi-brace on for the next week, just to check your vitals. No swimming or rock climbing during that time, please. Think of how embarrassing it would be for a curator to die because they fainted.'

Clio snorted, and I suspected she hadn't agreed with his choice of word either. Embarrassing. Honestly.

He glanced at her quickly and cleared his throat. 'A tragedy for yourselves, obviously, and we would all mourn, naturally.' And with that, he dashed out of the room before he said anything else to annoy Clio.

Rami placed his hands on the back of the chair and, looking at us, he sighed deeply. 'Well, the crocodiles are well and truly in the temple now.'

'Rami, this is entirely my fault.' I said.

'And yet it was Clio who brought the boys through. Having stopped you from getting to them, she grabbed them herself.'

He glanced across at her curiously, but she continued to look at the ceiling.

'What's the verdict of the meeting? Are we going to be censured?'

Rami shrugged and sat down. 'As it happens, you are not. There was even talk of you receiving a commendation. But not everyone agreed.'

'A commendation?' asked Clio in astonishment.

219

'Yes. You successfully retrieved the crown jewels, and, somehow, that timeline hasn't been erased as predicted. You jumped without splicing, and you repaired the splinter. The Beta timeline has returned to a lovely smooth line, and all is well. Plus, you have given the engineers so much data to play with, they are practically laughing.'

I raised my eyebrows at Clio, who continued to ignore me. I was certain she was simply thinking of the right words to say well done.

'And what of Neith?' said Clio. 'Have those older scrolls we retrieved fixed things?'

Rami looked around the room, then sat down.

'Not yet. The linguist department is thrilled with you. Through Neith's injuries and tentative recovery, they are learning so much about language acquisition. Really boundary pushing stuff.'

Given how remarkably advanced they were anyway, I thought it was astonishing there was still so much to learn.

'But what about Neith?' repeated Clio.

'Like I said, they are working on it. Tiresias is working round the clock trying to map models to Neith's brain schematics. They are operating on her later today with the solution, they hope. For now, she isn't allowed visitors. Her behaviour remains erratic, and they don't want to trigger any seizures before the operation.'

Everything we had done had been for nothing. If Neith wasn't fixed, what was the point?

'Incidentally, Clio's lack of splice has really fired up the engineers. Sorry about that, Clio. By the time they're done prodding you, you would probably welcome a splice.'

I looked across at her, then smiled at Rami.

'Oh dear, that is bad luck.'

She turned to me with a glare that could scorch granite. I waved back and gave her a cheery grin. Anticipating a fight, Rami leant back in the chair and placed his foot on his knee.

'And then there's the timeline. It's perfect. There isn't a crease anywhere. Tiresias was asked to analyse it on a micro level. And, so far, there's nothing. It would seem that, against all odds, the great mystery of the Princes in the Tower is solved. We removed them. A perfect and contained paradox. If the engineers could, they would make you two pharaohs for ever. They are so excited. First even clapped her hands and laughed.'

'And the princes themselves?'

He sighed and rubbed at his jaw. 'Ah yes, well they are a problem, aren't they? Pharaoh Cleeve is unimpressed. Considers them a threat to Alpha society. But what can we do? There was a discussion about leaving them in suspended animation, or of returning them to modern day Earth. Both were considered cruel or akin to death. Finally, it was decided that the princes will be woken up and adopted. The meeting ended a short while ago.'

He looked at me sadly. 'And it will not be easy, Julius, but you will be the person to explain to them what has happened.'

The enormity of my actions now pressed on me. I felt like someone was standing on my chest. Of course it was going to be me. I was the only Beta here, plus I had experienced exactly what they had. I knew what their next few weeks were going to feel like. The pain, the fear, the disbelief, the confusion. They were about to wake up into a nightmare.

I nodded, but couldn't speak.

'Can we go now?' said Clio, getting out of bed. 'I want to see Neith.'

'I just said, that's a no.'

Clio's jaw clenched and she fixed her eyes ahead. Everything she had done had been to save Neith. She hadn't saved the boys to rescue them, or heal the timeline. She had grabbed them so that I couldn't. She was ensuring that my splice with Neith remained clean. And now it seemed that Neith was as broken as ever. If this operation didn't work, I remembered Minju's warning. I might never see Neith again.

Chapter 29 - Julius

I had been given leave to return to my apartment to change clothes and shave. After that, it was straight back to the hospital to speak to the boys. As I headed home, I cut through the plaza I stepped aside to let a family pass me by and fainted.

I came to with a dog licking my face, and the father calling for an ambulance. Shaking my head, I waved my medi-brace at them. Having determined I was only out for a few seconds, I stood up. There was no dizziness or headache, just an unpleasant amount of drool. It was hard to decide if I would have preferred it to be mine or the dog's.

Once they were reassured I was not about to die, the family walked away. As they left, I could hear the mother complain of my behaviour as the children started to cry. 'Really. Right in front of us. What did he think he was playing at?'

I rolled my eyes and walked on. They were going to dine out on that "drama" for weeks to come. In the meantime, I considered the faints. There was no warning. No funny smells, no flickering lights. No sense of nausea or headache. Just a funny taste of fish in my mouth. And it was just the same when I came round. I wasn't convinced this was a quantum hangover. But what was it?

My medi-brace chimed. 'Julius. Are you okay?' asked Koda Bitsoi.

'All fine,' I tried to reassure him. I was desperate to get home and clean up. I had been in medieval England for days. A wash was something of a necessity. 'As you probably observed, just a tiny collapse.'

'Can you come back in now, please? I want to run some scans.'

I told him I was on my way, then jogged back to my apartment. Nothing was going to get in the way of my shower and shave, and some decent clothes.

When I returned, Koda looked at my face and tilted his head.

'What? If I'm going to meet the King of England, the least I could do is shave. Besides which, I stank.'

'You could have had a bacteria peel here?'

Now it was my turn to frown.

'They are revolting, and you know it.' A bacterial shower was one thing but a bacterial shave was something altogether different. I tried one once, and it was the most unnatural experience ever. Give me water, soap, and a blade and I was a happy man. Pat my face with a bacteria and hair munching scrub, and I was not going to thank you. Besides which, last time I lost an eyebrow, which the local kids thought was hilarious.

An hour later, after a quick set of scans and tests revealing nothing wrong with me, I left the cubicle with Koda.

Waiting for us in the corridor were Chancellor Sam Nymens and a stranger. The woman was short, about five feet, and just as wide. Given that I was usually surrounded by curators and custodians, her appearance stood out.

'Hello, Julius,' said Sam with a reassuring smile. 'This is Marte Speare. She's going to act as the boys' nanny and, if it works out, their mother.'

She stepped forward and shook my hand. 'Henry, that's my husband, will come on the next visit. We don't want to overwhelm them, but Chancellor Nymens felt my presence might be helpful. If you introduce me, it will offer them a chain of connections.'

I shook her hand and listened to her chatting as we walked towards quarantine. I didn't want to do this. With every step, I wanted to turn away. I knew exactly how they were about to feel, and I had done this to them. I felt like an executioner.

We stepped through the infrared showers, then got squirted with various nanobots, picking off any remaining germs that might weaken the boys.

'Their immune systems are nearly up to speed,' explained Koda, 'they'll be spending another week in here. However, we will encourage visitors.'

'I doubt they will want to see me again.' I winced as I heard how self-pitying I sounded. It was my responsibility to see them through it.

Koda shrugged and walked over to a workstation and started making some notes and reading their charts. Marte came and sat down beside me.

'You saved their lives, you know.'

'Not necessarily.'

'Curator Strathclyde, I have studied their timelines. I have studied your actions. And it's clear they either died or were brought here. Those two little boys, victims of a political battle that could only be won at the cost of their destruction.'

'Yes, but this! How are they going to adjust? That boy is the King of England. Now what is he?'

'Alive?' She patted my hand. 'Trust me. I understand it was hard for you to adapt, and I doubt it will be much easier for them. But they do have an advantage over you.'

I looked at her hopefully, anything to offset my appalling guilt.

'They are children. Children are far more adaptable. And they have each other.' Now she held my hand and gave it a squeeze. 'They will be fine. Trust me. Just be honest with them. Everything is going to be alright.'

I don't know where Sam had dug up Mary Poppins from, but she was already doing me the power of good. I hoped she and the boys clicked.

'Are we ready?' said Koda as he came over to us. 'They are waking up now.'

We walked into the room and stood by the door as the two small bodies began to fidget in their beds. We listened as they whispered to each other. Sam nodded at me.

I cleared my throat. 'Hello, Edward. Hello, Richard. My name is Julius. May I sit down?'

They looked across at each other. Then continued to look around the room. Their eyes darting everywhere. What must this be like? The electric lighting, the strangers, the shiny reflective surfaces. The windows were opaque. No doubt the doctors wanted to drip feed the shocks. Fifteenth century England to twenty-first century Egypt was going to be one hell of a jolt.

'Boys? Why don't you share a bed? Richard, go join your brother, and I'll explain what is happening.'

Richard slid out of his bed, then clambered up in Edward's as his brother helped pull him up. I was about to sit down on the side of the vacant bed when Edward spoke.

'I have not given you leave to sit.'

Well, he was scared, so this was fair enough, but it was unlikely to speed the process up.

'I am happy to stand if it pleases you. But I have a lot to say, and I keep fainting at the moment. Sitting might help me.'

Richard whispered to Edward, who whispered back, then looked at me again.

'You may sit. Those three can remain standing.'

Richard whispered again, and Edward looked at him crossly. I think he was trying not to cry.

'The lady may also sit.' He paused. 'As may the priest.' In his red scrubs, I suppose Koda could be mistaken for a cardinal.

'Explain yourself. You were in our rooms fighting with a Nubian warrior, and now we are here.'

I wasn't sure where to begin, but I thought I'd better put them straight on Clio. 'That was my colleague. Her name is Clio Masoud.'

'If she's a colleague, why was she fighting you?'

Smart kid.

'Because she was trying to save me. I'll explain that a bit later. For now, we were in your room to rescue you. Your lives were measured in days.'

'Buckingham?'

'Quite likely,' I nodded. At least he had been taking notes.

'Then we were at no risk. Uncle Dickie would have seen him off.'

'And yet that didn't happen.'

'Hasn't happened.'

God, he was quick. I took a deep breath.

'Didn't. Past tense. This is the future.'

I waited to see how they would respond. Now Richard piped up, looking at the three of us fearfully.

'Is this heaven?'

'No. Not at all. We are in Egypt.'

'Where Pompey was assassinated?'

'Yes.'

The boys looked around. Richard's eyes were brimming with tears, Edward's eyes shone but his jaw was clenched. Clearly, they didn't think much of their predicament.

'Are we safe here?'

'Yes.'

They relaxed a fraction. What had the past few months been like for them, locked away in their rooms, permitted no visitors?

'When will I be able to return and claim my throne?'

I turned at looked at Sam. 'Do we leave this for another day?'

'No, everything now. Then they have the information and can start asking more questions. It's the only way through.'

I turned back in my chair. Edward was frowning at me.

'You won't ever claim your crown. In order to rescue you, we had to bring you to another realm.' It was weak, but I wasn't sure how to express it.

'Another realm? If this isn't heaven, is it hell?' The boys shuffled closer together.

I shook my head, but Koda's voice interrupted. 'No heaven, no hell, no God, you are truly free.'

I jumped off the bed, and a second later he was pressed up against the wall as I went toe to toe with him.

'Don't you ever dismiss their God again.'

'But I was—'

'Ever! Am I clear? Those boys lost their father only months ago. They have been torn from their mother and imprisoned for months. Now they have lost their crown, their titles, everyone and everything they know and understand. You will not deny them their faith.'

Koda's hands were upraised, trying to keep a barrier between us. He might have had a point. I had never been so angry.

'But he doesn't exist,' pleaded Koda.

Sam told me to calm down. 'I know this is bringing back a lot of bad memories, lad, and I know you are worried about Neith, but this isn't helping the boys.'

I wondered if Sam was thinking about his own children right now, and inhaled deeply. Calming down, I addressed Koda again, taking a step back.

'Last year, you'd have sworn blind that Anubis didn't exist either, but we all saw him taking selfies on Pythagoras Avenue.'

Koda opened his mouth then closed it again.

I glared at Marte. 'You too. No taking anything else away from these boys.'

She nodded mutely, but didn't appear intimidated. Hopefully, she agreed with me. I turned around and sat back on the bed and took a few steadying breaths.

'Are you in charge?' asked Richard, his voice wavering.

I laughed. 'No, not a bit of it. But they thought I would be the best person to explain what has happened.'

'Because you brought us here?'

'No, because I'm an Englishman, like you. And like you, I also come from your realm. We are in the future, and we are on another version of Earth. You can never go home.'

There it was, as bald and as brutal as I could be. Rip off the plaster and all that.

'Are there camels?' asked Richard. Edward seemed to think if he could glare at me hard enough, I might change my mind and say he could go home.

'Camels?' I laughed at the unexpected question. 'Yes, there are camels.'

'Can I see them?' Richard wriggled in the bed, looking excited.

'You can even ride them, if you like. But honestly, they are not that impressive. They bite, they are as stubborn as mules, they stink like a midden and, once, one threw up over me. I was covered from head to toe in hot, smelly camel vomit.'

The little boy giggled, and I thought I saw Edward's lips twitch.

We talked a little bit more. I explained Marte would be taking care of them, and that I would call in on them daily. Edward remained hostile, but I could hardly blame him. Richard, on the other hand, three years younger, appeared to be rolling with the situation so far.

As I stepped out of the corridor, Clio was waiting. 'I thought you might be moping.'

I raised an eyebrow.

'You know. Guilt or something. Woe is me.' She glared at me. 'So, we're going to the stupid pub. Okay?'

She fainted twice along the way, and I fainted three times in the pub. Eventually, the others turned it into a drinking game and people were placing bets on how long we would black out. Oddly, the more we drank, the fewer the faints, so we proceeded to get trolleyed whilst we regaled our friends with our adventures, and I tried to shake off my guilt.

Chapter 30 - Neith

Day 202.

I had been monitoring from Day 160. Before that, I was in a coma. After that, my daily calibration was intermittent, but I had now recorded 25 days straight without omission. Some of those early recordings were below standard and hard for me to listen to, but I was improving. The last procedure really stabilised my mood swings, but not the pain.

The pain in my head was beyond anything I could comprehend. Earlier, I had caught myself whimpering and had to wipe tears from my face. It felt like my head was in a rough concrete clamp that throbbed and scratched. All rational thought was squeezed out of my head.

The operation had apparently gone without error, and yet I felt worse. I still couldn't be understood. I had no trouble in my head understanding what I was saying, but if I tried to write it down or speak out loud, it remained a jumbled mess.

I opened my eyes, glanced around the room, confirmed nothing had changed, and began my daily calibration.

My greatest concern with every brain procedure was my memory. So far, I appeared to be the only person who knew the truth about Minju. I had watched all the news and shows reviewing the attempted coup and Minju's betrayal was missing from everything. I even watched the tiresome biopics, the one on Minju was hilarious. A devoted archivist safe in the bowels of the mouseion guarding the treasures whilst the battle raged overhead.

It was bizarre to watch my own biopic. The actress who played me tended to shout a lot, then stop to shelter children. Where in the name of Bast had there been children in the battleground? At one point I also helped a cat escape with her kittens. I spat my drink out laughing at that bit. Apparently I had time to do all this whilst the gods and Grimaldi unleased terror from the skies and tried to obliterate us.

I watched feeling sick as Jack was abducted and I ran towards him, screaming at Grimaldi. And then he raised the gun and I fell. I stared at the screen numb with shock, then saw Clio chase after Grimaldi. The actress playing Clio didn't swear as much as Clio, but then who does? I knew she had killed Grimaldi but it was still sobering to watch her chase him. Right up until the last second, he thought she was with him. I felt uncomfortable as she avenged my death. Being in Clio's debt sat poorly on me.

No matter what I watched, nothing tallied with my recollection of Minju. I had seen her once since my shooting. She had come to my rooms and I had attacked her. As she cowered in the corner, I saw her study me. At the time I was insensible, but now I knew I had alerted her. I had given her reason to doubt me and from what I now knew of Minju I had made myself dangerously vulnerable.

There was a knock on the door, and Julius walked in. I told him to fuck off. He smiled and told me to fuck off myself. It seemed that some bits of Welsh never changed.

He poured us two glasses of water into soft beakers, handed one to me, then told me all about his recent steps. I wasn't sure if he was trying to entertain me or drive me insane.

That said, it was fascinating seeing Clio through someone else's eyes. I laughed as he told me about the *Queen of Sheba* routine, even though the pain left me gasping. Julius stopped talking for a while and asked if I needed anything. I waved at him to carry on. A conversation was impossible, but I could listen. I had read their formal account of each step, and it was fun to see what they left out. *The Queen of Sheba* was one of those details, as was little Alys. I wanted to ask if he had investigated her timeline yet, but this was a one-way conversation.

Then he moved onto his daily life. The faints were concerning, but apparently slowing down. But if he mentioned how lovely and considerate Minju Chen was one more time, I would scream.

Minju is an excellent cook. Minju pours a refreshing cup of tea. Minju and I love playing 'What if?' Yesterday we played What if Stamford Bridge had never happened?

What if I take my lunch tray and smash it against the side of your head to knock some sense into you?

I shook my head in frustration and set off a wave of pain akin to a drill plunging through my eyeballs. I hadn't seen Julius leave the room, but he returned with a doctor. She asked if I wanted to be sedated for a bit, and I blinked, tears welling up.

Chapter 31 - Neith

Day 203.

The following morning, Doctor Bitsoi came in smiling, as did three junior doctors. And they were all smiling as well. Something was very wrong.

'Excellent news, Neith. You have made an incredible recovery.'

A tall woman with long plaits from a central top knot nodded emphatically. 'Truly excellent. I am writing a paper on it.'

'Yes,' said her colleague, eager to chime in with a fawning smile. His tapered fingernails suggested an academic life. 'The way your brain and Tiresias worked together to create new neural linguistic pathways will greatly advance our research methodologies.' He looked at the others. 'We have learnt so much.' Everyone beamed back at him and continued to nod.

I stared at them blankly.

'The pain has gone, hasn't it?' They consulted their monitors and each other.

The taller woman looked across at me as an afterthought. 'Your cranial swelling has reduced to perfect levels.'

I continued to stare.

'Now, why don't you say something and we can all rejoice in the cure?'

I didn't want to speak. I didn't want to take this final test, because if this failed, that was it. I wasn't getting my voice back, and if I couldn't communicate, I couldn't be a curator. They fiddled with their clipboards and their stupid smiles slipped. I was spoiling their fun. Doctor Bitsoi cleared his throat.

'Repeat after me. "I am sitting in the quantum's infirmary facility and I am perfectly recovered."'

I took a deep breath and began to speak. It sounded fine to me, but as I watched their faces fall, I realised nothing had changed. The voice synthesisers were sprouting gibberish as they followed my garbled words. My voice petered out.

'Well, that's disappointing,' said the taller woman, and the short man wrote furiously on his tablet. Only Bitsoi looked at me, the sympathy on his face overwhelming my fragile state.

'Get out,' I mumbled.

Tiresias said something about airports. They wore the same disappointed expression, so I screamed at them to fuck off. As established, this was a phrase that Tiresias had fixed on, and the doctors started to get excited.

'Fascinating. See how the most emphatic and coarse of language remains focussed throughout history.' They looked at me, eyes sparkling, eager to play with their new lab rat. 'Neith, can you repeat a few more vulgar Beta phrases and let's see what works and what doesn't?'

I talked then, quickly and furiously, my voice rising as I swore and hurled every abuse under the sun at them. I used language that would make a camel driver blush. As I roared, they collectively took a step backwards. I flung the glass pitcher at them, followed by the chair, followed by the side table. As they fled, I rammed the bed into the doorway, took the broken monitor and hurled it at the window. It bounced off, and I slumped into the corner of the room, sobbing myself to sleep.

Day 204.

The following morning I was moved under armed guard into another room. As we stepped over the carnage I had created, I wasn't even ashamed of my outburst. Inside, I roiled and seethed. The guards surrounding me could sense this as well. We moved in silence, their fingers on their lasers, ready to stun me if I so much as twitched. This time, Doctor Bitsoi came on his own. The armed guards flanked him, but the other two doctors had sensibly chosen to stay away. Their smiles were no longer required.

'Neith Salah, your disappointment is understandable, but such destruction is not acceptable. We understand your frustration, and it has been decided the best course of treatment is a long-sleep.'

I jerked back. I should have seen this coming. Long-sleep was the ultimate solution for the currently incurable.

'We believe your rages are being caused by a cranial imbalance.'

'Of course they are, you cretin. I can't communicate.'

Tiresias blathered on about impatient sheep dogs and disobedient hedgehogs. I didn't know how to advocate for myself, and I didn't know anyone else who would. I paused. I could do this.

'Ramin Gamal.'

'You want Ramin Gamal?'

I shook my head. And slapped my chest, saying his name again. Maybe he would understand that I was asking for Ramin to be my advocate.

'You think your name is Ramin Gamal?'

I wanted to scream, but bit my tongue. Another outburst and they'd probably throw me in the ice locker without even a review.

I shook my head and fell silent.

'Okay. I know this seems scary, but we will have counsellors helping you through the process, and we will appoint an advocate to speak on your behalf.'

'Ramin Gamal!'

Suddenly, Bitsoi smiled, a huge beam across his face, and I smiled back. 'You want Ramin Gamal as your advocate?' I nodded through my stupid tears.

'Oh Neith, I know you are in there. I'll be advocating for you as well, but you have to get your outbursts under control. The pharaoh wants you on long-sleep, as do some of the other chancellors. We need to prove that you aren't a threat. You are a curator and are trained in combat. Had you been a red custodian behaving like this, there wouldn't have even been a debate.'

I nodded my head. He was right. I was acting like a toddler waving a gun around. It was time to come to terms with this. I was certain Minju was behind the pharaoh's viewpoint. That would be in line with everything I knew about her, pouring sand in the cracks. I couldn't let her win this. The fact that she was prepared to get rid of me with only a suspicion that I might be on to her was chilling. I was on the back foot and losing. I alone knew what she was, and if she shut me away, she would be unstoppable.

'I'll leave you now. There are no guards outside, but if you try to leave or attack anyone, then you will have effectively ended your own review.'

He looked at me and I said yes. Another word that Tiresias, the genius super-computer, could understand. Yay, technology.

On my bed were a collection of day clothes. On the wall was another monitor, behind bars. All the furniture in here was sealed to the floor. It took me a whole five minutes to explore the place and found not a single loose item beyond basic clothing. And even that was devoid of ties or fastenings. The bed, however, had the familiar restraints of my first room. I was going backwards.

241

Frustrated, I changed into the new garments just to have something to do, then looked out the window. Tiresias asked if I wanted to watch a Beta programme, but I silenced him and watched my fellow citizens go about their lives below. How could I become one of them? How did I become other than myself? For now, though, I needed to convince the other chancellors that I wasn't a threat.

There was a knock on the door and Julius entered, a guard by his side. The guard was carrying a laser. And Julius, for some reason, was carrying some plants and a bowl of figs.

He smiled at me tentatively. 'Flowers and grapes for the patient. Well, I say grapes, all I could find were figs.'

I watched as he placed them by my bedside. I had no idea why he would bring in things to decay. Was this his idea of a joke? *Let's all rot away together.* In addition, there was a box tied with a ribbon, which he placed at the foot of my bed with a smile. He was about to speak when I turned my back on him.

'Go away.' I continued to look out the window.

'I just came to say—'

'GO AWAY!' My words might make no sense, but my intent was clear. I was furious that he couldn't remember the truth and furious that in order to protect him I couldn't tell him either.

He stepped back, no doubt remembering his broken wrist, and quickly left the room, saying he would call again the following day.

Half an hour later, Clio came in and I threw the bowl of figs at her. As soon as she left, I ran around the room, picking up all evidence of my outburst.

The box sat at the end of my bed. I looked at it dubiously. More rotting produce? I pulled at the ribbon and lifted off the lid. Inside was a collection of maybe twenty brand new socks, all unpaired and all in a jumble. I pulled out the first sock then found its pair, folding them together, then folding them into a neat shape. I then tipped the box out and repeated my actions with the rest of them, calming down as I went. In the end, I placed them all neatly back in the box, except one pair, which I placed on my feet and smiled as I wiggled my toes back and forth.

Only Julius understood the nature of our splice, and I knew I had to save him, not for my sake, but for his. It was my fault that he was here, sailing too close to Minju's designs. I had to save him and save Alpha.

I spent the next hour looking at the ceiling, hatching plans and feeling sorry for myself.

'Hello.'

I turned my head away from the sea and looked over at a blonde headed child standing in the doorway in a hospital tunic. He looked around the room, then walked in, closing the door behind him. He sat down on the chair, then stood up and removed a fig.

'I believe this is yours?'

I held out my hand and he walked over, placing the fig on the bed, then returned to his seat.

'Thank you.'

'It's thank you, my liege.'

I looked at him. 'No, it's not. You are not my liege.'

'Yes, I am. I'm the King of England.'

'Not here, you're not.' I could have been kinder, but my head was throbbing.

'I am the King of England.' He stamped his foot. 'I will be the King of England until I die.'

Which is when it hit me like a bucket of icy water.

'You understand me?'

Chapter 32 - Neith

The young king looked at me and scoffed.

'Of course. Some words are hard to catch, but it's easy enough to fill in the gaps. When I resided in Ludlow as the Prince of Wales, I made it my goal to talk to the common labourers. However, I must say, some of the words I heard you shouting yesterday were not very ladylike. They weren't even becoming of a swineherd. You know an awful lot of swear words.'

He looked at me reprovingly, but all I could do was laugh.

'Are you a simpleton? Or maybe a holy fool?' he was asking with the blunt curiosity of a child.

I composed myself. 'No, it's simply that you are the first person to understand me in months.'

'You've been here that long? How many others have they stolen from my land?' He jumped out of his chair, a twelve-year-old boy not even hitting puberty, ready to fight the entire world to protect his kingdom. Well, it was what he was raised to do, I supposed.

I sighed. 'No. I'm one of them. One of these people. How much have they explained to you?'

I listened as he rattled off what they had told him, and was impressed that nothing had been hidden from him. I was also impressed that he was still planning on escaping.

He shrugged and composed himself, settling back into the chair. 'So they didn't steal you? They simply imprisoned you?'

'How do you mean, steal me?'

'As they did with my brother and myself. A tall blonde hero, with eyes like your own, and a dark warrior pretending to be a man.'

I grinned inwardly at the description as he hurried on.

'Never fear. I am working on a plan to escape. When I have finalised it, I will get us out and you, if you wish.'

'And where will we go?' I was more than a bit in awe of his attitude. This kid was a fighter.

'England, of course. Although, you may return to Wales if that is your wish. Now that I have told you my tale, will you share yours with me? How is it that I can understand you, but no one else can?'

I thought about it. All the texts that Tiresias had been using had been written, and because the oldest texts were so rare, the language used was the most formal version available. Tiresias had no vernacular language. The idioms, the swearing and jokes, all that made for everyday speech, were missing. King Edward VI of that name was the missing link.

'Tiresias. Start recording this conversation. For my use only.'

Nothing happened. I looked at Edward.

'Can you try what I just said, but make it as formal as possible?'

He tried a few times before Tiresias acknowledged and began recording.

'In fairness, you don't talk very well.'

I nodded. 'That has been brought to my attention.'

'Hang on.' The young king jumped from his chair. 'I told my brother I was going to see if you were safe. I'll be back in a minute. His common tongue isn't as good as mine, but we used to chat together in it whilst at the Tower. It felt like a code.'

With that, he ran out of the room, and a few seconds later returned with a smaller version of himself who looked at me in frank amazement.

'You know the worst words in all of Christendom,' said Richard in frank admiration. I tossed the fig towards him with a smile. At least this child seemed less complicated than his big brother. He sniffed the fruit before biting it, then grinned back at me. Clearly, he was the more trustworthy of the two. Or just younger. As he groaned in delight, juice dribbling down his chin, he smiled at his brother.

I offered him a second one, checking there was no dirt on it. 'It's not poisoned.' I took a bite out of it.

'You eat my food!' His outrage was particularly funny, and I threw a fig his way as I carried on eating. Richard was right, they were delicious. Edward, seeing the foolishness of his outrage, took a bite and gave me a tentative smile. For the first time in months, I savoured my food as I laughed and joked with the boys.

'So why are you locked away?' asked Edward reaching for the figs and passing one to his brother.

I held up my hand. 'Tiresias, stop recording.'

The light continued to blink. And I looked at Edward.

'Invisible Tiresias, desist your observation.' He spoke perfect medieval Latin, and the light went out. We had been chatting a while, and Richard had climbed up onto my bed and fallen asleep. I imagine he was still processing, his shock playing out, but it made things easier. He seemed more likely to inadvertently let things slip.

'I am here because I have angered someone who wants to dispose of me, but they can't work out how to do it without drawing attention to themselves.'

'Are they more powerful than you?'

'Yes, but they conceal their power.'

'To what ends?'

'They want to rule without limit or restraint.'

'They want the crown.'

I thought about it, then nodded. 'We don't have crowns, but the analogy works.'

'And how do you plan to evade them? Does your husband champion your cause?'

'Women are independent and equal to men here. I have no husband.'

He looked at me, astonished. Truly, I think of all he had heard so far, this was the most remarkable. I tried to help him out.

'If you make your astonishment known in public, or you address a man in return when a woman speaks to you, you will be acting in the most unseemly manner.'

Well, that caught his attention.

'The rules of your court are strange, but I can adapt.'

'So, what are your plans?' I was intrigued and wanted to know what he had in mind. 'May I lend assistance?'

'You doubt my abilities based on my age, I see. Is that not also considered unseemly?' His voice was haughty and I was reminded I was chatting with the King of England. 'I have been raised in the craft of kingship since the day I was born. I was born in sanctuary, as my father, the rightful king, was an exile in France. My mother was the daughter of a rebel and a traitor to the crown. The crown of England has been fought over viciously since before my birth, and continues to be. I was raised as the Prince of Wales, and have been making decisions about my household since the age of ten. I speak numerous languages, debate with the keenest tutors, and study warfare and politics on a daily basis. I clearly have much to learn. But I think I can help outwit someone who is foxed by a lady incapable of clear speech!'

He let his breath out in a rush and glared at me.

I tilted my head. 'I apologise, your highness. You have learnt much. Your father was no doubt very proud of your progress.'

That slowed him down. 'And my mother,' he said in a small voice. 'She was the brains between the two of them. I think you'd like her.'

Elizabeth Woodville, glamorous, clever and resourceful. Yes, I thought I would have liked her as well.

'She survives, you know.'

He looked at me closely. 'I don't want to know. The thought that she has been dead for centuries is too much.'

That broke my heart a bit. The King of England was only twelve years old, after all.

I decided to distract him. 'My enemy has a tail.'

He grinned at me, his curiosity piqued. 'Like a vestigial bone?'

'No, like that of a snow leopard!'

His eyes were like saucers, and I told him about Minju Chen and the recent coup, and subsequent memory block that everyone was suffering from. It was such a relief to finally have someone to talk to about it.

'But if and when you meet her, you must play the part of all others. You must take what everyone does and says at face value.'

'I am skilled at that. People mistake my years for a lack of intellect. Much is said in front of me that shouldn't.'

I could well imagine. 'You would do well to craft that skill. You are almost out of childhood. People will treat you differently here. But if you can watch and judge, you will do well. I'll let you in on a secret. My enemy, when she is unsettled or alarmed, her tail twitches. It's a tiny thing, and she tries to hide it, but just sometimes it twitches before she gets control.'

'Like Uncle Anthony, his eyelid pulses before he shouts. Normally, he is very reserved, but you can always tell when an explosion is coming.'

I nodded. 'Just like Uncle Anthony.'

'And my mother, the Queen, tucks a tendril of hair behind her ear if she doesn't respect the person who is talking to her.'

'You have the makings of a fine curator.'

He glared at me. 'I have the makings of a fine king.'

I let it go. It was not a point worth debating. The inevitability of his situation would soon sink onto his shoulders.

'Was she happy?' his voice was quiet.

'She was, I think.' And I explained what happened to his family after he left.

'Richard would have been a good king. Tudor was an upstart churl. And it sounds like my nephew was dreadful.'

'Yes, but your great niece was brilliant.'

'The Plantagenet women always are.'

Our conversation broke off as we heard shouting from beyond the door.

Chapter 33 - Neith

I sprang up, ready to defend the boys. I didn't know what was going on in the corridors, but if a fight had come to me, I was ready.

Edward shook his head and grinned. 'I think they have finally noticed our departure. We put pillows under the bed covering.' He had a wicked smile.

I chuckled as the adrenaline seeped away. 'Well, you had best open the door and let them know where you are. They can get very twitchy about jokes.'

'I won't be locked up again, will I?' he asked, his face falling.

'Not here. Here, you will be safe.'

He was about to get up when the door flew open. Bitsoi rushed in and stumbled to a halt. I put my finger to my lips and pointed to Richard asleep on the bed.

Bitsoi walked quickly across to the boy and, as his back was turned, I placed my finger on my lips and winked at Edward. I removed my finger just as Bitsoi turned round. With any luck, Edward would play along. I finally had the upper hand over Minju. No one knew I could be understood. Let Minju play out her game. If she over-reached, I would bite. I had no idea how to use this, but it was something that Minju didn't know and I needed every advantage I could muster. Remaining silent felt passive, but Minju had played in the shadows for years,

252

maybe I would do the same. However, for this to work I needed to keep Edward and Richard nearby.

'Edward, are you okay?' Bitsoi looked between the three of us, trying to gauge the situation.

'I am. I got bored and I thought I would come and listen to the ravings of this holy fool.' He turned and looked at me. 'Nothing she says makes any sense, but then nothing here makes any sense, anyway.'

Reassured that the children were safe, Bitsoi relaxed. 'Well, it's probably not a good idea to bother the other patients. If—'

'I wasn't bothering her. I think she too, is bored. I will return tomorrow. Please, could you arrange for us to have a chess board brought in?'

I watched, amused, as Edward took control of the situation. Bitsoi was about to concede to the child's demand. How easily we bow down before innate confidence and authority.

'Actually, I'm afraid that won't be possible. Neith has her review tomorrow.'

'And that is?'

'We will determine if it is in her own best interests to be placed into stasis, to await improvements in brain procedures.'

I jumped up. Tomorrow was too soon. I wasn't ready.

'Neith, stay calm. Remember, any outburst at this stage will be your undoing.'

As I paced, Edward cleared his throat.

'If this is the last I'll see of her, may I stay another hour? You may take my brother away now and I will join him presently.'

Shaking his head in surprise, Bitsoi carried Richard back to his bed.

As soon as the door was closed, Edward turned to me. 'What are you going to do?'

Bloody good question.

'I don't know. If I can show that I can communicate with you, it might be all I need.'

'Why didn't you tell that man you could talk just then?'

'Because I don't want to reveal my hand yet.'

'Will your enemy be present tomorrow?'

'Almost certainly. She'll want to be certain her plan goes through, but she'll be directing the proceedings through the pharaoh so she can keep her hands clean.'

'She's a puppet master then, your enemy? Enemies are easier to fight on the battlefield.'

'Nothing about Minju is easy.'

'Wait, did you say pharaoh? That's a king. Maybe I can address him, one ruler to another?'

'Our pharaoh is elected by all the people and is currently a woman. She is also one of Minju's puppets.'

Edward narrowed his eyes. 'Women are not born to lead.'

I cleared my throat, and he apologised quickly.

'I meant some weak people are not born to lead. Not that I'm saying women are weak. After all, the Maid of

Orleans led her troops into battle. There are also many queens who rule whilst their kings are at war.'

'You're right,' I smiled reassuringly. 'What I think you meant to say was some women, as well as some men, are not fit to lead.'

He looked relieved and nodded quickly, his mantle of authority wavering between king and child. 'So, you plan to give your enemy just enough rope?'

I frowned and tried to recall the Beta idiom.

'To hang herself,' he explained.

I huffed. 'Charming, but apt. Yes, I will invite Minju to place her head in the noose. And then I will tug on the rope.'

'Will that undo her?'

'No, but it will undo her plans and save my skin. Now, in the morning, you must make your way to my review. It will probably happen here, but I won't be able to summon you. None of them can understand me. You will need to fight through any obstacles and come to my side.' I looked at him intently. 'Can you do that?'

Bizarrely, he stood up, then knelt on one knee, looking up at me, his face solemn.

'My Lady Neith, I give you my word that I will come to your rescue at the appointed hour.' He stood up and bowed. 'And now I must retire.'

As he left, I found myself shaken by his sincerity. He was too young to be involved in my fight, but I was out of time and options.

Chapter 34 - Julius

The morning of Neith's review had arrived, and I was heading across the lawns to meet Rami. He was going to stand as her advocate. I was present only as her last working partner. Rami had told me quite explicitly that nothing I said would be considered. I was there purely as a courtesy. I wouldn't even have a vote. I had taken all this on board, but I still had a speech prepared.

As we arrived, we were ushered up to Neith's room. She was sitting in the corner, and everyone else was sitting awkwardly on chairs brought in for the occasion.

'From what I understand,' said Rami, 'the patient is normally in bed, either restrained or on life support. The rest of the panel then stands.'

He looked around the large room and nodded at everyone. I recognised the pharaoh, Dr Bitsoi, and several chancellors. There were a few more doctors I didn't recognise, and finally I saw the face I was looking for. Minju was sitting to one side, and I gave her an anxious look. She returned a small smile, and I hoped she had convinced the pharaoh to sway the vote.

'Will Minju be allowed to speak?' I muttered to Rami behind my hand.

He looked around then tilted his head in surprise. 'I shouldn't have thought so. I mean, she can't, anyway. But I'm not sure why she's here?' He thought about it, then shook his head. 'The fact that Neith is seated suggests she is trying to control the situation. Keep everyone wrong-footed.'

Koda was sitting in front of us, and now twisted in his seat, joining our conversation. 'It was her decision. But she hasn't spoken a word all morning. I don't know if silence is going to work for her. We all know she can't communicate. The focus of this panel will be her rages.'

He looked at Rami. 'That's what you need to focus on in her defence. Stress that it's a perfectly understandable and controllable response to her current predicament.'

Rami nodded as the bell chimed. Koda stood and joined the pharaoh.

Nolyny Cleeve cleared her throat, twisting a ring on her finger as she gathered her thoughts. Maybe she only liked delivering good news. 'We are gathered today to discuss the medical treatment of Curator Neith Salah, who was shot in the head and temporarily died. On her recovery, it became apparent that massive damage had been inflicted upon her language centres as well as those areas controlling her moods.'

The room was still as everyone considered their uncomfortable duty ahead. Neith sat in the chair and glared at each and every person. No one was under any doubt that she was taking mental notes, and no one wanted to be in Neith Salah's black books. But if she was put to sleep, they might be dead by the time she woke to take revenge. Camels or cockroaches.

In the silence, we could hear voices in the corridor as a child started shouting, demanding to be let in. I jumped to my feet and headed to the door. Something in the child's accent suggested Egyptian was not his first, or even fifth, language. My best guess was that the King of England was demanding admittance.

I opened the door to see a custodian cringing with mortification as a child shouted up at him. Properly behaved Alpha children would never dare harass a custodian. This one was more than harassing the poor man, he was tearing him to shreds.

'Hello, Edward,' I said. 'Do you remember me?'

He rolled his eyes. 'I'm a child, not an idiot.'

'Yes, well.' The damn child had caught me off-guard. I had so much sympathy for him, but this wasn't the place. 'We are in the middle of an important meeting, you see. If you wait in your room, I will come along presently.'

Edward put his fists on his waist and drew in a deep breath. 'I am not here to see you. I am here at the behest of the Lady Neith.'

That caught me out, and I looked over my shoulder where everyone was now looking my way. Which meant that no one saw Neith smile and give a quick nod of her head.

'You know Neith?'

'Of course. We are both captives here.'

I turned back to the room as the custodian continued to guard the door. 'I say we let him in and see what he has to say.'

Minju leant forward to speak to the pharaoh, no doubt encouraging her to agree with me, when Sam told the custodian to step aside.

Edward walked slowly into the room, looking neither left nor right as he waited for the crowd to break apart. He held his head high, ignoring everyone until he stood beside Neith.

His young voice rang out, clear and sharp. 'Attend me. My Lady Neith has something to say.' He looked her way and gave a small bow.

Neith smiled and remained sitting as she opened her mouth. 'Greetings to your heart and hearth.'

It took a split second before we realised she was speaking in Egyptian. Even Edward looked at her in surprise.

Ah, I thought, this has caught you out as well. What was going on?

'I am grateful to Edward for the gift he has given me. Yesterday, Edward and I discovered a common tongue. Medieval Welsh vulgate. The medieval slang was the final bridge that my brain needed to map the words and meanings. I had a mild headache, but that was nothing. I also noticed that I kept slipping back into Welsh, but it was coherent Welsh. Whether medieval or modern, I was

259

sticking to the right timeframes and definitions. And, with a bit of effort, Edward was able to follow me.'

The two linguist doctors in the front row were whispering to each other, scribbling furiously on their pads as they nodded along.

Neith gave a dry cough, and Edward looked around the room. 'Someone fetch the Lady Neith a glass of water. You in the back with the tail. Water, now.'

We all stared in astonishment as Edward gave an order to Minju. To her credit, she slowly rose, walked over to the guard, and requested the water. As she returned to her seat, her face was like thunder. I grimaced sympathetically.

Neith whispered to Edward, and he bowed in Minju's direction.

'My Lady Neith has informed me you are a highly valued and respected member of this society.'

He stopped short and waited for Neith to carry on talking. Instead, she whispered at him again and we watched as his small face screwed up in annoyance.

He straightened up and addressed Minju again. 'Apparently, my last apology did not sound like one.'

Neith coughed. His face was a picture of annoyance as she held his gaze.

He turned back to Minju. 'I apologise.'

For all his poise, he was still a kid, and one that had just got schooled. Minju tipped her head in acceptance. As the water was brought in, Neith took a large gulp and sighed deeply.

'Thank you. My throat is quite parched at the moment. Now, where was I?'

She shuffled in her chair and smiled across at me and Rami. His smile in return was as strong as mine.

'When I woke this morning, my language was restored. Just like that. I went to sleep, and this morning I was speaking clearly. I'll leave it to the linguists to work it out, but my guess is my brain and the neural implants were just waiting for those missing linguistic links to fire up the whole system.'

She sat back as the room started to talk amongst themselves in concern. They had been brought here to discuss the long-sleep of a dangerous patient, and yet they were listening to a celebrated hero talking loquaciously.

The pharaoh stood up. 'We are all delighted that you have your voice back, but your loss of language was never the issue.'

I was startled by her words. It was a massive part of the issue, or so I had been led to believe. Behind her, Minju looked over and gave a tiny shrug. She seemed as perplexed as me.

'What we need to consider today is whether Neith's rages are an indicator of a long-term brain affliction caused by the bullet and subsequent scar tissue.'

'That's bollocks,' I muttered to Rami. 'They can't be seriously going ahead with the review?'

Rami looked concerned. 'Don't worry, there were always two issues, but I think the solution to the first will also solve the second. Don't forget, my case will be even stronger now.'

Koda got to his feet. 'My Pharaoh. I am quite happy to suggest that Neith's outbursts were no more than manifestations of frustration. Such as we are all prone to. She is a curator, after all, and her frustration may have been that bit more emphatic. It is my judgement that we call off this review. Neith can stay with us a few more days as we run tests—' Neith groaned audibly. '-as much as Neith is looking forward to that. We will confirm that her language pathways are stable, and her impulses have returned to a normal framework.'

The two linguists nodded in agreement, and Neith gave them a sour smile. I couldn't help but grin as they flinched. The other chancellors looked at each other uncomfortably. It was clear that the pharaoh wanted Neith put to sleep, but Koda had put forward a good argument, and Neith herself was now smiling around the room. Polite, curious, and taking mental notes.

Edward stood beside her, the personification of youth and innocence. I didn't buy his act one bit. He coughed, and everyone looked his way. 'Did you have something more you wished to say, my lady?'

She raised an eyebrow.

'I was saying that I would very much like to get out of here and get back to work.'

There was a small laugh in the room as Neith broke the tension.

One of the linguists stood up and turned towards Sam. 'Chancellor Nymens. As discussed previously, there can be no question of Neith Salah returning to active service as a curator.'

Neith recoiled, then sat still.

'What?'

I stared at Rami, but he didn't appear shocked.

'The damage to your brain—' began Koda.

'You said was fully repaired.'

'For everyday life, yes. But we don't believe it will withstand the pressures of a quantum step. Our hypothesis is that it will rupture your brain, and we have advised the quantum facility that you can no longer travel through the stepper.'

'For how long?'

'We believe this to be a permanent situation.'

'That's rubbish,' scoffed Neith. 'I've travelled before with a splice.'

'This isn't a splice scenario. We have fresh data from the step that Curators Masoud and Strathclyde took where they merged with themselves on a time stream. We observed micro-fractures that, whilst giving them headaches and faints, we hypothesise would surely tear you apart.'

'Surely.' She pounced on the hesitancy. 'So there's doubt.'

'Yes, there is doubt, but not enough to risk your life.'

'But it's my life!'

'But not your facility.' Sam spoke kindly, but Neith just stared at him in horror.

'I'll appeal.'

'To whom? This has already been accepted by the pharaoh, First Engineer and myself. We have made this decision in your best interest.'

I stood up. I couldn't let this happen to Neith.

'Clio and I are fine. We haven't had an incident in days.'

Everyone was looking at me. I was determined that I could somehow sway their opinion. Which, of course, was when I blacked out and sealed Neith's fate.

When I came round, hardly anyone had moved. Minju was heading towards me with a glass of water, which I waved away.

I stared at Koda, panic stricken. 'This means nothing. I was barely out. A tiny seizure. I didn't even fall over.'

Koda shook his head in disbelief. 'You said the syncope events had stopped.'

Sam barked a laugh. 'You took the word of a curator regarding their physical health? I've seen them stagger back through the step with limbs hanging off and refer to it as a flesh wound. Even Minju is famously on record declaring that she had a hankering for milk after she was surrounded by the remains of a snow leopard and a spliced tail.'

Minju shrugged. 'He has a point,' she said. 'If you want the truth of a curator's health, you need to check your equipment.'

I looked at the medi-brace on my wrist and sagged. That would have recorded all the little micro-seizures I had been suffering.

'Strathclyde, you lied?' asked Koda.

I winced. He was a decent sort and he seemed genuinely distressed.

'I'm fine,' I repeated.

The linguist cleared his voice. 'Further evidence that Formerly Curator Neith Salah must find a new job.'

The appellation of Formerly was enough to shock the room. It was a formal renunciation either of a family name or a career and was never used lightly. It was a race as to who was going to hit him first. Rami's chair shot back as he sprang across the room, pinning the linguist up against the wall. Sam quickly stepped between the two, and I saw out of the corner of my eye Edward place his hand on Neith's shoulder and whisper in her ear. She looked fit to explode, and I noticed Minju was also aware of her response. She spoke quickly to the pharaoh. Cleeve moved to speak, when Bitsoi shouted over all of us.

'Enough. I think Neith has just demonstrated that even under the most extreme of circumstances she can now control her frustrations. We rule against long-sleep.'

The room stilled as Rami came and sat beside me, adjusting his clothing as if he hadn't just completely lost his cool. The linguist was muttering about disciplinary measures, and Sam was threatening him with his own set for provoking a potentially vulnerable patient. I should have been cheering at Neith's reprieve, but her face was broken. I saw nothing to celebrate.

She stood up and the room fell silent. 'Get out.'

I wanted to go over and console her. Her greatest victory lay in ashes around her feet.

No one moved.

'I'm going to count to three.'

Everyone left.

Chapter 35 - Neith

Day 207

There was a knock at the door and Ramin walked in.

'No Edward, Neith? I think you have a bit of a fan there.'

I shook my head. 'He and his brother have been moved to their foster home. I'll be visiting as soon as I get out of here. He's a great chess player.'

I got out of bed and walked over to give him a hug. To his credit, he didn't flinch.

'I'm happy your restraints have gone.' We settled down into the armchairs.

'Makes you happy?' I looked at him in disgust. 'Can you imagine how it's been for me?'

'You did keep breaking people.' Ramin's voice was softly admonishing. Not actually telling me off, but reminding me not to be an utter douche.

I groaned. 'You're right. You should have seen Julius's face. He was so contrite and apologetic. Like it was his fault that he had got too close to me. And honestly, at the time I was so out of my mind, I didn't even register it was him.'

'It was only a little break to the wrist. You snapped Clio's femur.' He looked at me slyly. 'Are you certain you didn't know who you were attacking?'

It was good to share a laugh, and I wiped a tear from my eye.

'Do you know the funniest thing? She looked so proud that I had been able to break her leg.'

'Well, that's Clio.'

'How are those two getting on?'

'Julius and Clio? Total headache. The minute they get back from a step, they are pulling me to one side to complain about the other.'

'Tell them to put it in their report.'

We both snorted. That was never going to happen. Julius had some sort of weird honour code that meant he would rather jeopardise a mission than highlight someone's issues in a formal report. And Clio didn't want to suggest she was anything other than the perfectly reformed team player who didn't have a bad word to say about anyone.

'How is she doing?'

'Honestly? She's fooling those that don't know her, or want to be fooled. Those that do know her can see she is actually trying really hard to turn over a new leaf.' He looked at me hopefully.

'She orchestrated the death of Paul Flint, the abduction of his sister, the theft of priceless artefacts. Let me see, I'm sure there was something else. Ah yes, overthrowing the government with Grimaldi.'

'*Attempting* to overthrow the government,' he corrected.

'So, I should revel in the fact she also can't complete a mission?'

He sighed and looked out the window. I wanted to talk more about the uprising, see if there were any chinks in his memory, but I knew all my conversations were being monitored. I had no issue with that, it was for my health. I just knew that Minju would also be able to listen in if she chose. Of course, the tapes were confidential. But this was the woman who had sat in the shadows for years, was the mastermind behind the thefts, and almost pulled off a regime change. Then she slid away back into the shadows and rewrote herself as the hero of the hour. Minju Chen would have no trouble tapping into my feed.

'You're going to have to forgive her, Neith.'

'Are you kidding?'

'Not for her sake, silly. For yours.'

I realised he was still talking about Clio. He turned back to the window and we watched as a glider came too close to a pair of giraffes in the park. Seconds later, a custodian glider came chasing after them.

'Someone's about to get read the riot act.'

'Remember when you first learnt to fly your glider?'

'And you grabbed the controls and we crashed into the side of an elephant?'

The impact force-field had saved all parties, but as we scrambled to safety, the elephant stomped on the glider and we were both grounded for half a year.

'I thought I'd never pay that off,' I said with a laugh.

The room chimed, and I glared at the ceiling.

My allotted stimulation time was drawing to a close.

'Seriously though, how is Julius? What was that blackout yesterday that spectacularly ruined my case for re-instatement?'

'He was so angry with himself yesterday about that. He and Clio got into a fight in the pub, and he even swore at her. Now it looks like they are both being dragged back in for another procedure.'

'If they get fixed, maybe I can return to work?'

His expression was serious, and my mood was crushed. I had been trying to keep my spirits up, but now it looked like he was about to squash them.

'I'm here as your friend, Neith. You can't be a curator.'

'Oh, do you have plans for me?' I winced at my sarcasm. 'Career advice, hey? I've already had loads of job offers. Linguistics Researcher. Curator Trainer.' I laughed at that suggestion. I would never go back into the quantum facility if I wasn't allowed to step.

'I thought you had already picked your new role?' His voice was dismissive and I looked across at him. 'Camel's arse.'

'Are you here to lecture me?' I asked in astonishment.

'Too bloody right. You are behaving like a spoilt brat. So what if you can't be a curator? You're alive, aren't you? You saved Jack's life. You prevented Grimaldi from staging a coup. And yet you sit here and blub like a baby. The whole bloody planet is grateful for your actions and your recovery. You evaded the long-sleep, but you're sulking. You embarrass me.'

I paced the room. I didn't want to hear this.

'What? Looking for something to throw at me? Are you going to scream at me to leave? What's it going to be, Neith? What sort of tantrum are you going to pull today? Balls, even Clio behaves with more restraint.'

That was cold. I felt tears prick my eyes, and I tried to wipe them away before he noticed.

'Oh, Neith.' Ramin sprang up out of his chair and dashed across the room. As he wrapped his arms around me, I leant into him and gave thanks for the fact that my best friend was by my side.

Wiping my eyes, I went and sat down in the armchair. 'I'm sorry.'

'Don't apologise. I'd be the same. We all would.'

'So what was that lecture, then?'

'A bit of tough love. Just trying to break through to you.'

I sighed. 'It's just—' I knew what I was going to say next would sound pathetic, but I just needed to say it and get it behind me. I started again. 'It's just so unfair.' I laughed. It *did* sound pathetic.

Ramin laughed alongside me. 'Yep. I think that about sums it up. Our greatest curator prevented from doing that which she excels at.'

I knocked his foot with mine. 'Greatest?'

'Yes. And stop fishing for compliments. I've been looking over all the rosters since the stepper first came online. In my mind, you are up there with Caractacus, Tensing, and Black.'

'They were greater than me.'

'They all died. You survived every mission. You died in the line of civic duty and you came back! And finally, you, Neith Salah, are my best friend and have been ever since you shared your sweets with me in playtime.'

I smiled, remembering all the times we had got into scrapes growing up. The time we had decided not to date the same bloke, and had to play cards to see who won the right to go after him. Our early missions together before it was decided we would do better in other teams. Namely Clio.

I groaned. 'Clio still gets to step.'

'Life's a bitch, isn't it?'

I looked at Ramin and huffed in surprise. 'Is that it? Are those your words of wisdom? *Life's a bitch*?'

'It's done, Neith. By all means, keep trying to find a way around it, but in the meantime, start living. Find a purpose. Get your head out of your arse and get on with it.'

We spent the next hour in small talk. Ramin had dismissed the chimes, telling the doctors that this was a greater cure. As he chattered about his newfound domestic bliss, I let his words wash over me. Ramin didn't know it, but I did have a mission. I was the only one that knew about Minju. I didn't know what I could do, but I knew I was the only one that could.

Chapter 36 - Neith

After Ramin left, the doctors said there would be no more visitors, but an hour later Minju knocked on the door.

'Hello, Director Chen.' I spoke warmly and saw that her smile matched mine.

'Please, call me Minju. And can I say how delightful it is to hear you speaking Egyptian again?'

'Pretty delightful for me too. And I'm honoured that the pharaoh is taking an interest in my recovery.'

Although I was far from delighted with how frequently Minju was in her company. Any state visit, public opening, official reception, there she was, smiling and advising. She had no official role, but she always seemed to be around. Everyone loved her calming presence.

'I understand I owe you an apology?'

Minju looked at me blankly.

And so the dance began. I knew she was bad, but I don't think she was sure if I knew it. Obviously, the last time we met, I screamed my bloody head off. That might have given her a clue. But, in my favour, the rest of the world had been conned, and I was delirious from having a bullet in my head. I guessed she was here to check me out. Now I had to convince her that I was a fully paid-up member of the Minju fan club. If I mis-stepped, I imagine that by tomorrow I would wake up in long-sleep. I didn't consider myself safe yet, despite Dr Bitsoi's judgement. If Minju wanted me out of the way, I'd be gone in a blink. So it was time to shine.

'I screamed at you and tried to attack you. Apparently I did that to lots of people.'

'Yes.' She relaxed into her seat, her tail curling around the base of the chair. 'I understand you broke poor Julius' wrist?'

'Ugh, don't. I feel dreadful about that. I don't even remember it. I think in my head I was still trying to get out and fight Grimaldi.'

'But that's all over now.'

'Is it, though?' I looked up at the cameras knowingly, then suggested we go over and sit by the window. I pulled my chair closer to hers and leant forwards. She was watching me carefully, but playing along. The very tip of her tail was twitching.

Lowering my voice, I began to speak. 'Is it all over? I haven't been able to speak to anyone, to voice my concerns, but you are so well connected I wondered…'

'Go on.'

'Well, is it really over? And even if it is, are we safe?'

Now she leant forwards. 'Safe?'

'We defeated Grimaldi, but his ability to take control shows a fundamental flaw in our society.'

'But he had the help of those other quantum beings?'

I leant closer still. 'And that's the other thing. What can we do about them?'

Minju sat back and looked concerned. 'But Julius got them to give us their word never to return.'

This was ridiculous. We were both leading each other down the same garden path, but at least I got the feeling that she was beginning to trust me.

'And do you trust them, Minju? Those quantum beings. I mean, do you even understand them?'

She looked at me. Her face was blank, and I wasn't certain if I had pushed my luck. She placed her hand on my knee. 'Can I ask you not to speak of this to anyone?'

I made a pretence of looking relieved. 'You share my feelings, don't you?'

Of course she did, the little psychopath. She was not at all impressed by the idea that someone bigger and stronger might try to take over her playground. It was that flaw I was hoping to exploit and ultimately expose.

'You do, don't you?' I said quickly. 'I can't tell you how relieved I am that someone else is paying attention. Everyone seems to be all relaxed now that Grimaldi has gone, but I'm not relaxed. Not one bit.'

Minju leant back in her armchair. Only this morning I'd been laughing with Ramin. Now I was fighting for my life.

'Leave it with me. When you're out of here, let's talk again. The pharaoh is monitoring things. She knows the threat. We don't want to alarm anyone, but clearly the sharpest minds will have already seen the danger.' She stood abruptly, catching me off-guard. 'And now, my dear, I must go. Artefacts to catalogue, media streams to sort out, lunch with Nolyny. Busy, busy, busy.'

I was puzzled. I wasn't aware of the media streams reference. Minju now cleared things up.

'The pharaoh has asked me to monitor the new Beta media offerings. All that SF, fantasy and historical stuff. Try to make sure that we don't alarm the populations too much.'

'Ah.' I smiled. 'I wondered about that show *Rome*.' I had been watching a lot of Beta television whilst I recovered. 'Blood thirsty lot, weren't they?'

She looked worried. 'Is it too much? Should I block it? I thought people might find it interesting, but if you think it's too much?'

'What on earth would I know about what the general population like?' I shrugged. 'If you get complaints, remove it.'

'Good idea. So I'll just let it run for now then?'

'I would,' I said, fully aware that if there were complaints, Minju had just nicely manoeuvred herself into a situation of non-culpability. She could say it was my suggestion. I needed to remember she was a damn sight better than me at being sneaky. I was going to have to really watch my step.

'I tell you what,' she said. 'If you want, I have a job for you?'

277

I looked at her. If I said yes, I could keep a better eye on her. But then, she'd also be able to keep a better eye on me. Again, I felt like a mouse trying to dodge Minju's paw. With no better idea, I said yes and watched as Minju smiled in genuine delight.

As she left, I climbed back into my bed. The exchange had genuinely exhausted me, as had the fact that Minju Chen was still plotting. Whatever it was, I was determined to be on the inside. If I could just hold my nerve.

Chapter 37 - Julius

It was a week after Neith's review. Tomorrow, there was a gala to mark seven months since the failed coup, the stepper had been successfully re-launched and to celebrate Neith's recovery. Her return felt like the event had been drawn to a close in people's minds. I still couldn't get over how much the population was desperate to act like nothing had happened.

For now, though, I was back in the hospital. Koda wasn't happy with our readings. I hoped that whatever the procedure involved, it would be over quickly. To tell the truth, I would be glad to be done with the intermittent taste of rotting fish in my mouth. It was far worse than the temporary blackouts. And they were nearly done. If it hadn't been for my stupid outburst the other day, we wouldn't even be here. We were almost healed as it was. Now the doctors had to prod and poke again.

'You understand why you are both here?' Koda looked at both of us.

'Yes. Julius can't keep his mouth shut.'

'I didn't say anything.'

'No, you just fainted in front of a room of chancellors and doctors who were determining if Neith could work again!'

'I did not do it del—'

'Enough!' said Koda in exasperation. 'Now listen. Neith would never be allowed to return to work with the current state her brain is in. You both have experienced these quantum seizures, and yet you would want your friend to experience them and die!'

Clio snarled. 'It would be her choice.'

'Happily,' snapped Bitsoi, 'the decision isn't hers. Or yours, Clio.'

He explained how a comprehensive mapping of our brains earlier had detected identical nubbins. Of course, he didn't say nubbin. He said something about protein plaques and membrane anomalies. But I reckon nubbin also worked.

'We are going to go in and remove it. After that, fingers crossed, no more quantum quakes.'

He meant fainting. Although, to be fair, suffering from quantum quakes sounded a damn sight better than a fit of the vapours. Even Great Aunt Agatha, who blamed her frequent collapses on too much ice in the whiskey, never called it fainting. Maybe the old girl was actually a time traveller as well?

To date, the best theory for these quakes was that not only had we travelled to a point that we already occupied, namely the corridor in the Tower, but that we then travelled back to Alexandria on the same timeline to merge with ourselves. Some theories suggested we do nothing, and that the symptoms would pass. And in fact, this was what we had been doing, as it looked like we were improving. That was blown out of the water, though, when they found this little matching anomaly in our brains. And God love them, Alphas do like to experiment.

So surgery it was.

I opened my eyes. Clio was sitting beside me in a hospital gown, looking frantic. She was about to speak when Bitsoi walked in.

'Hello, Julius.' He stared at Clio and shook his head.

'Clio, you should be in bed resting.'

'I'm fine. Not my first brain scrape. I was just concerned for my friend. Didn't want him waking up alone.'

Clearly Clio's procedure had gone massively wrong and given her a new personality.

'Most commendable.' Koda smiled benignly at us. 'Now, since you are both together, I can run a few questions past you. As far as we can see, everything was a success.'

Clio moved her chair closer to my bed and held my hand. Something was very wrong, but I continued to smile as he asked various questions. I tried not to be distracted by her fingers around my hand. I was certain she could break it if she chose to. We covered the princes, my visit to see them in their new home yesterday, our journey to Aberystwyth, my first arrival on Alpha Earth.

'And when you saw Neith get shot, how did that make you feel?'

'Furious, terrified. When I—'

I paused, playing the scene back in my head, and I felt sick. Bile burnt my throat and I started to sweat. Clio squeezed my hand carefully.

'But!' I looked at her. This was wrong. Everything was wrong.

'But what, Julius?'

Clio stared at me again and I realised what she was trying to tell me.

'But when I saw Clio run after Grimaldi, I knew she would take care of him, and I would take care of Neith.'

He looked at me as if expecting me to say more.

'I felt very conflicted about Clio,' I added lamely.

'Yes. Understandable, but Clio has made full restitution, don't you agree?'

'I do.' I couldn't help myself. 'And the—'

Clio's grip tightened.

'And the joy of it is, I have a new friend.'

She let go of my hand and smiled at me sweetly. 'Is he fit to leave, Doctor Bitsoi?' she asked. 'I thought the pair of us could use some fresh air. No offence, but I've never enjoyed being in here.'

'None taken. And Clio, can I just say how proud we all are by your rehabilitation?'

'The greater the shame, the greater the gain. That's the mantra, isn't it?'

He smiled warmly at her and put his stylus away. 'Okay, you both still have your medi-braces on. We'll be tracking you for another forty-eight hours, but you should be fine. Drop them in when they notify you the observation period is up.'

As they left, I got out of bed and headed for my clothes. I was trying to keep my face straight and my heartbeat under control. I could taste fish oil in my mouth and wanted to get out of here without another fainting episode. And I desperately needed to talk to Clio with no one listening.

Clio had left with Koda, but now returned in her day clothes.

Half an hour later, we had walked out to the boulder that Neith and I liked to sit on to discuss things away from prying ears.

'Clio—'

She held up her hand and quickly waved it at me. I noticed a ring on her finger, which was unusual, as she rarely bothered.

'A gift from Jack. I asked for something to check if we had any listening devices enabled or embedded. We're clear, and so is the area. Plus, the ring also emits a static field. Clever tech. It simply bounces the surrounding sound, so anyone listening will just hear waves and gulls and us murmuring. If anyone was listening, they'd simply assume their device needed recalibrating for focus. Here's yours.'

I listened to her waffling and decided I was fine with that. I had walked for half an hour, and I still didn't know what to say.

'Clio?'

She looked at me and snorted. 'Yes. Don't worry, you aren't going mad, or at least if you are I'm with you.'

'But Minju—'

'Exactly. Minju, not Grimaldi, was behind the whole uprising.'

'And we're certain about this. I remember finding out when we were first divided into two teams. Could she have been coerced?'

'No. I was on her team, remember? She was furious to have been outed by Anansi, but the minute she was, she went at it, guns blazing.'

'But Minju?'

I was feeling all the shock and disbelief that I felt the first time I found out. Oddly, realising I had felt all this before was helping me to believe my memories.

'And you don't think this is a side effect of the surgery? After all, no one else seems to have this memory.'

'No. I spent a bit of time searching the news feeds, waiting for you to wake up. We appear to be alone in this memory. The thing is, I just don't know how it could have happened.'

'I have an idea,' I said, my mind casting back to those final moments outside the quantum facility. The battle was raging, and the tide was turning in our favour.

'Towards the end of the battle, Minju ran up to Anansi and asked him something. I remember him being surprised, but he nodded. It looked like he had agreed to do something for her.'

'That's it!' Clio jumped off the boulder. 'Come on, let's walk. I can't sit still whilst I'm trying to think.'

We headed away from the city. All around us were sand dunes and the sea. Lizards darted away from our feet, and I took care to avoid any holes in the sand.

'Just after we had all developed those glyphs over our heads, Minju said, to balance things out, she should be allowed to ask for a godlike gift, just as Asha had. I think she asked Anansi for a smokescreen. And I think that little glitch they noticed on our brains was Anansi's work. It had nothing to do with the quantum anomalies.'

'Makes sense. I can still taste fish oil.'

'Same. We just have to hide our symptoms now. In case they wonder what else the nubbin could represent.'

'Well, isn't that a good thing? If they undo everyone's memory and expose Minju.'

'And do you honestly think she'll allow things to get that far?'

I was having trouble reconciling my mild, timid friend with the savage and ruthless mastermind I also knew her to be.

'We'd be dead before we could make a move.' I came to a halt. 'Oh, Jesus! What about Neith?'

Clio shook her head. 'How could she bring herself to work with someone as slow as you?'

'You've had this information for longer than I have.'

'So what? The minute I remembered, I realised Neith was working for her. My first thought!'

Again with the pissing contest.

'Yes, fine. You are smarter. You care for Neith more. You would never hurt her. Oh no, wait, that last one isn't quite right, is it? You are labouring under the most massive guilt complex going. If the only way you can find to cope with that is to pretend you are better than me, then go right ahead.'

We had come to a standstill, and I was poking her in the shoulder as I shouted at her. I dodged her first punch, but failed to get out of the way of a punch to the ribs.

Wincing, I grabbed her tunic and fell, throwing her over my shoulder. I turned and sprang back, but she lay on the floor staring at the sky. I felt instantly contrite. The one thing we shouldn't be doing right now was fighting.

'Are you okay?'

She started to shake. Was she crying?

'Clio, I'm sorry. I—'

Her breath hitched as she pulled herself up into a sitting position.

'I can't believe my luck.' It was hard to tell if she was crying or laughing. Her shoulders kept shuddering, and tears ran down her face. 'I have the opportunity to make amends. I have to save Neith, and the only person I can rely on is a stupid Beta.'

I sat down beside her. One of us was going to have to be the adult.

'Clio. You are singularly the most unpleasant, suspicious, aggressive person I have ever met. Your attitude stinks. You are selfish, vain, and dangerous. But...' I exhaled. 'You are, for better or worse, my partner. So I suggest you stop feeling sorry for yourself, or you can get out of my way.'

She laughed. 'Why? Do you have a plan? A way to take down Minju?'

I shook my head. 'No. Do you?'

'Okay, Shitfly.'

'Fair enough, Psycho.'

'I'm not a psycho.'

'And I'm not a Shitfly.'

She sighed and lay down again and looked up at the clouds racing past. 'So, now what, Julius?'

I shrugged and lay down and watched the clouds as well. Minju was powerful and dangerous, and no doubt still had plans to take over Alexandria, if not all of Egypt.

'I haven't got a clue, but we have a party to go to and try to act like we're having a good time.'

Chapter 38 - Neith

Day 212.

The party was in full swing. Servers were skating around the room, gliding in and out of the guests, their blue and green ribbons trailing out behind them. On their trays, they offered glasses of champagne and delicate nibbles. Depending on the nibbles you ate, the taste could change dramatically. The trick was not to eat from two blue trays at the same time. The result could be challenging.

From across the room, I watched Julius splutter and choke. He started trying to apologise for making a fuss. Clearly he had forgotten about the need to combine plates. Right now he was probably experiencing chilli magnified by chilli. As usual, there was no shortage of people rushing forward to help him. In fact, that was something I had noticed. Julius was no longer viewed with apprehension, and hardly anyone called him Blue anymore. People were suddenly fine with the name Julius. When had that started? I had been out of action for six months, but the world had continued to turn. I needed to catch up. Minju was six months ahead and light-years smarter than I was.

As I watched them laughing, I wanted to join them. The temptation was enormous, but the need to protect them was greater. Clio and Rami knew me so well, I worried they would sense me hiding something. I couldn't alert Minju in any way that there was a chink in her armour, a bubble in the glass.

Tonight's theme was fancy-dress in a Beta outfit. There were soldiers and ballgowns, but there were a lot of outfits I didn't recognise. These were no doubt inspired by the sudden flood of Beta SF and Fantasy. I recognised the Doctor Whos. Helpfully, most costumes also had numbers on them. Ten seemed rather popular, but I was quite drawn to the one with the silly scarf. Sam had come as a mermaid with clam shells on his chest and a long blonde wig. He kept singing *Let It Go*, and I was convinced his girls had pranked him into muddling the Disney heroines. But he seemed happy enough.

I was quite a fan of Disney when animals were involved, but the gender divide in the human stories could be a bit tiresome, and would get in the way of a great story. A hologram of a bunch of Dalmatians ran past, and I knew Khani from the yellow custodians had arrived. He always came as Cruella de Ville and gave out Turkish Delight to everyone he spoke to. Another mash-up that seemed to work.

'There's a lot of Romans, aren't there?' said Shui-hi, who had come over to join me. I had been introduced to her earlier that day as one of my new team. She was dressed in some sort of golden bikini, with plaits pinned in round buns to the sides of her head. I couldn't place the reference, but told her she looked excellent, anyway.

'Fuad's come as Chewie. Wait till you see him!'

I grinned and nodded, unaware of the reference but happy to play along. Dress up was never really my thing. I guess it was because it was part of my job. My old job. Tonight, as at every other party, I had come as a cat.

'What's that you said about Romans?'

'There're loads. Emperors, gladiators, senators, soldiers, even slaves! I mean, that one I don't get!'

I didn't get any of it. In the past six months, our attitudes towards Rome had changed dramatically. People still talked of them as brutal oppressors, but now it wasn't in hushed tones. Now it was, oh yes, bad guys those Romans, but they had a great work ethic. Stuff like that.

It reeked of Minju's manipulation, but to what end?

'Maybe by dressing as a slave, the individual is displaying their own personal and societal freedom? An ironic statement?'

Shui-hi thought about it and agreed. Then, having decided she'd done enough small talk with the boss, she excused herself, saying she wanted to get hairy with Fuad. I had no idea what she meant, but I had a lot of broadcasts to catch up on. I watched as Minju entered the room and headed towards Julius and Clio. Clio appeared to have come as the Queen of Sheba, and was doing her best to play the part of an enthusiastic party attendee. Julius wasn't in costume, which surprised me not a jot. Minju was dressed as a clown. I shivered.

'How are you coping?' A warm voice interrupted my thoughts.

I turned round, smiling up at Ramin. He was in his regular dog costume.

'Hello, you. I'm good. You know.'

'I know.' He smiled sympathetically. 'We've missed you.'

'Well, Minju has been keeping me busy this past week.'

'She sure has. I've seen the photos in the news reels.'

I groaned. 'You can imagine how much fun that was.'

'There was something stoic about your smiles.' He laughed and picked up two drinks from a passing tray. 'Here. Let's drown our sorrows together.' He took a sip and smiled at me. 'Shall we go join the others?'

I nodded, but as I looked across I saw Minju's tail spasm.

'Shit. Quick, Ramin, look over there,' I said, pointing in the opposite direction.

'What?' Ramin studied the band and looked back at me. 'What have you seen?'

'Not them.' I still wasn't looking at Minju. 'Don't look over, but Minju's tail just gave a massive flick. Whatever Julius was talking about has really disturbed her.'

'And we couldn't be seen looking, because?'

Because she's a homicidal genius who keeps her cards so close to her chest that no one knows what's on her mind. Such a massive slip would go down badly. But that's not what I said.

'Because she's proud of her ability to control her emotions. Such a public slip would embarrass her. She will be checking to see if anyone noticed.'

Ramin looked at me closely, then took another sip. 'You are a most considerate person, Neith. Come on, let's join them. Maybe steer Julius away from whatever he was saying to disturb her?'

I thought that was a bloody excellent idea, and we headed across. Whatever Julius had said, it seemed like I needed to save him from himself. Minju noticed our approach almost instantly and broke off her conversation to greet us. Calling for a bottle of champagne, she raised an impromptu toast to the heroes of the Grimaldi Insurgence. Spontaneous applause broke out around the room, then people went back to their own conversations.

I felt slightly ashamed of myself as I watched Clio squirm, but only slightly. Dear Minju managed to make everyone equally uncomfortable in the same toast. Quite a feat.

'Well, that's all in the past now, isn't it?' said Julius, having noticed Clio's discomfort, and quick to change the subject. Ever the gentleman, even towards Clio. 'I was just talking about how many familiar costumes I can see. Some chap has even come as Chewbacca. Lord knows how he is coping in this heat.'

'I see you've come as a Cambridge Professor,' teased Ramin.

'Rami, how many times do I have to tell you? A party where the dress code is obligatory is hardly a party.'

'What about funerals?'

'Hardly a party, old man!' exclaimed Julius. We all paused. The Betas had such an odd attitude to death and stopping.

'Okay, well, what about your "black tie" events? They can often be parties.' Ramin grinned triumphantly, waving his glass at Julius, and we all looked at him expectantly. Ramin had him there.

'Well, that's just a social etiquette,' said Julius with a grin. It was the same grin that he used when he was standing on a snake hole and swearing he couldn't hear the rattle. Eventually he couldn't hold it any longer and burst into a good-humoured laughter. 'Fair play.' He shook Ramin's hand. 'You've got me there. Next time I'll come to a fancy-dress party in black tie and pretend to be James Bond.'

We all agreed he'd make a terrible Bond. 'Can you imagine?' asked Ramin. 'The name's Bond, licensed to apologise and be terribly sweet about it.'

'Now hang on,' protested Julius. 'I can be mean and ruthless.'

Ramin looked crestfallen and looked down into his drink. 'It was just a joke.'

Julius looked appalled. 'Crap. I'm so sorry, Rami. I know it was. I didn't mean to upset you.'

At which point Ramin grinned mischievously and tipped his head. 'See!'

We all started laughing as Julius swung between apologising again and laughing along with us. Even Minju appeared relaxed. Whatever earlier conversation had angered her had passed. I couldn't think of a way to find out what had been said without getting Julius into further trouble.

'So, tomorrow's the big day, hey, Neith,' said Clio, her tone slightly challenging. Or normal, for Clio. I didn't want to get into a conversation with her, so I just nodded and sipped my drink, hoping someone else would step in.

'Quite the promotion you've had.' Clio sneered. 'Archivist in charge of Beta Artefact Repatriation. I wonder, you must have friends in high places.'

'Better than friends in low ones.'

'Well, we all have to get by.' She smiled at me. It was the crocodile smile.

'Careful, honey,' I said. 'Your mask is slipping.'

Amongst our group, I doubt anyone was taken in by Clio's rehabilitation, but it was a pleasure to see her snarl, if briefly.

'I'll forgive the barb, Neith. You are our superior, after all. I wonder what you had to do to climb the ladder so fast?'

'Clio!' snapped Julius and Ramin simultaneously. Minju just stood quietly, observing.

'Oh, my apologies,' said Clio, sweeping a low bow, her long black plaits sweeping down in front of her, the gold chains clinking. Then she pulled herself back to her full height. 'The Queen of Sheba bows to her superiors.'

I sighed. She wasn't going to goad me. 'And anyway, it's a temporary position, isn't it, Minju? This is only a proposal. It hasn't even been ratified. We are just drawing up lists.'

'Then, when you're finally healed, you can get back to work,' said Julius, raising his glass to me. 'I was just saying. You can't keep a good curator down. We'll be working together again before you know it.'

'Julius,' said Minju, 'I know you don't mean to be unkind, but such talk isn't helping our beloved Neith come to terms with her new life.'

Julius inhaled and took a swig of champagne. Then he nodded sharply. A server skated past, removing his glass, and he paused until we were alone again. Our own little bubble of misfits in a party of Alphas. As I looked around at Ramin, Minju, Clio and Julius, I realised that we were all on the outside. Except Ramin, and even he was a curator. Maybe that was why Ramin was so important to me. He was my bedrock. I so wanted to tell him what I knew, but then I would be placing his life at risk. Maybe Clio as well. Despite my feelings towards her, I didn't want to jeopardise her either.

Julius cleared his throat, then looked squarely at me. 'Whatever happens, Neith, you and I will always be partners. Together we will be unstoppable, whatever we do.'

I stepped forward and grabbed his hand, squeezing it tightly. 'Forever.'

He laughed and called for more champagne as he threw his arm around my shoulder. All eyes were on him, this beautiful, laughing Beta. Out of the corner of my eye, I saw Minju's tail flick again, and I realised that Julius was in even more danger than I had realised.

I had to retire from the party and work out a way to protect him from Minju. For some reason, she was not reacting well to talk of Julius and me working together. Maybe I would have to tell him the truth about her, I hope that he believed me. Maybe the truth would save him.

'If you'll excuse me, I have a busy day tomorrow.' Shaking Julius's arm off my shoulder, I turned and walked out of the room. His expression, hurt and confused, was my final image of him.

Chapter 39 - Neith

Day 213

My head throbbed.

I wish I hadn't drunk so much the night before. In a fit of self-loathing, I had slunk away from the party, grabbed a bottle from one of the stores, then headed home for a pity party for one. Julius' expression had hurt me, as had Clio's. I was an outsider by my own making and drinking wouldn't solve anything.

It took me a while to realise the banging I could hear was not in my head, but at my front door. I slid out of bed and shambled over to answer it.

Minju was standing in the doorway, and it honestly took me a second to recognise her, she was so dishevelled. Her grey hair had mostly fallen out of its bun, long strands and hair pins fell across her shoulders. She appeared to be wearing yesterday's clothes, and her blouse was untucked. She was panting heavily and her tail swung wildly from side to side.

'Neith, they've taken Julius. He's going to be repatriated.'

I ran back into my apartment and began pulling on clothes. 'When? Where are they holding him?'

I turned around as I pulled my top over my head. Minju was pacing the room, muttering to herself.

'Minju. Which station is he at?'

'He's already at the stepper. They're removing him now. He may have already gone.'

I dropped my shoe. 'What? Why the fuck didn't you call me?'

'You never wear your brace,' she wailed, as though this was my fault.

'The room alarm. You have the authority to override it!'

'I didn't think! Oh Neith, what can we do?'

She was still wringing her hands, but I'd had enough of her theatrics. I ran out of my apartment barefoot and sprinted towards the quantum buildings.

'Tiresias,' I shouted into my brace. 'What is the location of Curator Julius Strathclyde?'

'There is no Curator Julius Strathclyde.'

'Julius Strathclyde. My partner, where is he?'

I shoved an elderly couple out of my way and sprinted across the traffic. My brace was pinging fine after fine as I knocked over a rubbish bin. Litter spilt out onto the concourse, and I could hear people shouting at my back. Tiresias piped up.

'Angel Julius Strathclyde is at the quantum facility.'

My blood ran cold. Julius was a curator, not an angel. Angels were being repatriated under an initiative to calm public fears.

'Precise location.'

'Angel Strathclyde is in the stepper room.'

'Call Ramin. Call Sam,' I was screaming into the brace now. I ran through the ornamental garden. Cactus spikes dug into the soles of my feet, but I ran on.

'Connected.'

'Sam. Ramin. Julius is being repatriated right now. He's in the room. Stop it!'

I stopped shouting and sped up. Six months of hospital rest had left me soft and flabby. I just needed to get to Julius in time.

Ahead of me, I could see Sam running from the admin block across the plaza and into the quantum facility. He was shouting into his brace.

I slammed through the doors, taking the steps two at a time, then sprinted down the corridor. People had already been alerted by Sam's run ahead of me, and were now looking about them as I hurtled past.

Holding my brace up to the security door, I burst into the final division. I didn't bother heading towards the gantry, but ran straight into the stepper. The door bounced behind me as I flung it open and ran into an empty room.

Above me on the gantry, Sam and Ramin were both shouting at the terrified operatives.

'Sam! Where is he?' I was screaming up at them. Where was Julius? Where was my silly, goofy friend? Where was my mate, my brother? Tiresias's disembodied voice rang out across the speakers.

'Angel Julius Strathclyde is in Cambridge. He is home.'

I tore the brace off my wrist and hurled it, screaming at the wall opposite.

The next hour passed in a blur of angry recriminations. I was present to see Custodian Githumbi return through the step with Ludo Bianco. But it was hours later before I noted Githumbi's reddened eyes. Sam had finally got through to the pharaoh, who said she would explain the securities issues face to face. Ramin had ordered a day of mourning and was immediately countermanded by the pharaoh. Minju had finally made it to the facility and assured us all that she would get to the bottom of whatever had changed the pharaoh's mind.

I was still in a daze as she ushered me out of the facility.

We were standing in the open. Families were walking past, taking images of the facility, posing as curators about to step to a barbarous planet to save their treasures from their own neglect. I felt sick to my stomach of all that we had become. Minju was shaking my arm, trying to focus my attention. She was bloody lucky we were surrounded by families and children, as I wanted to rip her gutting head off. She had done this. I had seen the signs, but been too slow to react. I had failed Julius, but I wouldn't fail my country.

My greatest enemy had offered me her patronage, and I had said yes. Now I needed to get to work. The closer I got to Minju Chen, the more savage my revenge.

Coming Next

Book Five
The Quantum Curators and the Great Deceiver

Available for pre-order now or read on for a sneak peek…

The Quantum Curators and the Great Deceiver

Chapter One

Quite frankly, I blamed myself. I was a total bloody idiot. The thing was, I had been in the middle of a really good dream. When the summons came through for an emergency step, I stumbled into work bleary eyed and full of sleep.

Even when I saw I would be stepping with Ludo, no alarm bells rung. Apparently Clio was out getting drunk somewhere and I blindly accepted that. The fact that we were also stepping over with a custodian, and not just any custodian but Githumbi, Asha's right hand, also failed to alert me to an issue.

We all stepped through. I was probably even smiling.

Five seconds later I found myself in Charlie's house. Correction, my house. The disconnect was startling and yet I still didn't twig. I thought we were here for a Cambridge mission. I was annoyed though. The least they could have done would be to warn me. As I looked around the little study I was momentarily overcome with homesickness. And for a heartbeat I would have given everything to stay there. Well, they warn you not to wish for things, just in case your wish comes true.

'This is a bit rum, Githumbi? Might have been nice to warn a chap?'

Githumbi cleared her throat and looked at Ludo. 'If you will, please.'

Things were beginning to feel wrong. On reflection I can only wince at how long it took me to reach this conclusion.

'Angel Julius Strathclyde—'

I took a step away from her and found myself bumping into one of Charlie's many bookcases.

'Hang on a minute. I mean I'm not one for titles but it's Curator not Angel.'

The part of my brain that had been still happily resting on a pillow, dreaming of snowball fights, was rapidly waking up and panicking.

'We are pleased to repatriate you safely to your home.'

He was reciting words almost by rote and staring straight ahead, refusing to make eye contact. Githumbi was looking directly at me and her face was pained. I had seen her fight Medusa and hadn't seen such an expression on her face.

Ludo continued on, but I had stopped listening. My brain was awake and screaming.

'No, look, hang on. I think there's been some sort of mistake,' I said.

'These orders are directly from the pharaoh. We don't make mistakes,' said Ludo.

'You make mistakes all the bloody time! You allowed an uprising to occur under your bloody noses. You had thieves in the heart of your organisation.' My mouth was now running ahead of my brain. 'This is Minju's decision isn't it? She's fooled all of you. You all think she's the saviour of the day, but she's conning everyone. Anansi made you forget her role in the uprising. She was behind the thefts and the riots.'

The pair of them stared at me as I ranted and I realised my revelations were falling onto stony ground.

'Githumbi. This is a mistake. Let me go back, I can fix this.'

I slapped my emergency brace before she could stop me, but nothing happened. I tried again but Githumbi just looked at me sadly.

Ludo piped up. 'Angel Strathclyde, your brace has been rendered immobile. Please remove it from your wrist and return it to me. All equipment from the quantum facility is on loan only and remains the property of the quantum facility.'

'Make me.' I took a step towards him and then felt churlish as he stepped back. This wasn't me and I retreated.

He cleared his throat and continued. 'Fear not. A cover story for your past year has been established, your bank account has been generously enhanced and there is a job waiting for you back at your college. We are proud to inform you that your transition has been designed to be happy and pain-free.'

'Githumbi? Is this a joke?' I knew it wasn't. This was my fault. I knew other angels had been repatriated, but I hadn't done anything to investigate. To protect myself from a similar fate. Githumbi was about to speak when Ludo tried again.

'This is no joke, Angel Strathclyde, but a wonderful-'

'Fuck off!'

Now he really did recoil. I can't think if I had ever sworn at someone in anger but it felt appropriate.

'Julius,' Githumbi's voice was so sorrowful that I felt like bursting into tears. 'This isn't a joke. I wish it were, but the orders were very clear. We're to leave you here. In your home.'

Silence fell between us. It was the middle of the night and the silence from beyond the house was also complete. I strained to hear anything, anything that might herald a rescue party, a way out, but I was fooling myself. My brace was immobilised. Whoever was at the other end had closed my return. Githumbi was here to prevent me from doing anything stupid. Ludo was here to read me the terms and conditions. I didn't know what to do, so I fell back on my manners.

'Right. Well.' I cleared my throat and tried again. 'This can't be easy for you, either. What happens now? You just go home and I go to bed and resume my old life?'

'Pretty much,' said Githumbi, nodding slowly.

I tried to think about tomorrow. I could do this. So long as I didn't think about yesterday.

'Very well.' There was no need to make this harder for Githumbi than it already was. I removed my brace and held it out to Ludo without looking at him. I might feel sympathy for Githumbi, but if I had to engage with Ludo again, I might absolutely sodding lose it.

Tomorrow I would start planning a way to return. I had no idea how yet, but curators came here all the time. All I had to do was find one and... And what? I didn't have a clue, but that would be something to aim for.

Githumbi stepped forward, her hand stretched out, and I nodded.

'Quite right.' I shook her hand and smiled at her. 'It has been an absolute honour to know you. Please say goodbye to—'

And then I blacked out.

Pre-Order **The Quantum Curators and the Great Deceiver today**

Author's Note

This one was an absolute beast to write, especially when I realised I had managed to write two books in one. Having properly unpicked the two tales means that book five is almost ready and maybe even get released this year. Although first I need to collapse.

As ever the majority of events and artefacts are real. Llewellyn's Crown is real and was lost in the theft of the crown jewels. In one of those perfect moments of reality beating fiction, I discovered an artefact called the Cross of Neith. It seemed too preposterous to include, who would believe it?

The theft of the crown jewels was as ridiculous as I've described. In fact it was even worse but of course my curators had to leave the scene. It was a theft that took place over several days. It was not noticed until some fishermen found silver goblets in the Thames. Over the next few weeks treasures were found under beds and pillows, in vegetable patches, in midden heaps. It was as if the thieves had no idea what to do next. I wonder if little Alys was involved? If you want to read more about it I recommend *The Great Crown Jewels Robbery of 1303* by Paul Doherty.

To this day the mystery of the Princes in the Tower has challenged historians. I like my solution.

It was also lovely to return to my alma mater, the National Library of Wales. I received my Masters in Librarianship from the University of Wales, Aberystwyth.

It was great to go back. Well do I remember downing jelly shots and dancing on the tables. It's how we librarians roll!

With Thanks

As ever, this is a team effort. In particular, I need to thank Alexandra for reading through my first draft and not laughing too loudly at all the wrong bits. This time the first draft went fully off the rails and it took months to spot the problem. Once fixed the manuscript was further knocked into shape through various rounds of edits, and I'd like to thank my editors, Mark Stay and Julian Barr. Finally, my excellent ARC team went over it like the most diligent archivists on this side of the two Earths.

I also want to say thank you to my family. It's fair to say that this has been a mad year. Again. And I have so much to be grateful for, they have put up with many crises of faith. I owe them.

And finally, thank you. You have followed Neith and Julius across multiple Earths and met some fascinating characters but wait until you discover who they meet next. Minju won't know what hit her.

Thank you for reading

Getting to know my readers is incredibly rewarding, I get to know more about you and enjoy your feedback; it only seems fair that you get something in return, so if you sign up for my newsletter you will get various free downloads, depending on what I am currently working on, plus advance notice of new releases. I don't send out many newsletters, and I will never share your details. If this sounds good, click on the following:

https://www.thequantumcurators.com

I'm also on all the regular social media platforms so look me up.

@thequantumcurators

Printed in Great Britain
by Amazon

34914593R00180